'Answer me,' Garrett said, letting all his hostility out. 'Or I'll really hurt you. Now, who is Leila Jarhoun?'

Ibrahim shook his head. 'No,' he said. 'I tell you nothing. Nothing!' He spat blood. 'You kill me if you like.'

Garrett took out his ASP and held it down by his side.

'Go ahead!' the Arab shouted. 'Go ahead! I have no fear! I am nothing. The Struggle is all!'

'You're not worth a bullet,' Garrett spat. 'I'll save that for your lady friend.'

'You talk big!' Ibrahim sneered. 'But first you have to find her.'

'I'll find her, Ibrahim,' Garrett said. 'You can be sure of that. Wherever she is, whatever she plans to do, I'm going to find her.'

The Arab smiled. He had his courage back now, and this time the contempt was real.

'I hope you do,' he said. 'Every night at sunset I will pray you find her. And that she kills you!'

SWEET SISTER DEATH

Frederick Nolan

ARROW BOOKS

Arrow Books Limited
62–65 Chandos Place, London WC2N 4NW

An imprint of Century Hutchinson Ltd

London Melbourne Sydney Auckland
Johannesburg and agencies throughout the world

First published in Great Britain by Arrow 1989

Set in Plantin
by JH Graphics Ltd, Reading

Made and printed in Great Britain
by Courier International Ltd,
Tiptree, Essex

ISBN 0 09 960640 2

But sweet sister death has gone debauched today and stalks on this high ground with strumpet confidence, makes no coy veiling of her appetite but leers from you to me with all her parts discovered.

David Jones, *In Parenthesis*

Prologue

On an April day in 1988, two Lebanese businessmen, one of them accompanied by his wife, an attractive, dark-haired woman of perhaps forty, were among the hundred and twenty-eight passengers who got off the Tunis Air 737 arriving at Tunis international airport from Cairo. Passing through Immigration and Customs without incident, the single man, whose passport gave his name as Abdel al-Aqleeq, went straight to the car hire desk and hired a red Peugeot 305 saloon for a week. He took off his jacket and tie as he waited for the paperwork to be completed. There were dark perspiration stains beneath the arms of his dark blue shirt.

The other two, ostensibly husband and wife, took a taxi to the Africa Hotel, where a double room on the fourth floor, looking out over the lake, was already booked in their name. An hour or so later they left the hotel; the man, whose name was Ari, went to a car hire office, where he arranged to hire a Volkswagen twelve-seater minibus for a week. The following day he drove his wife, whom he addressed as Tsipa, to the airport; there she, too, hired a white minibus, which she drove back to town.

From the airport, Ari drove to the Abu Dawas hotel on the beach, where he rendezvoused with Abdel al-Aqleeq, who had driven straight to the hotel in his hired Peugeot. Over the next four days, the three of them mingled with the crowds thronging the cafés and beaches: it was the height of the season, and in their casual clothes they attracted no attention as they strolled along the palm-fringed seafront of Sidi Bou Said, a luxury beach resort not far from ancient Carthage. They arrived each day in one of the minibuses, driving up the quiet residential rue Abu El-Kasem Chebbi and then turning on to the seafront road that led to La Marsa and Raouad.

On the fifth day, the man who called himself al-Aqleeq drove northwards towards La Marsa in the red Peugeot; by midday he was in Sidi Bou Said. He parked on the seafront, lit a cigarette and leaned back in his seat to wait. About an hour later, a man in tan trousers and an open-necked shirt came over to the car and tapped on the window.

'Ready?' he said.

The man in the car nodded.

'The boats land at midnight,' the man in the open-necked shirt continued. 'Tsipa and Ari will take them to the rendezvous. We go in at oh one hundred.'

'Understood,' the man in the Peugeot said. He flicked his cigarette out of the window and drove back the way he had come.

At eight o'clock that evening, an El Al Boeing 707, ostensibly bound for Casablanca, took off from Tel Aviv's Ben Gurion airport. According to its filed flight plan it was to fly due west across the Mediterranean on flightpath Blue 21, between Sicily and Tunisia. Had anyone been observing the preflight preparations – in fact, no unauthorized person was allowed within five hundred yards of this or any other plane on the tarmac at Ben Gurion – they might have remarked upon the fact that no flight number was allocated to the plane, that it never appeared on the departures board inside the terminal, and that no civilian passengers either reported for the flight or boarded the plane.

There was a good reason for this, of course. This plane was no ordinary commercial jet; it was an electronic command post manned by Israeli military and intelligence chiefs, its destination a holding pattern seven thousand feet above the Mediterranean, a few miles off the coast of Tunisia. It took up station, while some of the officers operated the sophisticated equipment jamming telephone communications around the target house, and others were coordinating the activities of the commando squad that was even now being whisked in a fast missile boat from Haifa to the night-empty beach at Raouad, about ten miles west of Sidi Bou Said.

At eleven o'clock, the sleek ship hove to, and thirty black-clad commandos carrying 9mm Mini-Uzi sub-machine-guns with thirty two-round box magazines clambered down rope ladders into waiting rubber dinghies. They swept ashore like a black wave, running crouched low over the dunes; two quick flashes of the headlights revealed the location of the VW buses. Within twenty minutes the assault team was on its way to the rendezvous.

At eleven-thirty, the man al-Aqleeq, who would lead the operation, started the engine of the Peugeot 305 and reversed on to the road, turning right off the promenade and up a wide avenue lined with palm trees. About half a mile up the avenue, he saw the two Volkswagen minibuses parked by the roadside. He slowed down, and one of them pulled out in front of him; the second fell in line astern as he turned right into the rue Abu El-Kasem Chebbi.

As they approached a large white Moorish-style villa that stood alone in its private grounds about halfway up the street, the minibus bringing up the rear pulled over, park-ing crossways to the road. The Peugeot stopped just short of the main entrance to the villa. The leading VW went about twenty yards further and then also stopped, turning to block the street from that end.

The man in the Peugeot got out of the car, closing the door quietly. In his right hand, down beside his leg, he held a silenced .22 calibre Model 87 Beretta. He gave a signal and the greased doors of both Volkswagens slid back. Twenty of the commandos got out of the vans as silently as cats and formed a cordon along the six-foot-high perimeter wall of the villa. The remaining ten formed a tight sickle curve about six feet behind their leader. He opened the gate of the villa and went in ahead of them.

He had gone about twenty feet when a guard appeared, a frown on his face as he saw the stranger coming towards him. Then he saw the phalanx of men behind the intruder. As he opened his mouth to shout, the man in the blue shirt shot him between the eyes. The guard fell backwards over a low wall, one of his legs sticking up.

The leader made a signal with his left hand; five of the

men behind him moved off to his left, the other five to his right. They streamed through the orange grove between the walls and the house like hunting otters. A trio of the dark figures slid into the garage, where a driver sat in his car listening to the radio. There was a short, flat sound, like a slap, as one of the commandos shot him in the back of the head. He died without even knowing who had killed him.

Inside the house, Abu Jihad, military commander of the Palestine Liberation Organization and a close friend of its leader, Yasser Arafat, was watching a video of Palestinian youths throwing stones at Israeli troops in a village on the West Bank. He heard the flat, hard sound and frowned, looking at his watch. It was one-thirty. He scrambled to his feet, heart pounding. Kicking off his slippers, he eased out of the door, keeping close to the wall. Through a glass panel he saw shadows flicker between the trees in the orange grove outside. He raced across the hall to the bedroom, where his wife, Intissar, was sleeping with their two-year-old son Nidal in her arms.

'Get on the floor and stay there!' he hissed, grabbing the 9mm Heckler and Koch P7 automatic on his bedside table. Even as he spoke, the Israeli commandos kicked down the main door and boiled into the downstairs hall, mowing down a house guard who ran out of the kitchen with a gun in his hand. Abu Jihad burst out of the bedroom with the pistol in his hand. The intruders were bunched together at the foot of the staircase. He got off one shot at them before he was met by a solid wall of lead from their Uzis; the bullets tore off his gun hand and dropped him in a tattered heap halfway down the staircase. The woman who had driven one of the minivans came into the hall carrying a portable video camera. She took pictures of the scene, and kept turning as one by one each of the four commandos stepped forward and emptied his weapon into the inert body. When they were finished there were more than a hundred bullets in the corpse.

'All right!' snapped the leader. 'Out!'

The assassination squad moved out of the killing zone and ran through the gardens to the vehicles waiting in the street with their engines running. They piled aboard, and the convoy roared down the silent street and out along the road to the landing beach. Within twenty minutes, the entire unit was back on the missile boat, which moved away from the coast, with a dark throb of its powerful engines. High in the sky, the big jet banked to starboard and set a course for Tel Aviv.

1

The pay phone in the uncarpeted hall of the seedy house in Paddington rang at 4.30 p.m. A door opened on the upstairs landing; a young woman of about twenty-five ran down the linoleum-covered stairs. She wore a dressing gown and cheap slippers.

'Hello?' she listened for a moment, then nodded. 'Hold on. I'll just get him for you.'

She yelled up the stairs. 'Hank!'

A young man dressed in blue and white flannelette pyjamas stuck his head over the banisters on the floor above.

'It's them,' the woman said.

The dark-haired man nodded and bounded down the stairs. His brown eyes were alert and shining as he picked up the phone. He said something in Arabic. The woman watched, taking a packet of Silk Cut cigarettes from her dressing gown pocket and lighting one. The young man jerked his head. She sniffed and went back up the stairs, her slippers making a gritty sound on the dirty linoleum. When she was gone, the young man spoke for a few minutes with the caller, then hung up. He patted the phone, smiling, then ran up the stairs, calling the woman's name.

'May! May!'

They shared a rented two-roomed furnished flat on the first floor of a rundown old house in Whickham Terrace, Paddington, one of the hundreds of almost identical rows that had sprung up when Samuel Cubitt started developing the open fields north of Marble Arch around the turn of the century. It was now owned by an East African Indian, and had no identity, no personality. Each of its three floors was subdivided into flats with enough poor sticks of junk-shop furniture to enable the owner to let them as 'furnished' on the one hand, and to evade the requirements of the Rent Act on the other.

In the two front rooms occupied by May and Hank there were a couple of battered armchairs with greasy covers, a fourteen-inch television set, a gas fire with a worn rug in front of it, and some plywood shelves that had bowed beneath the weight of the dog-eared paperbacks piled on them. In one corner was a screened-off cooking area; it contained a gas cooker, an old Hotpoint Iced Diamond fridge and a sink. A pair of tights hung on a string line. Between the two big casement windows that looked out over the patch of garden at the rear of the house stood a cheap desk, cluttered with old newspapers. In the second room were a bed, a wardrobe and a chest of drawers, all of which looked as if they had come from church hall jumble sales. The bathroom was outside on the landing.

'I've got the job,' Hank said.

'You mean it?'

'I told you. They want me to come and see them. Tomorrow.'

'Brill!' she said. 'How much?'

'I don't know. At least two hundred a week.'

'Two hundred?'

'And a car.'

'Oh, Hank, that's brill!'

'It will be. You'll like Athens.'

'I hope so.'

'They said the flat is all ready; all you have to do is move in. Someone from head office will meet you at the airport and take you out there.'

'How long will it be before you come?'

'As soon as the training course is finished. A week, probably. You don't mind going on your own?'

'Course not. It'll be brill.' She looked around. 'I won't be sorry to leave this place.'

'Neither will I,' Hank said. He untied her dressing gown and put his strong hands on her buttocks, pulling her body against his.

'You at it again?' she giggled. 'You randy bugger.'

He pulled her on the bed and closed his mind, letting the sensations of his body take over. She wrapped her legs around his back and heaved up against him.

'Ooh,' she moaned. 'Ooh bloody hell that's nice.'

After it was over he lay awake and smoked a cigarette. May lay asleep on her back with her mouth open. Cow, he thought idly.

He had picked her up one night in the bar of The Crown on the Harrow Road; after a few drinks she agreed to go out with him. She told him her name was Mary Patricia Logan and she was a waitress in a hamburger bar on Tottenham Court Road. She had come to London from Ireland six months earlier, and was sharing a flat in Camden with three other single girls.

After a few more meetings he persuaded her to come back to his place. It was all he could do to go through with it. Her body was flabby, white and unattractive, her sagging breasts heavy. Nevertheless, he made love to her as ardently as if she were a Nablus virgin coming to her bridal bed; she moved in with him soon after.

The morning after the telephone call, he got up early and made instant coffee. He took a cup into the bedroom. She awoke, pawing blearily at her eyes. She had drunk a bottle of cheap red wine the night before, watching some stupid television thing.

'Wossa time?' she mumbled.

'Eight o'clock,' he said.

'I'll get up in a minute.'

'No, there's no need,' he said. 'You have a lie-in.'

'You spoil me, you do.'

He smiled to hide a grimace of distaste. 'I'll be back about six,' he told her. 'See you later.'

'Good luck, love,' she called.

He went out into the street and hailed a taxi. He was shivering with excitement. Chosen, he thought. At last.

Hank got out of the taxi on the corner of Wardour Street, and crossed the street into Leicester Square. It was already getting warm; it was going to be a nice day. There was a

9

queue of people waiting at the half-price ticket booth. When he reached the statue he stopped, as if to examine it. He didn't think it looked much like Charlie Chaplin.

'Are you Iman?' a voice said. He turned sharply. A man dressed in a blue tracksuit with white piping and Reebok running shoes, with a Duracell roll bag slung over his shoulder, was watching him warily.

'Yes,' Hank said. 'You are Hassan?'

The man nodded. 'Go and sit on a bench. In the garden.'

Hank did as he was bidden. An old man was feeding the pigeons with bits of bread. Somewhere a police car whooped its way through the traffic. Tourists milled around in the pedestrian area in front of the Empire. The man who had identified himself as Hassan came and sat next to Hank on the bench. The old man took no notice of them whatsoever. Two young girls in tight shorts walked by, eating ice cream. Hank watched their buttocks move.

'You know what you are to do,' Hassan said.

'I know,' Hank said, proudly.

'I have brought you everything you will need. Take the bag,' Hassan. 'Wait ten minutes after I leave.'

'Yes,' Hank said. 'Yes.'

Hassan got up and walked away. He was about thirty-five, Hank decided. Short, powerfully built, black hair, black moustache. He wondered who he was. It didn't really matter.

He waited, watching the seconds turn to minutes on his digital watch. When ten minutes had passed, he swung the bag on to his shoulder. Something hard and heavy banged against his back. He walked along Coventry Street and went into the Regent Palace Hotel. The toilets were through heavy swing doors and down the stairs. He went into one of the cubicles, locked the door and unzipped the roll bag. Inside was an Ingram automatic pistol, two magazines of ammunition, a slab of C4 plastic explosive and an envelope containing fifty twenty-pound notes.

He put everything except the money back into the bag and went out of the hotel and into the Boots the Chemist shop opposite, where he bought a Casio calculator. From there he walked along Piccadilly to the TWA office and paid cash for an Ambassador Class ticket to Athens in the name of May Logan. She might as well go in style, he thought. He was still smiling at his own gallows humour as he hailed a cab and told the driver to take him back to Whickham Terrace.

May was a nothing, a donkey, an unwitting means to a desired end. She had swallowed the story he had fed her about being interviewed for a job in Athens like the gooey chocolates she was always stuffing into herself. There was no job, no training course, no flat awaiting her, but the stupid cow knew none of that. She would bovinely do whatever he asked her to do because she loved him and believed that he loved her.

The plan was simple; foolproof, even. When she left for Athens, he would ask her to take a few of his things with her, packed in the Duracell roll bag that Hassan had given him. In it, rolled flat beneath the hardboard stiffener at the bottom of the bag, would be the plastic explosive, and on top of it the calculator, rigged as a miniature bomb set to go off when the plane reached thirty thousand feet. It would explode the C4 by sympathetic detonation and blow the plane out of the sky, taking to their deaths not only May Logan but everyone on board, including the men who were the real target of this action: a team of CIA counterterrorist experts led by Lieutenant Colonel Dennis Gurney, flying to the Greek capital from New York as representatives of a front company called the United States Agency for International Developments.

Gurney was a CIA hawk. It was he who, in March 1985, had trained the Lebanese hit team which detonated a car bomb in Beirut meant to kill Muslim leader Mohammed Hussein Fadlallah. In the event, Fadlallah was uninjured; but eighty people were killed and two hundred injured when the bomb went off. This was the first time Gurney had returned to the Middle East since then; his death, they had told Hank, would be an example and a deterrent. The man who killed him would be a hero.

* * *

11

May was very excited as they drove out to Heathrow, but Hank only half listened as she prattled on about what they would do when he joined her. He drove extra carefully, conscious of the catastrophic consequences of even a small accident. The traffic around Shepherds Bush was heavy, but he picked up the flyover without too much trouble. Once they were on the motorway he relaxed, becoming aware of the tension that had held his body in a vicelike grip. He flexed his hands on the steering wheel.

'What terminal does the plane go from?' she asked

'Three. We can park for a minute.'

He drove into the airport and round to the islands in front of Terminal Three. Everything May owned was in the one suitcase she had with her. he handed her the Duracell roll bag.

'Take it on as hand luggage,' he said. 'The camera is in there and everything. Don't want it stolen, do you?'

'Oh, Hank, I wish you were coming too.'

'I'll be there soon,' he said. 'Come on.'

He carried her case over to the automatic doors and suffered her smothering kisses; God, would she never go?

'See you next week, love,' she said. 'I'll call you as soon as I get there.'

'See you,' he replied. In Hell, he thought, and then she was gone. He watched through the doors as she put the suitcase on the scales and handed her ticket to the girl at the desk. The roll bag was on the floor at her feet. As far as Hank could see, no one was taking the remotest interest in her. Well, why should they? A woman travelling alone, British passport – why should anyone be interested in her? Smiling, he got into his Escort XR3i and headed back to London.

Inside the terminal, May Logan checked her bag and went upstairs to the mezzanine. She went through passport control and handed over her roll bag for a security check, passed through the metal detector and went into the departure lounge. She looked up at the board: the flight hadn't been called yet. She went over to the bookstall and browsed along the paperback shelves until she found a new

12

Catherine Cookson. She took it to the desk and paid for it, found a seat, and started to read.

Ten minutes later, a black Rover Sterling slid to a stop at the kerb outside Terminal Three. A big man wearing a Burberry and a Donegal tweed hat got out and walked purposefully into the building, going straight up the stairs to the departure lounge. He showed his ID to the security guard, who nodded and signalled to the uniformed policewomen to wave him through.

'My name is Garrett. Would one of you ladies come with me, please?' the big man said. His voice was deep and not unpleasant. One of the WPCs smiled and fell into step alongside him.

'Something up, sir?' she asked as they bypassed the security check and went into the departure lounge.

'We're look for an Irish woman named May Logan. About twenty-four, five feet two, dark hair, green eyes, sloppy plump. Flying TWA to Athens. Carrying a Duracell roll bag as hand luggage.'

'There she is,' the WPC said. May Logan was sitting on a bench by the window, smoking a cigarette. The Duracell bag was on the chair next to her.

'You take the woman,' Garrett said. 'I'll get the bag. What's your name, Constable?'

'Foster, sir,' the girl said. 'Emma Foster.'

'Go to it, Foster,' Garrett said.

As the young policewoman walked across the crowded lounge, Garrett veered away to one side. WPC Foster stopped in front of May Logan and smiled.

'Miss Logan, is it?'

'It is.'

'I'm afraid there's been a bit of a mix-up about your ticket,' the policewoman said brightly. 'If you'd like to come with me to the airline office, they'll fix it up. It won't take a jiffy.'

'Don't worry about your bag.' While the two women were talking, Garrett had eased around on May Logan's blind side and now had the Duracell roll bag firmly in his solid-looking fist. 'I'll bring that for you.'

13

Puzzled but not perturbed, May Logan plodded dutifully across the lounge behind the policewoman. People stared at her as she went by; her chin came up and she glared back at them, as much as to say, I've not done anything wrong. They took her to an interview room in the security wing. It was quite featureless: a formica-topped table, a few stacking chairs, a window that looked out at a blank red brick wall, fluorescent lights. Unfriendly and cheerless, it made May Logan nervous. She sensed there was something very wrong but she could not imagine what it was.

'This isn't an airline office,' she said.

'The man who brought you to the airport, Miss Logan,' Garrett said, ignoring her protest. 'What is his name?'

'Hank. Hank Malik. It's really Hanif, but everyone calls him Hank.'

'How long have you known him?'

'About four months. Look, what has this got to do with—'

'Bear with me, please,' Garrett said. 'Where did you meet this Malik?'

'In a pub in the Harrow Road. He come in one night, bought me and my friend drinks. Later on he asked me to go out with him. Look, who are you? What's all this about?'

'You are going to Athens?'

''ass right.'

'Business, or pleasure?'

'We're going to live there. Hank's got a job with Olympic Airways.'

'But you're not flying Olympic?'

'Hank bought the ticket.'

'You're travelling alone?'

''ass right. Hank has to go to a training school first. He'll be following me out there later.'

'Did you have any luggage?'

'Just one bag. I checked it in. Everything else is going air freight.'

'Is this bag yours?'

'Course.'

14

'What's in it?'

'You know, bits and pieces. Some of Hank's things.'

'Nothing else?'

'Course not.'

'Did you pack it yourself?'

'Yes,' she said, but she knew they had noticed the slight hesitation.

'Would you mind opening it?'

She unzipped the roll bag and pulled it open. It lay on the bench like a waiting mouth. Garrett carefully took out the clothes: a Vivitar Point-and-Shoot camera, a makeup kit, the *Daily Mirror*, a woman's raincoat. Beneath them was a cheap sports jacket, a pair of trousers, some books tied together with string. He lifted the slacks and saw a Casio calculator. He did not pick it up.

'What's the calculator for?' he asked the woman.

'Dunno,' she said. 'Hank must have put it in there.'

Garrett looked at WPC Foster. 'Go and tell them we've got a banger in here, will you?' he said. Her eyes widened; she went to the door and spoke sharply. Another WPC came into the room. Foster hurried away.

'Will this take long?' May Logan said. 'I don't want to miss my flight.'

'I'm afraid you already did,' Garret said.

The woman looked at him, her mouth slack with surprise. 'What you mean?' she said angrily.

Garrett ignored her, turning as the door opened and WPC Foster came back in with a tall, thin man carrying an attaché case. He looked at Garrett.

'I'm Henderson,' he said. 'Security. Got one past us, did she?'

'The roll bag,' Garrett said.

Henderson went across to the bench and looked inside the bag. He nodded, opened his briefcase and took out a mirror on a long articulated handle. Shining a powerful torch inside the bag, he used the mirror to examine the calculator from every angle. When he was satisfied that it was not wired to anything, he gingerly lifted it out of the bag and set it on one side. He ran his fingers through his

15

thinning blond hair, cleared his throat, then peeled back the hardboard stiffener to reveal the putty-like layer it concealed. He licked his finger and nodded.

'C4,' he said. 'About half a pound, by the look of it.'

He next turned his attention to the calculator, very carefully sliding aside the plastic strip covering the battery compartment. In it was a Duracell nine-volt alkaline battery. Henderson examined the connectors through a magnifying glass. When he was certain there were no additional wires, he disconnected the battery and put it in his pocket. Then he took a scientific screwdriver from a small case and removed the back of the calculator.

'Surprise, surprise,' he said, holding it out so Garrett could see. Two wires attached to the terminals were patched on to a small square of the putty-like plastic explosive and from it to a cylindrical metal detonator.

'Here,' May Logan said. 'Woss that?'

'It's a bomb, May,' Garrett said quietly. 'Your boyfriend gave you a bomb to carry on to the plane.'

She stared at him in utter disbelief.

'Show her,' Garrett told the bomb expert harshly. Henderson put the calculator on the table in front of May. He brought the bag across and took out the plastic explosive.

'The calculator's got a barometric detonator in it,' he said to her, as one might explain something to a child. 'When the plane got to about thirty thousand feet – somewhere over the Bavarian Alps – the pressure would set it off. That would explode this stuff: it's called C4. About one and a half times as powerful as TNT. If it had gone off it would have blown the side off that 747 you were booked on. Not that it would have made any difference to you, love. You'd have been scattered from Stuttgart to Munich by the explosion.'

'He wouldn't,' May breathed. 'Hank wouldn't of done that.'

'His name isn't Hank, or even Malik,' Garrett said. 'It's Hassan al-Kharran. He is not Jordanian, as he told you, but

16

Syrian. He belongs to a terrorist group which calls itself the West Bank Liberation Faction.'

'I don't believe you.'

'That doesn't alter the facts.'

'He wouldn't, I tell you.'

'He did, May,' Garrett repeated. 'You're carrying a bomb.'

'Oh, stop,' May Logan said, softly, 'please stop.' She started crying, her plump shoulders hunched, convulsive sobs shaking her body. WPC Foster went across and sat beside May, her arm around the weeping girl.

'He was going to kill me. Kill me,' May sobbed.

'Well, he didn't,' WPC Foster said soothingly. 'You'll be quite safe now.'

'Safe!' she wailed. 'That's a good one. I'm pregnant.'

Garrett looked at the policewoman. She shrugged and patted May consolingly. There didn't seem to be anything worth saying.

'Why'd he want to kill us?' the girl wailed. 'Why?'

'Where is he, May?' Garrett said.

'I dunno,' May sniffled. 'He's at the flat, I expect.'

'No,' Garrett said. 'We checked that. He's given us the slip. Where else would he go?'

'I don't know.'

'You want to help us, don't you? You don't want him to get away with this?'

'No. Yes. Oh, I don't know.'

'Try, May!' Garrett urged her. 'We've got to catch him or he'll do this again, to someone else. Try to think. Who does he know? Has he got any specially close friends?'

'No, not really. Not that I know of, anyway.'

'What about relatives?'

'No. I don't know. Wait. Yes. He mentioned a cousin.'

'A cousin,' Garrett said, his demeanour changing. 'What was the cousin's name, May?'

'Ahmed,' May sniffled. 'Ahmed Jibril.' The shock was passing. Garrett saw the anger kindling now in the watery green eyes. That's a good girl, he thought.

'Where does this Jibril live, May?' Garrett snapped.

17

'I don't know,' May said. 'The bastard never told me nothing. Wait a minute. I remember now. He lives in Maida Vale. Somewhere in Maida Vale.'

'Have her taken to Paddington Green,' Garrett told WPC Foster. 'Tell them I'll be there later.'

Ahmed Jibril. The name beat in his mind as he hurried to a phone in the special operations room set aside for the security services at Terminal Three. From there he called his own office and told them what he wanted. He paced up and down impatiently, cursing the necessary minutes it must take for the relevant details on Ahmed Jibril to be located in Home Office records by the computer at Euston Tower. The phone rang; he snatched it up.

'Have you got it?' he said. 'Good. Fax it to me here. Yes, now, dammit!'

A few minutes later he was driving up the M4 towards London in the unmarked Sterling, a facsimile of the DI5 file on Ahmed Jibril on the seat beside him. He took the Ealing exit, expertly threading his way through the mid-morning traffic to Ladbroke Grove and Kensal Green. Barnlock Road was on the north side of the Harrow Road, the base of an inverted isosceles triangle formed by two other identical streets. There were only a few people about. He parked opposite the target address and used his car radio to contact Lonsdale House. Then he waited.

After perhaps fifteen minutes had elapsed he saw a dark blue Ford Sierra turn into Barnlock Road at the far end. It stopped opposite where Garrett was parked. A solidly built young man got out, went up the steps of the house and, after peering at the names beneath the numerous bells on the door frame, rang one and waited. Garrett was already on the move, easing the big car round the block. He got out of the car just as the young man May Logan knew as Hank Malik came over the garden wall behind the target house. He looked right and left, brushed down his clothes and set off towards the Harrow Road, walking rapidly.

Garrett crossed the street, moving diagonally so that his path would intersect that of the hurrying figure. Simultaneously, the man who had called himself Hank

Malik felt rather than saw the big man moving towards him. Their eyes met.

'Hassan al-Kharran,' Garrett said.

It wasn't a question. The Syrian felt icy fingers close inside his belly. Nobody knew him by that name. He averted his eyes and veered away from Garrett, walking purposefully as if to indicate that the name meant nothing to him. At the same time, he slid his hand inside his jacket; his fingers were actually touching the gun stuck into his belt before the big man moved. An automatic pistol appeared in his hand; without visible hesitation he fired seven shots into al-Kharran's body, the gun barrel following him down. The Syrian collapsed like dropped washing beside the Escort XR3i that he had driven from the airport.

"ere,' a passer-by said, gawping at Garrett. 'Woss goin' on, then?'

'Keep out of this,' the big man snapped. He knelt beside the body and checked for a pulse in the throat; there was none. The gun he had used was already out of sight. He removed the automatic weapon from the dead man's waistband and tucked it under his jacket. A small huddle of spectators had formed; they stood watching, talking in whispers. Garrett heard the crunch of tyres and looked up; the stocky young man who had gone to the front door of the house in Barnlock Road was getting out of the Sierra. In the back seat, handcuffed, was a swarthy, balding man in a gaudy cotton shirt.

'Hello, Jamesie. Is that the other one?' Garrett asked.

'Yes, sir,' the younger man replied. 'Cleveland Street says there's an ambulance on the way.'

Almost as if on cue, an ambulance turned into the street and drew up alongside the prone body. Two stretcher-bearers got out. They looked at the body in the gutter and then turned to stare wide-eyed at Garrett.

'Don't gawp!' Garett growled, his voice harsh. 'Get him out of here!'

The two bearers hastily lifted the body on to a stretcher and slid it into the back of the ambulance. They slammed the doors shut and then leaped into the cab, moving away at high speed, the sound of their siren bouncing off the walls. A few minutes later, a police Rover slid into the space the ambulance had occupied. Two officers jumped out and began herding the knot of onlookers away from the scene. After a moment, a tall man wearing a brown Harris tweed sports jacket and tan trousers got out of the back seat of the car and came over. He stood next to Garrett for a moment, looking at the bloodstains in the gutter. His expression hovered somewhere between annoyance and resignation.

'Another one, Garrett?' he said.

Garrett took the automatic out of his waistband and handed it over.

'Another one, Inspector,' he said. 'And he was carrying this.'

The policeman took the weapon and sniffed the muzzle.

'Hasn't been fired,' he observed.

'That's the whole idea,' Garrett replied. 'Isn't it?'

2

The young man who arrived on British Airways flight BA 156 from Cairo was about twenty-five, with a fleshy face and swarthy skin. His hair and eyes were dark, his lips beneath the heavy moustache thick and sensual. As he walked towards Immigration from the bay where the TriStar had docked, he amused himself by trying to identify the Special Branch watchers in the crowd.

He presented his passport, which showed him to be a citizen of Iraq. The Immigration officer, whose name was Robert Groves, deftly punched the visa details into the computer concealed in his desk without the passenger seeing him do so.

'How long do you plan to stay in England, Mr Hosseyn?' he asked.

'Ten days,' the man said.

'Business or pleasure?'

'A little of both, I hope.'

Immigration officer Robert Groves nodded. The computer check had shown that the passport was clean. He stamped the visa, handed back the passport and, waving, the man through, turned to the next person in the line. Another twenty minutes, he thought, and it's coffee time.

By the time Robert Groves finished his half-hour coffee break, the man whose passport had identified him as Khaled Abu-Hosseyn of Basra, Iraq, was in a taxi on his way to central London. He checked into the Inn on the Park, shaved and showered, then ordered sandwiches and a bucket of ice from room service. He unpacked the litre bottle of Johnnie Walker Black Label whisky he had bought at the duty-free shop and put it on the bedside table. Then he called the unlisted number on the 245 exchange that he had been given.

'Yes?'

'This is Ibrahim. I am in place. Room 1412.'

'Very good,' said the male voice. 'You will be contacted.'

Nothing more was said; the connection was broken. The Syrian smiled. A discreet knock on the door announced the arrival of the food and ice. He tipped the waiter, closed the door and walked across to the window. London looked shabby and dirty, the way it always did. He lit a cigarette and picked up the telephone again. This time he called a number he knew by heart.

'Starlight Escorts.'

He told the woman his name and waited while she checked it. When she came back on the line he told her what he wanted. She said she could have someone with him in about half an hour. He said that was fine and hung up. He took off his clothes and put on a silk dressing gown. He was pouring his second drink when the woman arrived. She was about twenty-five, tall, full-breasted, blonde.

'Mr Hussein?' she said.

'Hosseyn,' he replied. 'And you are. . . ?'

'Patricia.'

'They told you what I want?'

'Yes,' she said.

He fucked her three times and sent her away with four hundred pounds. When she was gone he drank some more whisky and watched a movie on cable TV. It was good to be back.

Next morning Hosseyn rose early, putting on a warm jacket and trousers. Spring had arrived in London, and the parks were yellow with daffodils and narcissus, but the air was thin and chill after the balmy warmth of the Middle East. He walked through town to Leicester Square, then took the Tube to the Angel.

The house he was looking for was on Islington Green. It was a decrepit-looking terrace with Georgian windows; a tarnished brass plate beside the wide-open front door identified it as the North London Academy of English. He went inside, down an unswept corridor. A fat woman in a duffel coat, a cigarette drooping from her lips, looked at him aggressively.

'Something I can do for you?' she asked.

'I wanted to inquire—'

'About courses?'

'That's—'

'English? Business management? What?' Her voice was impatient, as though she was angry at him for taking so much of her time.

'Business manage—'

'Second floor. Room Fourteen. Mr King.'

'Thank you.'

The woman had already turned away, as if he no longer existed. Hosseyn climbed the linoleum-covered stairs to the second floor. The banisters wobbled under his hand. The flaking walls were covered with crude Social Services posters.

The door of Room 14 was closed. He knocked, and a thin voice told him to come in. It was a classroom. At a desk on a dais raised perhaps a foot higher than the floor sat a thin man with steel-rimmed glasses perched on the end of a narrow nose. His eyes were small and rodent-like. He wore a Harris tweed jacket with leather elbow patches, brown twill trousers and scuffed dark brown suede shoes.

'Mr King?'

'Yes, what is it now?' His voice was thin, irascible, like a man interrupted while doing something important.

'I'd like to inquire about a business management course.'

King looked at him, and Hosseyn could see him guessing his nationality, pricing his clothes.

'I see,' he said. 'And you are Mr. . . ?'

'Hosseyn.'

'Egyptian, is it?'

'Iraqi.'

'Ah. Well. Have you got a work permit?'

'No.'

'Ah,' King said, sighing noisily. 'Makes it difficult, that. Very difficult. Not to say' – he paused, almost theatrically – 'expensive.'

'I don't think that would be a problem,' Hosseyn said. 'If you could help me.'

'It's the admin, you see,' King said. 'The admin. Smoke, do you?'

'Not just now, thanks,' Hosseyn said. King took a packet of Marlboro from his pocket and lit one, inhaling gratefully.

'Here's the way it goes,' he said. 'We give you a letter to the Home Office, d'ye see? It says you've registered with us for a course. A year. You don't want to stay longer than a year?'

'I don't think so.'

'If you change your mind, we can probably fix it up. Say you've signed up for three years, if you like. Then when your time's up, say you've signed up for another course – English, philosophy, history. But if it's only a year. . . .'

'What do I have to do?'

'You register with us. We give you a letter confirming you're a student, and you take it to the Home Office. They check with us. We tell them enough to make them happy.'

'And that's all?'

'No, no, course not. You're supposed to come here to school, three hours a day, five days a week.'

'Oh,' Hosseyn said, 'as much as that?'

'It's the attendance records, Mr. . . ?'

'Hosseyn.'

'Sorry. Terrible head for names. It's the attendance records, d'ye see? If they come round, checking, we wouldn't have a leg to stand on, would we?'

'Is there no other way? It would be very difficult for me to attend so frequently.'

'I see,' King said. 'Mm. Makes it tricky, that. Very tricky.'

'If it's a matter of money, I'm not worried about what it costs.'

'Well. There is a way. Very pricey, mind you.' He smiled encouragingly, showing bad teeth. 'Private tuition.'

'You have private classes?'

'Look at it like this. If you can't attend classes every day, we have to charge you personal tuition. One to one, we call it. We have to put fifteen hours on the Home Office form, d'ye see. Nothing we can do about that.'

'What would private tuition cost?'

King looked around, as if he was afraid of being overheard. 'I warned you it was pricey,' he said.

'How much?'

'Six thousand,' King said, as if saying it quickly would make it sound less.

'Six thousand pounds?'

King looked annoyed, as though the challenge was an insult. 'I don't make the rules,' he said, his voice almost petulant. 'Go and talk to the Home Office if you don't like it.'

'How long does it take to go through?'

'Ah,' King said, straightening up and smiling like a salesman who has made an unexpected deal, 'you're serious, then. I shouldn't think it would take long.'

'Could we do it now?'

'Right away? If you like. How would you, ah, be paying?'

'Cash.'

'Yes. Well. That will be just. . . .' He stood up, his voice trailing away, and looked at Hosseyn over the steel rims of his glasses. 'You do realize you'll have to come in and sign the register every now and then, I suppose?' he said sternly.

'No problem,' Hosseyn said. 'No problem at all.'

Three days later Hosseyn began the work he had really come to England to do. Now that he knew he could remain in England as long as he wished, he checked out of the Inn on the Park, moved into a bedsitter in Ealing Common that he rented on a monthly basis through an agency, and began to plan how he was going to kill the first of the men he had been sent to assassinate.

Henry Kitchen was thirty-eight years old. He lived with his wife Kathy and their two children – Deborah, twelve, and Mark, nine – in a 1930's terrace house in Wendell Road, Chiswick. He was a member, presently unassigned, of a Special Branch police unit whose headquarters were in an anonymous-looking building in Northumberland

Avenue, not far from the old Scotland Yard. Hosseyn knew a lot about Henry Kitchen: the results of two months' intensive surveillance were in one of the dossiers that had been delivered to the Inn on the Park the day after Hosseyn arrived in England.

Like most men, Kitchen was a creature of unconscious habit. He went to work by the same route every day, bought his cigarettes at the same newsagent's, parked his car in the identical spot outside his house every night – his wife Kathy, used the garage for her X-registered Fiat 127 – and went to bed most nights at ten-thirty.

Kitchen was a member of his local pub's darts team. Matches were played on Friday nights, one week at home, the next away. His other hobby was gardening; most nights he pottered about in his little greenhouse in the back garden. On Saturday mornings he usually took the kids out somewhere, the Natural History Museum or Greenwich. On the way back he always bought flowers for his wife. Once in a while Kathy Kitchen's mother baby-sat for them and they went out, to see a film or have a meal at a tandoori restaurant. Every Sunday morning, Henry Kitchen washed and waxed his car, a white Vauxhall Cavalier, then went down to the pub with his next-door neighbour, a man named Atherton.

Kathy Kitchen took the kids to school every morning and picked them up every afternoon. Monday, washing. Tuesday, a weekly trip to an osteopath. Wednesday, housework. Every Thursday afternoon she did her shopping at Sainsbury's, and on Friday, visited her mother in Hanwell. It was the work of only a few days to confirm that the Kitchen family's patterns were unchanged, and to make the other arrangements necessary to the successful conclusion of his task.

On the Friday following his arrival in England, Hosseyn left his bedsitter in Ealing Common wearing a tan anorak, faded Levis and Adidas running shoes. In the holdall he was carrying were a twelve-inch steel ruler, a slide hammer, a screwdriver, a pair of rubber gloves, a plastic case containing a hypodermic syringe, and a packet of heavy-duty plastic bin liners. Tucked into the waistband of his jeans under the Marks & Spencer anorak was a British Sterling .357 Magnum.

He looked at his watch, a cheap Japanese LCD that kept impeccable time. It was five-twenty. He crossed over the Uxbridge Road and walked along to Ealing Common station. In Tring Avenue, he used the steel ruler to open the door of a parked Ford Escort, removed the ignition lock with the slide hammer, and switched on the ignition with the screwdriver. He was moving away from the kerb within a minute of approaching the car.

He drove to Chiswick and parked outside Henry Kitchen's house. He looked at his watch: six-thirty. Kitchen would be home any time now. Hosseyn had already established by his departure time that Kitchen was on 'earlies' this week: eight in the morning until five in the afternoon. He got home about ninety minutes later, depending on traffic. Today was Friday. Kathy Kitchen would have picked up the children from school and taken them to see her mother in Hanwell. She would be back around seven.

At six-forty, Kitchen's white Cavalier turned into the road and coasted to a stop. He saw the Ford parked outside his house and pulled in behind it; by about seven it would be gone, and he could park in his own spot. He got out of the car to discover a young, dark-haired man in a tan anorak waiting for him.

'Yes?' he said.

'You see the blue Escort?' Hosseyn said. 'Get in it.'

Kitchen frowned, about to remonstrate. Hosseyn took his hand out of the pocket of his anorak and let the other man see the pistol. Kitchen's eyes widened.

'What's all this about?' he said, hoarsely.

'Shut up!' Hosseyn said. 'And move!'

They walked the few yards to the car. Hosseyn jammed the barrel of the pistol into the man's ribs as Kitchen got into the passenger seat.

'Fasten the seat belt!' he hissed. Kitchen stretched the belt around his body and turned his head to find the

27

mooring. Using his left hand, Hosseyn took from his pocket a hypodermic wrapped in a wad of Kleenex, stuck it into Kitchen's thigh and depressed the plunger. Kitchen recoiled in alarm; his mouth opened as if to call out. Hosseyn put the barrel of the gun on the man's upper lip.

'Don't!' he hissed, and held the gun there for a few moments. Whatever the stuff in the hypodermic was, it acted fast. Kitchen's eyes rolled back, showing the whites; his head lolled. Hosseyn ran around to the driving side and drove off, heading for the A4, the old Great West Road. When he got to Brentford he turned left into Syon Lane, and on south through Isleworth to the Chertsey Road. In another ten minutes he was at the entrance to the Richmond rubbish dump, or to give it its full title, the London Borough of Richmond Council Depot. It was situated in Craneford Way in an angle formed where the Duke of Northumberland's River joined the River Crane from the north.

The entrance to the dump was barred by a metal pole barrier, padlocked to the upright on which it rested. Hosseyn used the jack lever to snap it open, and drove in. It was getting dark; the college playing fields to the north and east were deserted. He parked the car near one of the huge skips, noting with satisfaction that it was about half full with black plastic sacks of rubbish. Kitchen groaned and stirred: he was regaining consciousness. How considerate, Hosseyn thought, with a grim smile.

He got Kitchen out of the car and half dragged, half frogmarched him over to the nearest skip, dumping him flat on the jumbled mess of garbage. He wrestled one of the bin liners over the man's head and shoulders, another up from his feet to his hips. When the entire body was covered, he felt beneath the plastic for Kitchen's head, jammed the muzzle of the revolver against his temple and pulled the trigger. The gun made a flat hard noise. Kitchen's body stiffened briefly and then went limp. Hosseyn clambered out of the skip and got back into the car. He looked around, but there was no one in sight. Easy, he thought, and drove away.

3

Charles Garrett checked the time; it was five to ten, and Bleke was scrupulous about punctuality. He took the lift to the third-floor offices of Diversified Corporate Facilities; there were no stairs in the front of the building. The flush, blank oak doors facing the otherwise empty hall opposite the lifts bore no nameplate. Garrett inserted his keycard into a slot in the wall and waited for the buzzer that signalled clearance.

The security lock clacked open, admitting him to a parqueted hall with a semi-circular desk at the far side. Swing doors to the right and left led to a brightly lit inner foyer; the soft whirr of electronic machinery could be heard. At the desk an athletic-looking security man took a thumbprint, put it in his desktop scanner and waited for the bleep. He knew perfectly well who Garrett was; but at DCF, no chances were taken, no exceptions allowed.

'Thank you, sir,' he said. 'Right-hand door, please.'

When the buzzer sounded, Garrett went through to the inner foyer. There were three doors: one to his left, one to his right and one straight ahead. The left led through to the South Aisle, which housed Administration, Finance and the library. The right-hand corridor led to the North Aisle, on which were Registry, Computers, and the five divisional offices, amongst them his own. Garrett went through the door straight ahead of him. It led into a grey-carpeted corridor with double doors at its far end. There he pushed the buzzer beside the heavy oak doors, standing in the centre of a square set into the carpeting so that the CCTV camera could log his entry.

Once again electronic locks buzzed. He entered an office decorated in muted greys and browns. A bright Hockney swimming pool painting hung on the wall. Beneath the window stood a long leather sofa; beside it was a circular glass table. On the right-hand wall were two doors; between them was a modern L-shaped desk unit with a PC console to the left. Behind it sat Elizabeth James, Bleke's executive assistant.

She was an attractive woman of perhaps forty-five, wearing a houndstooth Jaeger suit and a white shirt. Her blonde hair was greying, but attractively styled, her skin smooth and unlined. She smiled as Garrett came into the room.

'Good morning, Charles,' she said. 'Go right in.'

If anyone had asked him, Garrett could have described every stick of furniture in Nicholas Bleke's office as if each belonged to him personally. A huge desk, placed diagonally in a corner near one of the two large windows looking out over Berkeley Square, dominated the room. Behind it stood a breakfront bookcase; piled into it, every which way but tidy, were government publications and journals, books on criminology and drugs, psychology and law, forensics and ballistics, espionage and foreign affairs. On top of them, between them, and alongside them were stacks of situation and assessment papers, military digests and intelligence reports. It looked untidy and disorganized, but Garrett knew Bleke could almost at once find anything he wanted in his chaotic-looking reference library.

Two leather armchairs stood before the desk. A small dropleaf table at which Bleke often took lunch, a few upright chairs, and an old oak cupboard with some family photographs on top were the only other furniture, except for a harmonium which stood in the far corner of the room. A long time ago, Bleke had discovered that playing Bach aided his mental processes; the old harmonium had followed him from office to office ever since. To the left of the bookcase behind his desk was a door that led into an austere and functional briefing room.

'Sit down, Charles,' Bleke said. He was a short, stockily built man with a large head. His grey-white hair was cut very close to the scalp. His eyes were shrewd and alert, his mouth firm, his jawline resolute. He might have been a high-ranking naval officer, the governor of a public school, the senior consultant in a major hospital; there was about him an air that inspired respect, invited confidences. Garrett took the chair on the right, as he always did, and waited. Bleke had a file on the desk in front of him. The diagonal red stripe told Garrett it was highly restricted.

'This al-Kharran business,' Bleke said, wasting no time on preliminaries. 'Any further developments?'

'I doubt we'll get much more,' Garrett replied. 'We know al-Kharran was born in the Ghor valley in 1959. Came to London as a student in 1981, made a contact at the People's Bureau, sold them names, phone numbers or car registrations of enemies of the State. Low-level stuff. When we kicked them out, he was back on the street.'

'Didn't like working for a living, that it?'

'His ambition was to be a terrorist. He went to Damascus with the idea of getting them to finance him. Quite by coincidence, they had just learned from Washington that Gurney's A-team were going to be travelling to Athens on 17 April, Syria's national day. Al-Kharran was a natural: no record, not even a parking ticket. Just what they wanted: what their intelligence people call a *rifa'at*, a bullet. They took him to the Beka'a Valley, trained him specifically for this one job, promised him a quarter of a million dollars if he pulled it off. They wouldn't have paid him, of course. Probably planned to kill him when it was over.'

'Do we know his control?'

'Yes. His control is Mahmoud Sayeed, a major in air force intelligence. He arranged for Al-Kharran to be given cover as a mechanic with the national airline and posted to London; they do it all the time. Curzon lets them: that way at least they know who to watch. When he arrived in England, they put al-Kharran into the H Section mainframe at Euston Tower and gave him the business: mail, phones, pavement artists, the lot. He did nothing to indicate he was anything other than what he was supposed to be, an airline mechanic, so they put him on a twicer.'

A 'twicer' was a twice weekly check designed principally to watch possible 'sleeper' agents, to confirm that there had been no significant change in the habits, contacts or circumstances of a surveillance subject during the preceding three or four days. The demands on Curzon's resources being what they were, more intensive scrutiny was only undertaken if the subject gave cause for it. There had been no such cause in the case of Hassan al-Kharran.

'He found himself a flat in Paddington, went to work at Heathrow, did all the things he was supposed to do. There was a flurry of excitement when May Logan moved in with him, because she was Irish, but there wasn't so much as a whiff of IRA about her or any of her people. Curzon lost interest.'

'You checked her yourself?'

'Of course. She's just what she says she is.'

'Decent but not very bright.'

'Al-Kharran told her he'd swung a well-paid job with Olympic Airways, a flat in Athens, good money. She was over the moon. Meanwhile one of Sayeed's people, posing as an airline steward, smuggled the explosives in and showed al-Kharran how to rig the bomb. He also brought him ten per cent of the blood money.'

'You recovered that, I trust?'

'Special Branch found most of it in the cousin's flat in Maida Vale. With your approval, Finance will use some of it to make an ex gratia payment to May Logan – turns out she's pregnant.'

'Go ahead,' Bleke said gruffly. 'I gather she's been very cooperative. What about the cousin?'

'He's being very cooperative, too,' Garrett said, with a thin smile. 'But we're not paying him anything.'

Bleke nodded, cleared his throat and looked uncomfortable. Here it comes, Garrett thought.

'I have to tell you that the Met isn't best pleased with you, Charles,' he said. 'I've had a note from the Commissioner. Something on the lines of Maida Vale not being the place to restage the gunfight at the OK Corral. BBC and ITN clamouring for details. Bad for PR.'

'Yes, sir.'

'I told them you had no alternative, but I'd like you to confirm it,' Bleke said. 'Was there no other way?'

Garrett met his chief's eyes. 'Absolutely none,' he said.

32

'Very well,' Bleke said. 'Let's move on. I've got something I want you to look at. Bit outlandish. Come over here.'

He got up and walked across to his luncheon table, bringing with him the security file Garrett had noticed earlier.

'A8 referred this to us,' he said. 'I want you to take a look at it.' A8 was the counterterrorism arm of the Metropolitan Police. Garrett's interest sharpened. 'Special Branch have lost some of their people,' Bleke continued. 'It's bothering them.'

Special Branch is the executive arm of the security services, none of which has even so much as powers of arrest. An élite force within each regional police force, the main duty of Special Branch is defined as 'the preservation of the Queen's Peace'. For that purpose SB gathers information about threats to public order, espionage, terrorism, sabotage and subversion; its officers are empowered to act as armed personal protection for persons at risk.

The London Metropolitan Police Special Branch numbers about four hundred officers, of who about eighty are normally engaged on port duties at Heathrow and Gatwick airports, and a further sixty or seventy on personal-protection duties which include guarding domestic and visiting VIPs during their public appearances in the United Kingdom and abroad. If the Queen goes to a film premiere, MPSB is there; if the British ambassador to France attends a ceremony at the tomb of the Unknown Warrior, MPSB carries the wreath; if the Home Secretary visits the scene of an IRA bomb outrage, Special Branch are responsible for making sure he is not the victim of another.

'What were the circumstances?'

'The details are in the dossier. Four men missing, apparently. Good men, men who knew their jobs. Lifted off the street like rent boys. One of them was found on a rubbish tip in Richmond. Another out in Buckinghamshire, and so on. Same MO, by the look of it.'

'Four of them?'

'Exactly. If it were one or two, I'd leave it to the Yard. But four: it smells, Charles. It smells to high heaven.'

'It's a bit bizarre, I'll grant you,' Garrett commented. 'But what's it got to do with us?'

He had the highest regard for Bleke's intuition, but he was reluctant to commit his time and energies to something Special Branch were perfectly capable of handling themselves. Garrett's job was counterterrorism: finding its perpetrators, infiltrating their organizations, neutralizing their plans. The movements of Iranian killer squads, the forward plans of IRA terrorists, the activities of well-known organizations like Action Directe and Abu Nidal and the lesser known ones like the Islamic Jihad and The Call, these were what he was interested in. He had no desire to play Hercule Poirot, and even less inclination to commit PACT to it.

The PACT organization was only a few years old, but it already had a number of significant successes under its belt. It was born immediately subsequent to the bombing of the Grand Hotel, Brighton, in October 1984, when the IRA nearly succeeded in assassinating Margaret Thatcher and most of her Cabinet. A high-level secret meeting to review the government's security and counterterrorism capabilities had been called at Chequers.

Among those present were the Home Secretary; the heads of the Security Services, DI5 and DI6; the coordinator of intelligence and security at the Foreign Office; a representative of the Joint Intelligence Chiefs; the Deputy Assistant Commissioner in charge of Special Branch; the Commissioner of Metropolitan Police; the President of the Association of Chief Police Officers; and the Colonel Commandant of the Special Air Services Regiment.

The result of their weekend deliberations was the establishment of a new executive, designated PACT – Punitive Actions, Counter-Terrorism. Working in close cooperation not only with British law-enforcement and security agencies, but also the Europolice network TREVI, its special brief would be to detect, counter and neutralize, using any means at its disposal, the planners and perpetrators of terrorist strikes and political assassinations.

It was implicit that the phrase 'by any means' meant quite literally what it said.

In January 1985, a front company, Diversified Corporate Facilities, was established; its offices were in Lonsdale House, Berkeley Square, a Ministry of Defence building situated within walking distance of DI5 headquarters in Curzon Street. Early in February, Brigadier Nicholas Bleke, a senior officer in K-7, the counter-espionage arm of DI5, was appointed its Chief Executive Officer and, ex officio, Director of PACT.

It was the Prime Minister's wish – which was the same as a directive – that Bleke be given carte blanche in his selection of personnel; she had the highest regard for this dedicated and ruthless spycatcher. Bleke knew exactly what was wanted and exactly the kind of men he would need. He begun by calling in from Registry the service jackets of the men who would become his executive officers: Harry Loeb, the best financial man at Curzon Street House; Tom Ashley, a computer genius at the Royal Armaments R & D Establishment in Chertsey, whose job it would be to set up the links between PACT and the TREVI computers in West Germany. There were others; but the most important of them all was a man Bleke had himself recruited into the service a decade earlier, and whose career he had discreetly promulgated: Charles Garrett.

He was aware that there were those who thought Garrett a burnt-out case after his experiences in Ulster, but Bleke knew his man better than that. Garrett had been at the sharp end before: in Aden, then Beirut, and later, Berlin. He had always come back. When he received Garrett's service jacket, Bleke was surprised to learn that Garrett was on secondment to Special Branch. The DI5 notation preceding this posting – 'Special Duties, Ulster' – gave no hint what Garrett had been through there. After six months' compassionate leave, he had been placed in charge of training operatives for security work in Ulster. It made sense – anyone being sent undercover in Northern Ireland needed the best training he could get, and Garrett's experiences there qualified him better than most to give it — but it was a waste of the man's considerable abilities.

What was more likely, Bleke concluded, was that upon his return to duty Garrett had been too outspoken for the liking of some Curzon Street mandarin: he had a reputation for being 'difficult', and of not caring a damn about whose toes he trod on. Neither did Bleke; it ought to make them a good team, he thought. If PACT was going to succeed in its job, it was going to need men who could play rough and dirty; and nobody played rougher, or dirtier, than Garrett when the chips were down.

'Well, Charles?' he asked now, gauging Garrett's reaction from the expression in his eyes. 'You think I'm wasting your time, don't you?'

Garrett avoided answering directly by asking a question of his own. 'You really think we ought to take an interest in this, sir?'

'Read the dossier,' Bleke said. 'Then tell me what you think. My nose is itching, Charles. I could be wrong, of course.'

I have my faults, but being wrong isn't one of them. Diana had bought a poster of a charging rhinoceros and tacked it to the kitchen door. He laughed when he saw it.

'What's that for?' he said.

'Just so you understand,' she told him. 'No more Mrs Nice Wife. This is the new, no-nonsense me.'

'What was wrong with the old, no-nonsense you?'

'She always let you win.' He saw the shine of tears in her eyes.

'Hey,' he said softly. 'You're serious.'

'Get us out of here, Garrett,' she said. 'Get us out of this hellhole.'

'I can't leave now. It's taken too long to set up. We've almost got them, Di. A few more weeks . . .'

'I hate this place,' she said vehemently. 'I hate its narrow streets and its narrow minds. I want to go home.'

'So does every boy in battledress,' Garrett agreed. 'But they don't have a choice. And neither do we.'

'You,' she said. 'You don't have a choice. But I do.'

Better not start thinking about that again. He took the

file and went out of Bleke's office via the Conference Room, which debouched on to the North Aisle, another brightly lit corridor. Outside each of the offices lining it was a metal slot with a card showing the name and rank of the occupant, and whether he or she was on duty or off. At the end of the corridor was Garrett's office.

It was a functional room, with few personal touches: no pictures on the wall, no photographs on the desk. Just filing cabinets, a Fax machine, a whisper telex and an IBM PC. A pair of louvre doors concealed a small dressing room and shower; in it, on a low table, stood a Braun coffee machine. Garrett opened the coffee tin, savouring the rich, dark aroma of the beans he bought fresh each week at the Algerian Coffee Shop in Soho. He got the Moulinex grinder out of the bathroom cabinet, put the beans into it, and ground them medium fine. He put enough water for eight cups into the machine, emptied the ground coffee into the filter and switched on. After a few minutes the sharp tang of fresh coffee filled his office.

He filled his Liverpool FC souvenir mug and added a spoonful of sugar, then took the coffee to his desk, where he opened the dossier Bleke had given him and began reading. A young computer analyst at New Scotland Yard had done an AKF (All Known Facts) dossier on the missing officers, combining material from the spread of information available in their APD (All Personal Details) and AKA (All Known Associates) files, and mainframed them together with details of all assignments, postings, even holidays, looking for common denominators. There were a number: all, for instance, had at one time or another been an escort to the Princess Royal, holidayed in France, worked in America. Whether there was anything significant about these facts was another matter. Generally speaking, computers were like accountants: what they told you was a hundred per cent accurate and a hundred per cent useless.

More interesting to Garrett was the fact that each of the bodies had been found stripped naked, every stitch of clothing and all personal possessions removed. To what purpose? Did the assassin think the police might put the killings down to robbery? If you killed a man, you might steal his watch and his wallet: but his clothes?

'See what you can come up with,' Bleke had said. Thanks a bundle, Chief. Garrett picked up the phone and dialled the unlisted number that would put him straight through to Jessica Goldman.

'Spring is here,' he said, when she answered. 'Why doesn't my heart go dancing?'

'Is that a serious question?' she said. Her voice was low-pitched, almost throaty.

'It was to Larry Hart,' Garrett said. 'Are you free for dinner?'

'I can be. Why?'

'I am in desperate need of counselling,' Garrett said. 'Is there any chance you could help me?'

'Who is this again?'

'How quickly they forget. Suppose I mention charisma, charm, rugged masculine good looks?'

'Ah,' she said, and he could hear her smiling. 'Robert Redford.'

'Close,' Garrett said. 'About dinner. Seven-thirty at the Connaught?'

'The Connaught?'

'Impressed, huh?'

'In a pig's eye,' she said inelegantly. 'You must want something pretty badly.'

'That's just your way of telling me I'm irresistible, isn't it?' Garrett said, and hung up before Jessica could reply. He picked the phone up again and called the Connaught to reserve a table. That done, he turned back to the dossier on the missing policemen. The first body to be found was that of Detective Constable Henry Kitchen, thirty-eight. It was discovered lying half-buried among the sacks of rubbish in the Richmond council depot at Craneford Way, Twickenham. He had been shot through the head: a .357 magnum, according to the police surgeon. The postmortem also revealed traces of a psychotropic substance in the bloodstream, suggesting Kitchen had been drugged before he was killed. There were no other clues, no witnesses. Nothing.

The second body, that of DC Leslie Garvey, thirty-five, was found four days later. He had left his home in Muswell Hill at the usual time on a Friday morning, but had never arrived at the office. When MPSB made its routine check with Garvey's wife she was unable to offer even a suggestion as to where he might have gone. At the end of the day she had telephoned to report that he had not returned home, and he was posted Absent Unexplained. Kathy Kitchen, wife of Detective Constable Henry Kitchen had also reported that same evening that her husband had not arrived home from work.

Ten days after Garvey's body was discovered, yet another naked body was found on a council rubbish tip just off the A413 near Amersham in Buckinghamshire. The finder was an old lady who had gone there very early to get rid of her sherry bottles while no one was around. The body was identified as that of yet another Special Branch officer, Mark Howell. He appeared to have been killed with the same pistol, and traces of the same drug were found in his body.

By now MPSB was in some disarray, because yet another of its officers had gone missing, this time Ralph Leverett, a thirty-two-year-old sergeant whose home was in West Norwood. Like the others, he had left his home – a maisonette in Gipsy Road – and disappeared without trace. Leverett had a happy family life, no financial worries and a good service record. It was eight days before his body was found on the council tip next to the Leyton Orient football ground. The manner of his death was identical to the others: the same gunshot wound in the head, the same drug in the bloodstream, and the same complete absence of clues or witnesses.

'All right,' Garrett said to himself grimly. 'What the hell were they killed for?' Revenge? Hardly likely: not one of them had ever killed in the line of duty; none had served consecutively with any other. The R2 computer analysts at Euston Tower had covered all that. Grudge? The same rules applied: the analysts had checked the caseload dossiers of all four officers through the VAX computer at Hendon looking for just such common denominators. Apart from coincidences of posting, there were none.

They why kill them?

'Shooters?' Garrett said to himself. MPSB officers were armed with the standard .38 Smith and Wesson used throughout the police force. He keyed question after question into the PC, getting negative after negative reply. None of the officers had been armed at the time of his death: their weapons had been found at, and since removed from, their homes. Garrett frowned angrily. There had to be something; but what, *what?*

He was no nearer an answer when he left the office and walked across Berkeley Square and up into Carlos Place. He was very fond of the Connaught. After he was shown to his table in the restaurant, Garrett ordered a bottle of Clos du Chêne Marchand, sipping a glass while he waited. Jessica was never late.

She turned heads as she walked in. Although she was not by any means a conventional beauty, she stood out in any company, a tall, willowy woman with a tumbling mane of black hair and lustrous eyes. Her face was thin; high cheekbones made her look more Arabic than Jewish. She was wearing a three-quarter-length navy blue double-breasted wool and cashmere jacket with brass buttons over a boldly striped blouse and plain woollen skirt. Her smile was a miracle.

'This is an unexpected pleasure,' she said. 'Or am I being optimistic?'

'I thought you deserved a break from my cooking.'

'Your cooking is fine.'

'Man wants to show off once in a while.'

'You look tired.'

'Hard day at the office.'

'Doing what?'

'The usual.'

'In other words, mind your own business.'

'Isn't that what you do at Kelvin House?'

She smiled; and he felt the same sudden attraction that he always felt; as always, it took him just a little bit by surprise. The wine waiter came over and poured some wine into Jessica's glass.

'Who taught you about wine, Garrett?' she asked.

'Ernest Hemingway,' he replied. 'Are you hungry?'

They ordered cold pâté of turbot with a lobster sauce to start, followed by noisettes of lamb cooked in the house style with fresh broccoli and sauté potatoes. While they were eating the fish, Garrett asked the wine waiter to open the bottle of the '82 Siran.

'I thought you secret service types only ate at the Mirabelle and drank cheap whisky,' Jessica said.

'Nah,' Garrett said. 'Some of us got clarse, en't we?'

'Don't ask me,' Jessica grinned. 'This Sancerre is good.'

'Wait till you try the Margaux.'

'Why are you being so good to me?'

'I want to pick your brain.'

'Aha. The ulterior motive emerges.'

'No such thing as a free lunch, my dear,' Garrett grinned. 'Tell me, what's new at CME?'

Jessica Goldman worked as a psychotherapeutic guidance counsellor at the Ministry of Defence Central Medical Establishment in Cleveland Street. What exactly she did there he was unsure. At the time of their first meeting, over dinner at Bleke's house in Ebury Street, she had evaded conversation about her work by saying that it was confidential all the time and classified most of it. He kept on intending to check her file in Registry but he had never got round to it. Maybe he knew why.

'Oh, the usual,' she said. 'Behavioural problems, mostly.'

'Can you answer a question for me?'

'Officially or unofficially?'

'I can make it official if you want me to. I just need to know whether you've had any Special Branch officers in recently. As clients.'

'Has this got anything to do with the four who were murdered?'

'This fish is good.'

'You want me to talk, but you won't, is that it?'

'How did you hear about the murders? There's been nothing in the papers.'

She shrugged. 'The autopsies were done at Kelvin. You hear things. Why are you interested?'

'I'm puzzled. It's like one of those damned silly riddles, where you know there's a simple answer but you just can't figure out what it is. Who would want to kidnap four Specials, kill them, steal all their clothes, and leave them to rot on a garbage dump?'

'Is that what is known as a rhetorical question?'

'Okay, okay, never mind who for a moment. Why would do just as well.'

'There could be a dozen reasons. Why are you asking me all this?'

'Bleke has asked me to take a look at the case.'

'Bleke,' she said, and there was a lot more in the word than one syllable.

'Let's not start on that.'

'We'll have to one day, you know.'

'Fine,' he said, just a thread of anger in his voice. 'But not now. Right now I need a break on this case.'

'If you really want me to help, I need to know a lot more than I do at the moment,' Jessica said.

'There isn't all that much to tell.'

'You're hedging,' she said. 'Don't you trust me yet?'

'Of course I do.'

'I wonder.'

'That's not fair,' he said.

'Who said it had to be?'

'Tough, huh?' Garrett said, breaking the mood with a grin.

'Not tough,' she said. 'Honest. I'm thirty-two years of age, happily divorced, financially independent. I don't have to take dishonesty any more from anyone. And I won't. Especially not from you.'

'You think I'm a liar?' he said.

'A lot of men are,' she said, and for a moment vulnerability showed through the self-sufficiency. They paused while the waiters did their performance with the serving dishes and the wine. They talked little as they ate. The Margaux was splendid, fragrant and perfumed. Come to that, he thought, so was Jessica Goldman. There was no strain to the silence. Jessica was one of those rare women who did not feel the need to make conversation. She ate with an evident pleasure that Garrett found equally pleasing.

'Look,' she said finally. 'I understand. It's the world you live in, the things you have to do to live in it. I know there are rules you have to obey. But they don't apply to me, Charles.'

'You're right, Jess,' he said, 'and I'm wrong. I'm sorry.'

She smiled forgiveness; but she had not forgotten, he knew. Well, that was something he understood. It had been the same with Diana. There was always a part of yourself you kept locked away. It was difficult to open that door; and the longer it stayed locked, the wider grew the void that even love could not bridge. He knew that now, knew that if he was to avoid ending up just another burnt-out case, he must trust Jessica; but that didn't make it any easier. The journey of a thousand miles begins with one step, he thought. Just make sure you're pointing in the right direction before you take it.

Over coffee, he outlined what was known about the four murders.

'The only common denominators look irrelevant,' he said, at the end of his exposition. 'All of them had been posted to Germany and the States at one time or another. In each case their bodies were found stripped naked on rubbish dumps. There doesn't appear to be anything else to go on.'

'It can't just be because they were policeman,' Jessica said. 'It has to be something else.'

'The computer boys have tried every combination known to man and modern science,' Garrett told her. 'There just isn't anything.'

'You say you've tried everything else and it didn't work. But there must be something you've missed.'

'I know,' he said. 'That's what's driving me mad.'

'Could it be something so obvious you haven't even considered it, Charles?'

'Like what?'

'Well . . . could they have been killed specifically because of what they were? Is there something unique to Special Branch officers, something no other policemen have?'

Garrett froze, his coffee cup halfway to his mouth.

'Jessica Goldman,' he said softly. 'You are a bloody genius.'

4

In the six weeks he had been in England, the man who called himself Hosseyn had lived at five different addresses. It was quite easy to find accommodation as long as you were prepared to pay the small fortune demanded by the crooks who rented such places for the cheap curtains and threadbare carpets they called 'furnishings and fittings', or that other illicit game they played called 'key money'. Hosseyn cheerfully signed leases, made agreements, paid deposits, whatever they wanted. He knew he was never going to see any of them a second time.

There had been no mention of the killings in the newspapers; this had puzzled him at first until he remembered the English system of censorship, called 'D-notices', by means of which the government suppressed news it did not wish published. The serial murder of four Special Branch officers would certainly qualify under that heading.

With the disposal of the fourth target, Leverett, Hosseyn's assignment was ended. He put the passport with which he had entered the country into a Jiffy bag with the Sterling pistol and dropped the package into the Thames. Then he went to a call box and phoned the contact number on the 245 exchange that he had been given before he left Iraq.

'This is Ibrahim,' he said. 'It is finished.'

'No difficulties?'

'None whatsoever.'

'You have disposed of the hardware?'

'And the software.'

'Have you any other requirements?'

'Payment.'

'Of course. Return to where you were before. A room will be reserved for you.'

After he made the call, Hosseyn went back to the place he had rented, a two-roomed flatlet on the ground floor of a block in Anerley Park. It was as bare now as the day he had moved in. His clothes hung on wire hangers from a length of rope he had strung across the room. He packed them all into a cheap suitcase and put on his only decent clothes, the anorak and trousers he had bought when he first arrived. He walked out of the place without a backward glance, putting the keys through the letterbox of the old biddy who acted as a sort of caretaker. Give the old cow something to do, he thought.

He walked up to the High Street and bought a bottle of Glenfiddich at an off-licence, then took a taxi to the West End. He checked into the Inn on the Park, collecting the package that had been left for him at the desk. In the room, he opened it to find it contained an Egyptian passport, the Immigration entry stamp dated five days earlier, a one-way club class ticket to Cairo on British Airways Flight BA 157 dated three days hence, and an envelope containing fifty twenty-pound notes. He put the passport and ticket into his inside pocket, then folded the money into two bundles, one going into each of his jacket pockets. Then he left the hotel to do some shopping.

He spent a couple of hours in Simpson's and Fortnum's, returning to the hotel with a seersucker jacket, a pair of trousers, four sports shirts, two sets of Jockey underwear, four pairs of socks, a pair of Nike shoes, a towelling bathrobe, a Braun electric razor, Aramis preshave and aftershave, shampoo and bath oil, a comb, hairbrush and nail clippers, two toothbrushes, and a tube of toothpaste. He was humming as he took the lift up to his room.

When he got to the room, he ran a bath and put some of the bath oil into it. While it was running, he called Starlight Escorts. He asked them to send someone younger this time. He bathed lazily, then shaved, patting Aramis on his face afterwards. Then he put on the towelling robe, switched on the television set, put some ice cubes into a glass and poured himself a drink, watching the news programmes without interest until the door buzzer sounded. The girl had shoulder-length blonde hair, blue eyes, and skin like a baby. She looked about fourteen.

'Mr Hosseyn?'

'Come in,' he said. His voice felt thick in his throat. Just the sight of her excited him. 'You want a drink?'

'Yer, why not?' she said. She was wearing a black leather mini skirt and a tight sleeveless bodice with three buttons at the front. She took off her coat and stood with her legs apart. He felt another giant throb of lust.

'Turn around,' he said. She turned. Her buttocks were firm, high and tight. She saw what he was looking at and grinned at him over her shoulder.

'Doggies, is it?' she said. He nodded, unable to speak. She flipped the skirt off and tossed it to one side. She was not wearing panties. She walked across the room towards the bed and climbed on to it on her hands and knees, pulling the pillow from beneath the counterpane and laying her head on it.

'Well,' she said. 'What you waiting for, darlin'?'

He ran at her like a lemming at a cliff.

At eleven the next morning, Hosseyn's phone rang. He was still in bed, eating breakfast. He frowned.

'Hello?'

'Ibrahim?'

'Who is this?'

'This is Sayeed. Your payment is ready.'

'How do I collect it?'

'Check out of the hotel. Be at the corner of Seymour Place and Marylebone Road at one o'clock this afternoon. A blue BMW will pick you up.'

'What—'

The connection was already broken. Hosseyn banged the phone on the cradle irritably and got out of bed. He poured some more coffee and walked across to the window. It was a bright, sunny morning. He got dressed, shaved, then called down to tell the desk he was checking out. He put his possessions into the Simpsons bag, checked the drawers and closet to make sure he had not overlooked anything, then looked at his watch. Already past midday. He went down to the desk, paid his bill in cash, and left. The doorman saluted him into a taxi and he told the driver to take him to the rendezvous. He got there at exactly twelve-fifty.

At one o'clock a blue BMW 525 injection slid to the kerb. He opened the passenger door. The driver was a young man with black hair and swarthy skin. He had never seen him before in his life.

'You have something for me?'

'On the seat,' the driver said, indicating a flat brown package about the size of a shoebox. Hosseyn reached for it. The driver put his hand on it.

'Sayeed wants to see you,' he said.

'Where is he?'

'A safe house, outside London.'

'Why didn't he come himself?'

'Get in,' the driver said. 'Put your bag in the back.'

Hosseyn got into the car, frowning. 'What does he want to see me about?' he asked.

The driver shrugged, concentrating on the traffic. They sped along Westway and through Acton, heading west on the A40. The drab suburbs of London all looked identical to Hosseyn. They passed an airport of some kind and he asked the driver what it was.

'Northolt,' the man said. He did not speak again until they reached Beaconsfield, where he swung off the motorway. They passed through the old town with its half-timbered frontages and furniture shops, then turned left down a suburban road. Hosseyn saw a sign that said 'Egypt', and then they were whipping along a winding lane between high banks that shut out the light. Then the lane widened and they entered a heavily forested area. Hosseyn began to feel uneasy.

'Not long now,' the driver said, as if sensing Hosseyn's nervousness. After about another mile or so, he pulled into an unmarked opening and followed an unmade road that curved between the trees.

'Where are we?' Hosseyn asked.

'This is rear entrance to the embassy safe house,' the driver said. 'You can see it through the trees.'

He stopped the car and got out. Hosseyn followed suit. He started to say something as the driver came round the car. Instead, his mouth fell open in silent terror. The driver had a silenced automatic pistol in his hand. He pointed it at Hosseyn. It looked like a cannon.

'No!' Hosseyn shouted, putting his hands out in front of his body as if by doing so he could somehow stop the bullet hitting him. The gun made its coughing bark. The bullet took off the tip of Hosseyn's left index finger, then drove through his forehead just left of the median line and above the left eyebrow, turning him sideways to fall in a crumpled heap on his left side. He kicked once or twice, dying almost immediately.

The driver, whose name was Nidal Faour, took off his jacket and threw it into the car. He opened the trunk of the car and brought out a pair of rubberized sailing trousers, a matching jacket and a pair of rubber gloves, all of which he put on. Then he lifted a flat steel toolbox out of the boot. He laid a four-foot-square sheet of clear plastic on the ground and weighted down the corners with rocks.

He went over to where the dead man lay and methodically went through his pockets, removing the airline ticket, the passport and the money, which he tossed into the BMW. Then he dragged Hosseyn's body on to the plastic. Using a Sabatier chef's knife, he swiftly and efficiently cut off the dead man's clothing, stuffing it into a large plastic bin liner. That done, Nidal took a hacksaw and a blowtorch from the toolbox. Having lit the blowtorch and laid it to one side, he picked up the heavy steel knife and stolidly began work. He started with the head.

At about ten o'clock that night, after several stops en route, Nidal Faour reached Portsmouth. He drove to the Brittany Ferries terminal, where he bought an overnight ticket for the eleven-thirty sailing to Caen. When he left the blue BMW in the car hold, he was carrying a cheap plastic grip. He took it directly to the cabin he had booked, stowing it in the cupboard there and locking the door. Then he went up to the restaurant and had a sandwich and some coffee. He stayed in the restaurant until around two in the morning, by which time the ship had reached the middle of the English Channel. Then he went down to the cabin, took the bag from the locker and went back up on deck. Checking carefully that there was no one around to see him, he lifted the bag over the rail and dropped it into the sea. It sank without a sound.

When the ship docked at Ouistreham next morning, Nidal drove off in the blue BMW and headed for the Caen *périphérique*. There was little traffic so early in the morning, and he had a fast run on the Autoroute Normande to Paris, 240 kilometres away. When he reached the capital, he headed for an hotel in the twentieth arrondissement. The BMW was taken away; resprayed, with new plates and papers, it was resold ten days later to a textile manufacturer's representative in Düsseldorf.

Leila was waiting for him in an upstairs room that smelled of perfume. He had forgotten how beautiful she was.

'Well?' she said.

He nodded. 'It is done.'

'They are all dead?'

'Every one. Just as we planned it. Tomorrow I will go to Frankfurt. Then it will be finished.'

'Come,' she said. 'Come to me.'

She took him to the bed and made him lie face down while she knelt astride him, strong hands massaging his back and neck muscles, the base of his spine, his buttocks and thighs, until he could stand it no more and he turned over and reached up for her. She eeled alongside him, taking him in both hands, her tongue flickering against his flesh like a taunt. Then she swung astride him again, moving the soft wetness of herself against his hardness, lifting herself so that he arched his body upwards to remain in warm succulent contact with her, and then her eyes widened and she made a guttural sound deep in her throat and sank down hard upon him and he cried out aloud in ecstasy and surrender.

5

His phone rang. Garrett had no secretary; there was no need to screen the few people who knew his personal number.

'Tony Dodgson here. Have you got a moment?'

'Of course, Tony.'

Dodgson was the head of A8, the counter-terrorist arm of the Metropolitan Police, with whom Garrett's organization worked in close cooperation. He was, to Garrett's way of thinking, one of the very best coppers on the force.

'We've run across something that might interest you,' Dodgson said. 'Want to come over?'

'Can you tell me what you've got?'

'We've got a headless male body. Hands and feet amputated. All identifying scars burned off, probably with a blowtorch. Somebody's gone to a lot of trouble to make sure we don't find out who he is.'

'No personal possessions?'

'The corpse was naked.'

'How long dead?'

'About a week. Someone walking a dog found it in a wood in Surrey. I'll tell you about that when I see you.'

'What makes you think we'd be interested?'

'Forensic think he's Middle Eastern. Normally I'd say so what, but this one is intriguing. We can't get any sort of a lead on him at all.'

'Tried the embassies?'

'First thing we thought of. Nobody's lost any Arabs. Not the Syrians, not the Lebanese, the Egyptians, Israelis, Jordanians, Iranians, Iraqis, Bahrainis, Kuwaitis or anyone else.'

'Go on.'

'This isn't a mad axeman job. Whoever cut this fellow up knew what he was doing, and you know as well as I do that when somebody goes to those lengths to prevent identification, it's not your run-of-the-mill domestic.'

'So: you've got a dead Middle Eastern man somebody doesn't want identified, and nobody wants to know about him. What else have you got?'

'We put out a request for information on that Sue Cook programme on TV.'

'Crimewatch.'

'There wasn't much to go on, but I think we've got something. A woman in Farnham Common saw two men who looked like Arabs in a car in Burnham, going into the drive of a house owned by Arabs which she knew was unoccupied. She went in to check. Apparently she talked to one of the men, who said he had dropped off a friend. He put her at her ease, and drove off on his own. She didn't think any more about it until she saw the *Crimewatch* item.'

'I don't see the connection yet.'

'You will. The woman had the car registration number. We checked: it was a rental, and it's ten days overdue.'

'Ah. That sounds a bit more interesting.'

'That's what I said.'

'You're checking ports and ferries?'

'Should have an answer any time now.'

'I'll come over. I've got to do something first. Half-past four suit you?'

'See you then,' Dodgson said, and hung up.

Garrett's next stop was the Foreign Office library, where he talked to a sharply intelligent young Arab girl who had formerly worked in B4, the press section of DI6. Her name was Suheila Zhamir, and her job was to manage the team of readers who daily gutted every single newspaper published in the Arab world. It was an enormous task, which Suheila managed with great panache. She was about forty, although her dark eyes and smooth skin could have been those of a woman half her age. She listened attentively as Garrett told her what he was looking for, her head cocked to one side like an intelligent bird, the bright dark eyes shining.

'There was something in *Haaretz* a few weeks ago,' she said. 'Or was it *As-Shiraa*? One of them, anyway. Something to do with selective killings. Hold on, I'll find it.'

She went away; Garrett scanned a copy of the Israeli paper *Davar* while he was waiting. Its headlines screamed the details of the assassination of Khalil al-Wazir, the PLO leader know as Abu Jihad, 'father of the Holy War', killed in his blue and white Tunis villa some weeks ago. An inevitable death, Garrett thought: it wasn't the first time that Shin Bet had sent their killers after Jihad. By all accounts it had been a textbook operation: the man had never had a chance.

Suheila came back with a large leatherette-bound book; in it were headline digests of articles which had appeared in the Middle Eastern press, cross-referenced by subject, by country, by source, and by the names of those mentioned in the stories. Using this, Garrett could call up on the microfilm reader any article which had appeared within the last decade. He remained in the library for over an hour, searching for any hint of a clue. When he was finished, he took a taxi up to Tottenham Court Road.

Tony Dodgson was a tall, thin man in his mid forties, with thinning brown hair and large, soulful brown eyes. Although he had been in London for as long as Garrett could remember, there was still a trace of his native Dorset in Dodgson's voice. His office was on the second floor of the station, a cluttered cream and green painted room that always reminded Garrett of a children's hospital ward. All that was missing was the toys.

'Hello, Pat,' Dodgson said. Tony was a bit of a western movie buff. Calling Garrett by the name of the sheriff who had killed Billy the Kid in 1881 was a small levity which Garrett had long since ceased to notice. 'Want some tea? Somethin' stronger?'

'Nothing, thanks. Anything new?'

'We've nailed the car. It was rented by someone who called himself Alexander Duval. French passport and driving licence. Brittany Ferries clocked it leaving on the night ferry from Southampton to Caen last Friday.'

'Kiss that goodbye, then,' Garrett said. 'He could be anywhere in Europe by now.'

'It's the French passport that interested me,' Dodgson said. 'The lady in Farnham Common insisted he was an Arab, and the photofit she did certainly looks that way.'

'Algerian, maybe,' Garrett said.

'The house is owned by a man named Hatem al-Sisi,' Dodgson said. 'He's an Iraqi businessman. DI5 have an interest.'

'Do they, indeed?'

'This al-Sisi is apparently a front man for the PLO. They use the place as a safe house.'

'And Alexander Duval would have had to know that,' Garrett mused. 'So what we have now is Duval taking someone out to the safe house, killing him there – where was the body found, by the way?'

'Micheldever Wood,' Dodgson said.

'Smack bang on the M3.'

'Main route to Southampton.'

'It fits,' Garrett said. 'Duval kills him, dumps the torso in Surrey, and exits via Southampton.'

'Dropping all the bits of our mystery man into the Channel en route,' Dodgson said gloomily. 'I know.'

'So what have we got here?' Garrett said. 'An unidentified Middle Eastern male who nobody claims, nobody misses. What looks like a professional hit. What's your theory?'

'I haven't got one. I thought you might have.'

'I might, at that.'

'Sit down,' Dodgson said. 'Talk to me.'

'I think there's an operation underway,' Garrett said. 'I don't know what it is, but I've got the faintest smell of a scenario. Let me try it out on you and see if it sets off any bells.'

'Fire away,' the detective said.

'Special Branch loses four officers,' Garrett began. 'All very efficiently murdered. Same MO each time: abducted on the street near their homes, drugged, taken to a municipal dump somewhere in London, shot once in the head with a .357 Magnum, stripped naked. All their possessions and personal effects removed from the scene of crime. No witnesses, no leads, no nothing.'

'Correct. Your conclusion?'

'They were killed for their warrant cards.'

'How do you work that out?'

'There was no common denominator at all, yet I knew there had to be one. I was talking to someone, a friend. She said, what if the reason they were killed was because they were Special Branch officers? I checked. The first two killed didn't have their warrant cards on them.'

'So it could just as easily have been three. Or seven?'

'That's my guess.'

'Let's suppose you're right, and someone killed them for their ID. Why?'

'That's what I wanted to know. Now all of a sudden we've got a headless, handless, footless torso, probably Middle Eastern.'

'Ah,' Dodgson said. 'Now I'm receiving you. You think Abdul might be the killer?'

'Abdul?'

'It's the name we've given to our mystery man. But if Abdul was hired to kill the Specials, why kill Abdul?'

'It's the way some Middle Eastern minds work. Let's say there's a "they" out there who are setting up a terrorist hit. Whatever they're planning to do, they need Special Branch ID cards. They send in a hit man. He kills four officers, then reports in: I've got what you want. They say, well done, go to rendezvous X, someone will be waiting. Let's call that someone Alexander Duval. His job is to get rid of the assassin and make sure he's never identified. That accounts for the butcher's shop job. When he's done that, he takes the head and the hands, buried them, or drops them overboard in the Channel somewhere.'

'All right, let's follow this through,' Dodgson said, leaning forward, elbows on the desk, chin on hands. 'We're them, whoever they are. We've got our warrant cards, we've killed our killer. What are we doing it for?'

'I don't know, Tony. I'm groping around in the dark.'

'But somebody somewhere is shaping up to play naughty games?'

Garrett smiled. 'I sometimes think practically everybody in the bloody world is shaping up to play naughty games, as you so charmingly put it.'

'Have you got anyone particular in mind?'

'I did some research before I came over here, checking out the possibilities,' Garrett said. 'I hate to tell you this, but there are a hell of a lot of them.'

'Make my day,' Dodgson said. 'Tell me about them.'

'Well, to begin with there's our friend the Ayatollah,' Garrett said. 'God knows, it's almost impossible to predict what he'll get up to next. At last report he was sending out assassination squads to infiltrate European capitals. A new campaign to eliminate dissidents abroad.'

'Good sources?'

'Very good.'

'They say anything about London?'

'Nothing specific. Indications are that the targets are in Germany, France and possibly Sweden.'

'Has TREVI got it?'

'Of course.'

'There aren't too many Iranians in the UK,' Dodgson said reflectively. 'We keep an eye on most of them. In fact, the Home Office is making me an up-to-date list right now.'

'Then there's the Syrians. But they're pretty quiet at the moment.'

'Especially since the al-Kharran business.'

'That's why we do it the way we do.'

'I know. But keep it off-street next time, okay?'

'Right,' Garrett said. 'I'll ask them nicely if they'd please only carry guns in places where shooting them won't embarrass the Commissioner.'

'You do go out of your way to be loveable, don't you?' Dodgson said.

'I know,' Garrett agreed. 'It's a habit I've got. Tell me,

are there any high-ups coming to London in the not too distant?'

'You mean Middle Eastern high-ups?' Dodgson said. 'Not that I know of. The Iron Lady isn't mad about Islam.'

'No state visits, no high-level conferences?'

'I can check,' Dodgson said. 'But I can't think of anything offhand that would be big enough to attract terrorist attention.'

'I don't know that that's any criterion,' Garrett said. 'But I suppose it will have to do.'

'All right, Pat, cards on the table,' Dodgson said. 'Who do you think is behind this?'

'My money's on the Palestinians.'

'Why?'

'The Irish are keeping a low profile. They've been taking a lot of punishment, and they're very much preoccupied since Gibraltar, trying to find the mole who's giving us our information. The Palestinians are different. I've got a gut feeling that something's brewing there. In the wake of the Abu Jihad killing.'

'I read about that. You think they'll retaliate?'

'It's called a "punitive response" these days,' Garrett told the detective. 'And the answer to your question is, yes. Our moles in the West Bank camps are telling us about a new group, a top-secret hit squad trained in the Bekaa Valley. It's called *Al Iqab*.'

'What does that mean?'

' "The Punishment",' Garrett translated.

'Is there any indication who they intend to punish?'

'Not yet,' Garrett said. 'But the obvious target is the Israelis.'

'Here, in London?'

'Who the hell knows?' Garrett said exasperatedly. 'As I said, I'm groping around in the dark. It could still be the IRA we're dealing with. And in spite of the fact that they're keeping a low profile, we've had a whisper they're up to something. A big arms buy behind the Iron Curtain.'

'Bastard Bulgarians,' Dodgson snapped. 'Why don't you people close their bloody arms trade down?'

'Better the devil we know than the devil we don't,' Garrett said. 'By the way, where have you got Abdul?'

'He's in the morgue. Why?'

'Theories are fine, Tony, but they won't get us anywhere. What we need are some facts. Let's go and see that lady in Farnham Common.'

6

Bulgaria is famous for four things. The first is that it exports more than ninety-five per cent of the world supply of attar of roses. The second is that two Bulgarian monks, St Cyril and St Methodius, invented the Cyrillic alphabet. The third is that it is the legendary home of Orpheus, who with his lute made trees, and the mountain-tops that freeze, bow themselves. The fourth, and perhaps most important, is that Bulgaria is the arms centre of the world. Whoever you are, whatever you want, from a shipload of shining new Soviet Kalashnikov AK-47s to a snug crate of Polish fragmentation grenades, you can buy it in Sofia.

The capital of Bulgaria is a pleasant, cosmopolitan, modern city of about a million souls. It provides, for a great many people, a taste of Russia made all the more pleasant by the fact that they do not have to go to Russia to experience it. The city is full of trees and pleasant green spaces; in fact, there are more than eighty parks. Visitors find its streets constantly interesting. Around every corner is another surprise, a Byzantine monastery, a Roman ruin, a Greek church, a Russian cathedral. Sofia is like Rome without the traffic, London without the tourists, Athens without the smog, Madrid without the muggers, Paris without the prices.

The heart of Sofia is Lenin Square, where Vitosha Boulevard meets Georgi Dimitrov Boulevard. Here, across flowerbeds ablaze with geraniums, the TSOUM department store faces the old Balkan Hotel as if each were disputing the other's seniority. The hotel's facade has an air of belonging to an earlier, more leisured time; but, these days, the old place has been fitted out with all the accoutrements such places need to attract the high-flying business traveller: conference facilities and a fitness centre and a Corecom shop selling Bulgarian embroidery and sheepskin coats. Although the foyer is no longer redolent of a time when ladies with hourglass figures in long dresses and ostrich feather headdresses arrived at its portals in open carriages, escorted by men in outrageous uniforms, it is still the most convenient location in the city, and one of the last great bargains in Europe.

Sean Hennessy savoured the day. The sun was already warm. The three-day-old *Daily Telegraph* he had read over breakfast said it was raining in Belfast. He saw in his mind's eye the rain-slick streets of Ballymacarrett, the heavy grey sky hanging low over the sullen waters of Donegal Quay, the dispirited crowds shuffling through the security gate in Victoria Street. There were a lot worse places in the world to be on a bright morning in June than Sofia.

Between the hotel and the store was an underground walkway, in which the Roman ruins discovered while it was being excavated are displayed behind protective glass. Hennessy strolled along it; short, sturdy, red-haired, blue-eyed, not unhandsome, a few months short of his thirty-fifth birthday, he looked tough and intelligent. He wore a tan leather jacket, a casual shirt, dark grey trousers and Nike running shoes. He was in no hurry; the meeting was set for ten-thirty.

In the middle of the underpass was a square, open to the sky, with souvenir shops and a café with white tables beneath bright yellow umbrellas. At this time of day, the little café was half-empty. Hennessy chose a table by the wall near the flower shop.

At ten-thirty on the dot, Vasclav Gurko materialized from the crowd and sat down beside Hennessy at the table. He wore a well-cut dark suit, a white silk shirt, a red silk tie, good-quality leather shoes: he looked as if he might be a government official, perhaps, or even a member of the secret police. Although this was not the first time they had done business together, Hennessy still did not know Gurko's exact status in the Bulgarian hierarchy, but he was *the* man you saw if you wanted what Hennessy had come to Sofia for.

'What time do we meet Gulikov?' he asked, in English.

'This evening. For dinner,' the man in the dark suit said.

'Dinner! Sweet-scented Jesus, Gurko, do you people have to eat a bloody meal every time you do business?'

'It's the way things are done, Sean. You know that,' Gurko said. He ran a hand over his silver hair, newly washed and cut that morning at a salon on Georgi Dimitrov Boulevard. He was vain about his hair, which he wore unfashionably long.

'I know it. I just don't know why.'

The silver-haired man shrugged, and a flicker of annoyance touched the younger man's expression.

'Don't bring me problems, Vasclav,' he said angrily. 'I don't want any problems. There's a lot of money involved. And a lot of people.'

'Don't worry so much,' Gurko said smoothly. 'Gulikov said he will bring the papers, and he will, I promise.'

'If you say so,' Sean said, mollified. 'You sure he'll have everything I need?'

'Yes,' Gurko said. 'Everything. Don't worry.'

'The price is what we agreed?'

'Of course, comrade.'

'Don't call me that. I'm not your bloody comrade.'

Gurko smiled forbearingly. 'In Bulgaria you are, whether you like it or not. You might as well get used to it. This isn't Switzerland.'

They had first met four years ago through a Swiss intermediary, an anonymous bank official named Herbert Aegerter. Nobody talked about guns, of course. There was a matter of establishing mutual trust to be taken care of first; there were a lot of cowboys in the arms game, con artists looking for a quick rip-off who made dealing even more dangerous than it already was. The first meeting was in a suite at the Churchill Hotel in London; then another in Paris, at the Plaza Athenée. They got down to business the third time they met.

Paddy McCaffery was in charge of the unit that went to Zürich. Sean Hennessy was the bagman; three-quarters of a million Swiss francs in a briefcase manacled to his left wrist, and a .45 Detonics Combat Master Mark VI in a shoulder holster under his arm. A stretch Mercedes with smoked glass windows took them to an isolated farm to inspect the merchandise. McCaffery had taken one of the guns out and tested it: an Ingram Model 11 with a MAC suppressor that emptied a thirty-two-round magazine in a fraction over one and half seconds. Paddy McCaffery. Dead long since, thanks to a treacherous bastard Englishman.

Will I ever see you again?

No. Never.

Gurko was looking at him expectantly. Hennessy realized the man had asked him a question.

'Sorry?'

'I said, where would you like to eat tonight?'

'Not in town.'

'Of course not. You know Bojana?'

'No.'

'It's south of town, about ten minutes in a taxi. Just tell the driver you want to go to the Kopitoto Hotel. There's a good restaurant there, with a wonderful view out over the city. You'll like it.'

'I'll like it better when Gulikov tells me my guns are on the water.'

'Don't upset yourself so much,' Gurko said. 'You know who you're dealing with. We're not in the double-cross business.'

'Everybody is in the double-cross business, *comrade*,' Hennessy growled. 'Especially when they're talking these kind of figures.'

'You would do better to concentrate on making sure that your security arrangements for the landing of the consignment are in order. We have no desire to share the publicity for any . . . misadventures you may have.'

'What's that supposed to mean?' Hennessy rasped.

'Your people have made some signal errors in the last year or so,' Gurko said urbanely. He took another Russian cigarette from the packet on the table and lit it. 'Blowing themselves up with their own bombs. That business in Gibraltar. . . .'

63

'They were betrayed,' Hennessy said. 'Betrayed by a bloody spy in our midst.'

'Whom you have not yet located,' Gurko said.

'How come you know so much about us?' Hennessy asked.

'It's in the nature of my business.' Gurko smiled. 'I like to know as much as possible about my clients. Some of them are less . . . forthcoming than others.'

'You're just a fucking fixer,' Hennessy said. 'What's so wonderful about that?'

'Nothing at all,' Gurko agreed. 'You are absolutely right, I'm just a middleman. If you don't care to deal with me, tell me to forget the whole thing. I'll find another customer for what I have to sell. And you can try to find someone who will give you the kind of credit you are asking for.'

'No, no, I'm sorry, Vasclav,' Hennessy said hastily. 'I apologize. I'm just wound up tight about his damned deal. I don't want anything to go wrong with it.'

'Nothing will go wrong,' Gurko said. 'Have some coffee.'

'I don't want any more of that damned stuff,' Hennessy said. 'What I need is some good Irish whiskey.'

'That's a little harder to come by. Will you settle for a slivovitz?'

'Twist my arm,' Hennessy said.

The Kopitoto Hotel was a big, curving modern building set on the crown of a timbered hill that looked out across the glittering city. Far below, the golden onion domes of the cathedral shone in the evening sun. Hennessy paid the driver two leva and went into the foyer. At the desk they told him that Comrade Gulikov and his guest had already gone into the restaurant. A bellboy escorted him.

'Comrade Hennessy,' Gulikov said expansively. He waved to a seat. 'Sit, sit, sit. We are so pleased to see you once more. A great pleasure, yes. You will drink something?'

'Give him some Kamchia,' Gurko told the waiter. 'And bring us another bottle.'

The waiter nodded and hurried away. Gulikov leaned

back in his chair and smiled his melon smile. He was a big fat man with a huge head, thin strands of white hair pasted across an otherwise bald pate. His eyes were small and close set. His skin was pasty and unhealthy-looking, and his thin lips were almost bloodless. There was always a thin sheen of perspiration on his upper lip; from time to time he dabbed it away with his napkin, but after ten minutes it was there again. Gulikov wore a grey lightweight three-piece suit, a pale blue shirt and a red silk tie. A matching handkerchief peeked over the lip of his breast pocket. On his right wrist he wore a heavy gold Longines watch. His fat fingers fiddled with it constantly, as if it were a talisman.

'You will eat?' he said, waving for a menu. 'Vasclav and I have already ordered.'

'Why don't you order for me?' Hennessy said. Gulikov looked pleased. He liked to play the generous host, nothing too good for his friends, all that shit. Did he seriously believe nobody knew who paid for everything? Hennessy wondered. Gulikov was a bastard, but he had to be tolerated because he worked in the State Bureau of Export Control, and as such was a vital component in Gurko's deals. Well, as long as he came through with the necessary export documentation, on demand, he could play-act all he liked, Hennessy thought.

The food came. Gulikov had ordered Shopska salad: roasted red peppers, cucumbers, tomatoes and onions topped with feta cheese. For Hennessy he had chosen Tarator soup, made of yogurt, walnuts, garlic, dill and cucumber to start. Hennessy didn't care what he ate. The damned stuff all tasted the same anyway: these bloody people ate nothing but muck. There was something on the menu called 'hotch potch'. The main dish was roast lamb. Gurko ordered a bottle of the 1980 Oriahovitza Cabernet Reserve from Nova Zagora, most of which he drank himself.

Gulikov seemed to be in an expansive mood. He had been watching football on TV. He was a soccer freak, a fanatical fan of the Spanish team, Real Madrid. He travelled all over the world to see them play: UEFA games, everything. He had said on more than one occasion that a good football match was the only thing he did not care how much he paid to see. His other passion was ice cream. He was a connoisseur, he said; he had sampled the ice cream in forty-two different countries, and could fairly claim to know more about ice cream than anyone else alive. Hennessy wondered whether there were another ten men in the world who gave a fart in a high wind either way.

'You're not interested in football?' he said to Hennessy. 'Not interested at all?'

'No,' Hennessy said shortly. 'Not at all.'

'What sport do you like?' Gulikov asked.

'Shooting,' Hennessy told him.

'Ah!' Gulikov smiled. 'You hunting! What you shoot?'

'Englishmen,' Hennessy said. 'Soldiers. RUC spies. Informers. There's all sorts to choose from.'

Gulikov made a noise as if some of the lamb he was shovelling into his mouth had stuck in his throat. It was all Hennessy could do not to laugh out loud. What did the stupid bastard think he wanted guns for? To shoot pigeons?

'The Irish have a strange sense of humour, Dimitri,' Gurko said. 'Don't pay any attention to our friend. He is a little . . . tense. I think he will be more relaxed when you tell him what you have to tell him.'

'Ah, yes,' Gulikov said. 'The shipment, you mean? Yes. Yes.'

'You've got the papers?' Hennessy asked.

'Of course,' Gulikov said, his tone of voice that of a man who could take offence, but would not. 'Bills of lading, export licences, everything.'

'How will the shipment be routed?'

'By steamer from Varna. Stated destination is Oslo. Eight crates of riveting machinery. It is genuine shipment. But inside each of these cases is a second case: these will contain the weapons.'

'Everything you asked for,' Vasclav Gurko told

Hennessy. 'Twenty EWS 5.56mm rifles. Five thousand rounds of ammunition. Ten 7.62mm Mauser Model SP66 sniper's rifles fitted with Smith and Wesson night sights. One thousand rounds of ammunition. Ten 9mm Heckler and Koch model MP5KA sub-machine-guns. Ten 9mm Heckler and Koch P7 M13 pistols. Ten thousand rounds of ammunition. And seven hundred and fifty pounds of C4 plastic explosive.'

'You got it, then,' Hennessy said to Gurko. 'Where from?'

Gurko smiled and said nothing. Off the fucking Libyans, I'll bet, Hennessy thought.

'What are the delivery arrangements?' he asked Gulikov.

'The freighter leaves Varna two days' time,' the Bulgarian said. 'She is directed Piraeus, Naples, Marseilles, then direct Oslo.'

'You know the arrangements,' Gurko said. 'The ship will heave to in the Somme estuary at high tide on the nineteenth, ready to transfer the weapons. The responsibility of providing the landing boat is yours.'

'That's already taken care of,' Hennessy said.

'Your timing must be meticulous, comrade,' Gulikov said. 'You must be alongside no earlier than one a.m. and no later than two.'

'What?' Hennessy snapped. 'What's this you're giving me?'

'Please, comrade,' Gurko said, placing a soft hand on Hennessy's clenched fist. 'Not so loud.'

Hennessy scowled; diners at neighbouring tables were ostentatiously pretending no interest in them.

'Let's have some more coffee in the lounge,' Gurko said. 'And some cognac.'

The waiters fawned over Gurko as they left the restaurant; five-leva notes slipped into waiting hands, everyone was smiling. Hennessy struggled with his anger until they were in the plush lounge with its dark bookcases and open fire.

'All right,' he said. 'What the hell is all this about?'

'We are making another shipment,' Gurko said. 'It is

imperative it arrives at the same time. A priority matter.'

'Priorities come in two varieties, Gurko,' Hennessy said. 'Yours and mine. This isn't what we arranged. And I won't sit still for it.'

'Believe me, as long as you adhere to the arrangements, there will not be the slightest risk,' Gurko said smoothly. 'The other shipment will be collected and taken ashore between two and three. It will not interfere with your movements in any way. You will not even see the parties concerned.'

'Comrade Hennessy,' Gulikov said apologetically. 'The documents are prepared. The shipment is on the quayside at Varna. To alter arrangements would create . . . complications.'

Hennessy made an angry, impatient sound. Gurko held up a hand as a waiter appeared carrying a silver tray on which were three glasses of cognac. He waited until the waiter put the drinks beside them, gave the man a tip, then turned to Hennessy.

'Let me make something clear to you, Comrade Hennessy,' he said, his tone flat and uncompromising. 'We have others beside yourself to consider, people who spend more in a month than you do in a year. If you force us to choose between you, you will be the loser. You understand?'

Hennessy fought back the angry urge to tell the Bulgarian to shove his fucking guns where the sun never shone; but he could not, he dared not. And Gurko knew it.

'Comrade Gulikov has gone to a very great deal of trouble to accommodate your shipment,' Gurko went on, like a judge pronouncing sentence. 'To unmake them would, ah, embarrass him.'

Gulikov stared at Hennessy; for the first time the Irishman saw the fear shimmering behind the fat man's eyes. Poor pathetic bastard, Hennessy thought. If he got it wrong and screwed up the contract, the people he was dealing with might take umbrage and blow him away. And even if they didn't, his own lot would probably stick him in a labour camp and throw away his number.

'All right,' he said angrily. 'But I still don't like it.' He glowered at Gulikov; the fat man's relief was obvious. As for Gurko, his expression remained aloof, imperturbable. Hennessy knew what that meant. Gurko didn't give a shit whether he liked it or not.

7

Rosemary Duckworth lived in a large detached house in Monckton Park, one of the older roads in the area; it lay on the west side of The Broadway, skirting the southern edge of East Burnham Common, a substantial prewar detached house with a Peugeot 205 parked at the front door. Garrett and Dodgson left the Jaguar at the kerb and walked up the curved gravel path. A golden Labrador came bounding out, barking furiously.

'Sam, Sam, stop that!' a woman's voice shouted.

'Here, Sam,' Garrett said. The dog's attitude changed. Its tail went down and started wagging. It came across towards them and allowed Garrett to scratch its ears before bounding off; seconds later it came back with a rubber ring in its mouth, shaking it and growling.

'He always wants to play.' Rosemary Duckworth said, coming round the side of the house. She was a small woman, dressed in jeans and a T-shirt; she had on some old gardening gloves, and carried a small trowel. She was about fifty, give or take a few years, Garrett decided, smooth-skinned, her fair hair cut short in a practical style.

'Mrs Duckworth, I'm Charles Garrett. This is Detective Inspector Dodgson, Metropolitan Police. We called you from London.'

'Yes, Mr Garrett, I've been expecting you,' the woman said. 'Won't you come round to the garden?'

She led the way around the house to a patio from which wide stone steps led down to a wide, beautifully kept lawn. Off to one side stood a big, handsome magnolia tree in full bloom. A path ran down the right-hand side of the garden to where lush rhododendrons nestled against the high fence. On the left-hand side, two huge horse chestnut trees, at least eighty feet high, dominated the lower end of the garden. As the erratic breeze blew, the branches moved and the leaves sighed and whispered like a waterfall.

'Lovely garden,' Dodgson said. 'You do it all yourself?'

'Good heavens, no,' Rosemary Duckworth smiled. 'There's more than an acre here. I've got a nice old gentleman who comes in twice a week to help me. Would you like some tea?'

'That would be very pleasant,' Garrett said.

'Then you sit here at the table while I make it,' she said. 'I'll only be a jiff.'

They sat at the teak table until Mrs Duckworth came out carrying a big oak tray on which were set a silver-plated teapot and hot-water jug, milk jug and sugar basin. The teacups, saucers and plates were Crown Derby. Chocolate chip cookies and wafer biscuits were neatly laid out in a small silver dish.

'Sugar, milk?' Mrs Duckworth asked.

'Just milk,' Garrett said.

'Me, too,' Dodgson told her.

When the ritual of pouring tea was over, and Mrs Duckworth sat down with them, Garrett asked her to tell him again what she had seen that day in Burnham Beeches.

'I had to return some books to a friend of mine at Littleworth Common,' she said. 'I took the car, so I could take Sam for his walk. I usually go during the afternoon. Across the common, as far as Pumpkin Hill. Or . . . well, you're not interested in where I walk the dog. This particular day I parked the car near Joyce's and Sam and I walked down past the pub towards Brook End Farm. I was just crossing the lane when I saw this car.'

'A BMW, you said, Mrs Duckworth?'

'Metallic blue 525 injection, registration B418 JXL.'

'You sound very sure of the details.'

'My husband is a car dealer,' she said. 'Duckworth's of Maidenhead. I know quite a lot about cars.'

'So it appears,' Garrett said. 'How many people were in the car?'

'Two men. Both Arabs, I'd say.'

'How far away from them were you?'

'I was standing on the corner of the lane as they turned in to Hassocks – that's the name of the house. I'd say about ten feet, maybe a little less.'

'What makes you think they were Arabs?'

'I talked to one of them later. He was definitely an Arab. I just assumed the other one must have been. But you're right, of course. He could just as easily have been South American. Or even Southeast Asian.'

'There were just two men in the car. No one else?'

'No.'

'And they went into the drive of this house?'

'Hassocks. No, not the proper drive. There's a little lane that goes around the rear of the house to the stables. It used to belong to Lady Penhallow. Then it was bought by Arabs. They're hardly ever there. Occasional weekends. And Ramadan, of course.'

'Stables, you say? Do they keep horses?'

'I don't think so.'

'You said the house was unoccupied at the time?'

'I thought it must be, it being a weekday. There's rarely anyone there on weekdays. That was what made me suspicious. I waited to see if they would come out, or what. I must have waited at least half an hour, maybe longer. Then I thought, I'll go and have a look. So I went up the path to see what was going on.'

'Go on.'

'The car was just standing there, on the path, turned round ready to leave. It was locked. There was no sign of the two men. I wondered about going up to the house. Then I heard someone coming.'

'Who was it?'

'The man who'd been driving the car. He was very surprised to see me.'

'How did he react, Mrs Duckworth? Think carefully, please,' Dodgson said. 'Did he appear nervous or uneasy?'

'No, not at all,' Rosemary Duckworth said. 'He asked me what I was doing there, it was private property.'

'Did he speak good English?'

'Not perfect, of course. But quite adequate.'

'What did you say?'

'I told him I was a neighbour. I said I was just checking to make sure the place wasn't being burgled. He smiled and said there was no need for me to worry. He had driven a friend out from London. "Then why didn't you use the front gate?" I said. He said his instructions were to come in the rear entrance. I thought, well, it's none of my business. He seemed perfectly respectable.'

'And that's why you didn't call the police?'

'There didn't seem any real reason to. I mean, it was a little unusual, but nothing more than that.'

'Can you describe the man you talked to?'

'But of course,' she said. 'I helped your people to make one of those computerized pictures. He was in his mid-twenties, skin, well, coffee-coloured, I'd say. Dark hair and eyes, full lips. He was wearing one of those casual jackets all the young men wear now, light blue. An open-necked shirt. I checked the registration number of the car as he drove away and wrote it down in my notebook. I thought, if I hear later that anything is amiss, I can always give the number to the police.'

'But you heard nothing more.'

'That's right. It was only when I saw the appeal for information on TV that I realized there might be a connection. I phoned in. You know the rest.'

'Mrs Duckworth, is this the drawing you helped the police artist to make?' Dodgson said, taking a photograph from his briefcase. Rosemary Duckworth held it at arm's length and looked at it with her head cocked on one side.

'That's the one,' she said. 'That's him.'

'You don't want to alter anything?'

'No,' she said. 'It's a good likeness.'

'And there's nothing else you want to tell us?'

'I can't think of anything,' she said. 'Unless. . . .'

'Unless?'

'I've just thought of it,' she said. 'In the car. There was one of those French parking discs. You know, the ones that show what time you arrived and what time you'll be leaving.'

'Go on.'

'It had the name of an hotel on it. I remember wondering where it was.'

'You remember the name of the hotel?' Garrett said, glancing at Dodgson. This was too good to be true.

Rosemary Duckworth frowned. 'No,' she said, 'I can't remember. But . . . there was a street name on it. Rue François. In Paris.'

'Paris?' Garrett said tensely. 'You're sure?'

'Yes,' Rosemary Duckworth said. 'Quite sure. I have a cousin called François. That's why it must have stuck in my mind. I'm awfully sorry I didn't think of it till now.'

'You're forgiven,' Dodgson said. 'May I use your phone, Mrs Duckworth?'

'In the hall,' she said. 'I'll show you.'

Garrett leaned back in the garden chair, listening to Rosemary Duckworth explaining where the telephone was. The horse chestnut trees moved in the breeze like fan dancers. Nice day for a sail, he thought. It was easy to imagine the cool feel of the wide stainless steel wheel in his hands, the buck of the boat as she punched into the waves, the Needles off to starboard, Hurst Castle a small flat lozenge on the northeastern horizon as he beat up the Solent towards the Hamble and home. All he had to do was close his eyes and he could see Diana in her yellow oilies, old Tom and Ross McTaggart jamming the jib as Garrett pushed the engine-control lever forward, bringing the 'iron topsail' into full play to counter the turning tide, Rosie down in the galley making egg and bacon sandwiches.

'That's it,' he heard Dodgson say, snapping out of his reverie. 'Thank you again, Mrs Duckworth.'

'I hope it was some help,' she said. She stood with one hand on her hip as they walked up the drive, and waved as they drove off. Dodgson turned south on the Farnham Road and sped through Farnham Royal and the Slough Trading Estate to the Chalvey interchange. Garrett said nothing the whole way. At Chalvey, Dodgson turned east on the M4 and headed for London, nineteen miles away.

'Well?' he said, exasperatedly.

'Well, what?'

'Well, what do you make of it?'

'I think Mrs Duckworth is a very lucky lady,' Garrett said. 'If she hadn't waited before she went up that path. . . .'

'She would have walked in on Chummy carving Abdul up. And he would have killed her on the spot.'

'I'm surprised he didn't anyway.'

'She believed him. If she'd given him so much as a hint she didn't. . . .' Garrett drew a finger across his throat.

'What about the parking disc?'

'A hotel in the rue François, Paris. We can check it out.'

'I've already put it on to the wire. If they get anything before we get back to London they'll fax it to me in the car.'

'Worth a try, I suppose,' Garrett said.

'You're too much of a bloody pessimist for me, Charles,' Dodgson said. 'Want to make a bet this comes out right?'

'I don't bet,' Garrett said.

'What are you so bad-tempered about?'

'I was thinking about sailing. On the Solent.'

'Oh,' Dodgson said. He knew about Diana, of course. There'd been no way to keep that under wraps. 'Still got the boat, then?'

'*Sunday Girl*? Yes. She's moored down at the Hamble.'

'Still sail her at weekends, do you?'

'Not any more.'

The fax machine on the back seat buzzed; Garrett frowned and turned to watch it feed out a piece of paper. On it were four lines of typing.

'No rue François in Paris. Rue Aristide François in the twentieth arrondissement. Hotel Liban at 66 categorized at TREVI by DST as a designated location,' Garrett read.

'Hotel Liban,' Dodgson said. 'That's French for Lebanon, isn't it?'

'Yes,' Garrett said.

'What's a designated location?'

'It's TREVI jargon for a terrorist hangout,' Garrett said. His eyes were glittering with contained emotion. 'Put the siren on, Tony. Get this bloody crate moving.'

8

It was raining in Paris.

Shrugging into his Burberry, Garrett skirted the crowd of waiting relatives and chauffeurs, and hurried out of the terminal building. The blue Peugeot 405 Mi16 was waiting exactly where Simion had said it would be. Garrett identified himself and got in the back. The driver swung the car out of Charles de Gaulle airport and on to the autoroute, heading south at a steady 120kph. At the Porte de la Chapelle interchange he turned east on to the *périphérique*. The mid-morning traffic was moving at its usual insane speed. Garrett smiled, remembering the honking traffic on the old cobblestoned ring road, the dubious perfumes from the abattoir and cattle market at La Villette, the days it could take three-quarters of an hour to get from the Porte d'Italie to the Pont National on the cobblestoned Boulevard Massena.

The driver took the slip road down to the roundabout at the Porte de Lilas and parked outside the old building on the Boulevard Mortier – once the Caserne de Tourelles – that housed DGSE, Direction Générale de Securité Extérieure, the French secret service. Because it overlooked the municipal swimming pool, the Stade Nautique, in the rue des Tourelles opposite, DGSE headquarters was referred to as 'La Piscine' by everyone in the trade, Parisian argot used in affectionate, downbeat mockery. Garrett thanked the driver and went inside, gave his name to the armed gendarme at the desk, and asked for Eugène Simion.

Simion worked for DST – Direction de la Surveillance du Territoire – which was something between MI5 and Special Branch, and probably nearer to the FBI than either. Most of its executives were former policemen, like Simion, who had done his time as a *flic* in the fifties, and cut his antiterrorist squad teeth on the assassination of Fadi Dani, assistant director of the PLO in Paris, in 1982.

Garrett was escorted to a featureless waiting room, told Simion was expected *'tout à l'heure'*, offered coffee – which he declined, having choked on their coffee before – and left alone. He pictured Simion bucking the traffic; DST headquarters was the other side of Paris, near the Invalides. It would never occur to the DST man to come by Métro: Parisians spent half their lives either in a traffic jam or searching for somewhere to park. He leafed desultorily through the copy of *Le Monde* lying on the table; after about fifteen minutes the door opened and Simion bustled in. He was about medium height, thickset, with wiry black hair and bright, alert green eyes. He looked compact and fit; Garrett recalled that Simion, a karate third dan, spent two hours every morning doing t'ai ch'i ch'tuan.

'Charles!' he said, embracing Garrett. 'Sorry I'm late. The bloody traffic.'

'It's good to see you,' Garrett said. 'How's Yvette?'

'Good, good. She hopes for a visit this time. And Diana?'

'Diana . . . died, Eugène. A couple of years ago.'

'Merde!' Simion said. 'I'm sorry, Charles. I didn't know. How. . . ?'

He saw Garrett's face and didn't bother to complete the question. Garrett spoke into the awkward silence.

'What's the news from the stakeout?'

'No sign of your pigeon,' Simion said. 'We've had the cameras going nonstop since you called.'

'What about identification?'

'My people are working on that now. Let's go downstairs and play with some of General Izbot's toys.'

They went out into the corridor and turned right, going through swing doors to a central foyer. On the far side was a bank of lifts; they got into one and Simion pushed a button marked U2. The lift dropped like a stone; the doors slid open silently to reveal a well-lit foyer. Before them was a security booth; it looked not unlike a passport control booth. Two armed guards watched impassively as their clearances were checked. The security man waved them through into the air-conditioned computer complex.

The place was as bright as an aircraft hangar, intersected, grid plan, by aisles of oatmeal-coloured carpet flanked by serried rows of hardware: front end interfaces, mass storage units, quad-redundant IBM 3033s attached to laser printers that could produce hard copy at the rate of sixty thousand lines a minute. Here inside the micro-circuitry of this humming, buzzing, whirring, beeping monster, its little lights flashing, its incredible inhuman brain moving faster than the human mind could conceive, were stored all the secret secrets of France. At the far end of the aisle was a suite of offices, open-plan affairs with glass panelling. Simion went into the first cubicle and said something in rapid French to the man sitting at the console. The man nodded.

'Charles,' Simion said, urgently. 'Come. *Vite!* We have something for you!'

The programmer turned and nodded to Garrett, then gestured at the screen. The photofit picture put together by Rosemary Duckworth was on the right-hand side. On the left was a blurred photograph of a dark-haired young man.

'There he is,' Simion said.

'Is that the only picture you've got?'

'We'll put it through ME. Sharpen it up.' Maximum Entropy is a technique devised by two scientists at Cambridge which uses computer technology to sharpen blurred surveillance photographs.

'What have you got on him?'

'Give me the RG dossier, Paul,' Simion said. The specialist nodded and started punching keys. The screen cleared, then line after line of information flowed across it, much faster than Garrett could read.

'There's quite a lot here, by the look of it,' Paul said. 'Do you want a print-out?'

'Naturally,' Simion said. Paul nodded again. When the information had finished feeding on to the screen, he tapped a few more keys and Garrett heard the humming zip of a laser printer. Paul reached down and tore off the continuous stationery sheets and handed them to Simion. The Frenchman passed it to Garrett.

'*Merci,*' he said absently, scanning intently. Nidal Faour, twenty-eight, born in Deir al-Balah, a graduate of the Islamic University, came to France as a student in 1985. Sharing an apartment in the twentieth arrondissement with two others, both Palestinian Arabs. None of them 'known'. Faour had come to DST notice as a suspected 'camel' – a runner used by extremist organizations to deliver forged documents – because of frequency of travel: Rome, Athens, London, Tel Aviv, Nicosia, Cairo in 1986, Berlin, Vienna, Rome again, Athens twice, Karachi in 1987. His contacts in all these places were listed; DGSE surveillance was very thorough.

'You see he left Paris for London on 12 June,' Simion said. 'We haven't sighted him since.'

'He's back,' Garrett said. 'But not using that name. He came across on a ferry, driving a car he rented in London.'

'What was the name?'

'Duval. Alexander Duval.'

'*Bon.*' Simion grinned. 'Paul, check that.'

'What's he doing?' Garrett asked.

'A manifest check,' Simion said. 'We've been requiring the cross-Channel ferries to log passengers since a few years. If that car came to France, we'll have it.'

'Eh,' Paul said, gesturing at the screen.

Garrett stared at the VDU. The cursor was blinking on the fourth line down, which Paul had video'd to make it stand out.

B418JXL:
23/6: BrittF PO-CAEN a0630.
BMW Bleu/met UK: B418JXL. +1. Nom: DUVAL,
ALEXANDER.

'*Voilà!*' Simion said. 'There's our boy. He came into Caen from Portsmouth on Brittany Ferries at six-thirty, 23 June. The car was a BMW, metallic blue, UK registration B418 JXL. One passenger. You see the name.'

'Does your computer know him?'

'Paul?'

Paul's busy fingers had already keyed the name into the machine. Once again the screen blinked, and once again information flooded it.

'Oh, this is much more interesting,' Simion said. 'Give me a hard copy, please, Paul.'

The laser printer buzzed and zizzed, and paper eeled out of the slot beside it, stacking neatly.

'The name Alexander Duval has been used by a man named Abu Hosseyn,' Simion said, reading out loud. 'Wanted for questioning in connection with the assassin-ation of General Oveissy and his brother in the rue de Passy, February 1984. Suspect in assassination of Michel Namari, publisher of the *Arab News Letter* in Athens, and an aborted attempt to murder the American Ambassador in August 1986.'

'Abdul,' Garrett said.

Simion looked up sharply. 'Abdul?'

'Hosseyn is dead, Eugene,' the Englishman said. 'Faour killed him in England, took his passport and used it to cross into France. So where does that leave us??'

'If he's still using the name Duval . . . Paul, would you kindly check the departures from Orly between the twenty-fifth and today – Syria, Lebanon, and so on?'

'*D'accord,*' Paul said, fingers flickering over the keyboard. The screen blinked blank, then beeped. Lines of information zipped across.

DUVAL, ALEXANDER:
25 rien
26 rien
27 rien
28 rien
29 rien
autres?

'Well, if he's gone, he didn't go by air,' Simion said. 'He

could have gone by road, of course. That will take longer to check.'

'Try Hosseyn,' Garrett said. 'Faour, too.' Simion nodded to Paul, who shrugged.

'Okay,' he said. 'Where will you be?'

'Call my office,' Simion said. 'They'll patch you through. Come on, Charles.'

They went up in the lift to the ground floor. Simion took him into a room with racks like a school cloakroom.

'You're too well dressed for where we're going,' he told Garrett. He looked around until he found what he wanted, a battered leather jacket, faded jeans and scuffed suede shoes not unlike his own.

'Put these on.'

Garrett took off his own jacket, trousers and shoes and did as he was told. The leather jacket was a reasonable enough fit. The shoes were tight, but he could live with that.

'Give you a packet of Gauloises, and Chabrol would sign you up tomorrow,' Simion grinned. 'Let's go.'

He led the way to the garage, where his unmarked Peugeot 405 was standing in a no-parking slot. The rain had stopped; they checked out and drove south on Boulevard Mortier.

'Now that I'm suitably dressed, where are we going?' Garrett asked.

Simion grinned. 'To see a friend of mine. It's not far. A nice little place in the twentieth.'

'Who's the friend?'

'*Un ver*. Isn't that what you British say?'

'No, we call them moles, not worms.'

'Very well, a mole. His codename is Sayeed. We've had him in deep cover for a couple of years. He killed an Israeli soldier on the West Bank. The PLO got him out. We turned him soon after he arrived. I told him to see what he could find out about your business.'

Square Severine slid past on their left. Eugene swung right on to the rue de Bagnolet and left again into the place de la Réunion. Down the rue de Vignoles; another turn.

The houses in the side streets were old and shabby, the pavements crowded with swarthy men in cheap suits, women wearing the veil, barefoot children in dirty cotton robes. At every corner pushcart peddlers sold old clothes, junk, poor-quality vegetables and fruit.

Eugene pulled into the kerb and parked the car.

'We'll go on foot from here,' he said.

They walked downhill, and round a corner into a small cul de sac. Simion crossed the street, checking to right and left that no one was following them. He stopped at a building that was decrepit, unpainted for decades. The shutters on the ground floor windows had been torn off, those higher up were peeling and rotten. An old crone sat on a wooden chair beside the open door.

'Hello, grandmother,' Simion said, in French. 'How are you today?'

'Me?' she cackled. 'Who cares about an old woman?'

'Is he in, the upstairs?' Simion jerked a thumb to indicate who he meant.

'That one. He'll be in the bar. Down the street.'

'We'll wait inside,' Simion said, slipping her a twenty-franc note. 'You tell him there's a friend to see him. Have one yourself.'

He led the way into the house. A long corridor led to an uncarpeted staircase; dirt gritted beneath their shoes as they climbed to the second floor. The banister was loose and sticky to the touch. On the landing a black-haired Arab girl of about four, dressed only in a T-shirt, was playing with a skinny cat. Tinny music blared from the open doorway of the apartment. A woman's voice shouted something; the child screeched a defiant reply.

Simion banged on the door. They heard feet sliding on the linoleum floor. A woman came to the open door. She looked forty; Garrett guessed she was about twenty-five. She wore a cheap cotton dress with little or nothing underneath it. She was dark-skinned, with long black hair. There were dark circles beneath her eyes.

'Hello, Zufila,' Simion said. She looked at him and shrugged.

'Do I know you?' she said. Her voice was flat, heavily accented. She put her hand on her hip, leaned against the doorpost.

'Aren't you going to ask us in?'

'He's not here,' she said, in the same uninterested voice. 'He's never here.'

'The grandmother has gone to fetch him,' Simion said. 'We'll wait.'

He pushed past her into the apartment. It was dark and drab. In the centre of the room was a bare wooden table on which stood a large box of cornflakes, a sugar basin and a coffee pot. Beside the table were three rickety upright chairs. A tap dripped into a stained earthenware sink filled with dirty dishes; several packets of detergent stood on a shelf above it. A door opposite stood far enough ajar for Garrett to see the unmade bed in the next room. Ignoring them, the woman lit a cigarette and sat down on the stained sofa in front of the flickering black and white TV.

'That's Zufila,' Simion said. 'She's a whore, and she doesn't like *flics*. As you may have gathered. A real charmer, eh?'

He sat down on one of the kitchen chairs; Garrett followed suit. The little girl who had been playing with the cat came in and stared at them with huge dark unreadable eyes.

'Mama,' she said. 'Who is it, Mama?'

'Go and play,' Zufila said, without taking her eyes off the TV set. They heard someone coming up the stairs. The woman did not look up. The man who came in was dressed in rough working clothes, scuffed shoes, a collarless shirt. He was big for an Arab, five nine or ten, heavily built, with capable-looking hands. The little girl went across to him; he picked her up and held her in his right arm. He stood in the doorway looking speculatively at Simion and Garrett for a moment, running his free hand over the two-day stubble on his chin.

'Go in the other room, Zufila,' he said. 'Take the baby.'

'I'm watching something,' the woman said petulantly.

'Do what I tell you.'

Zufila got up off the sofa and snapped off the TV. She glared at Simion and Garrett, then snatched the child out of the man's arms and went into the bedroom, slamming the door.

'Bitch,' he said, without anger. He looked at Garrett, then at Simion. 'Who's this?'

'A friend,' Simion said.

'I don't like your coming here. You should have arranged a meet.'

'There wasn't time,' Simion said. 'It's all right. We haven't got anyone on our backs.'

He pulled a half bottle of Scotch out of his pocket and put it on the table. The man looked at it eagerly, but did not touch it.

'What have you got for me, Sayeed?' Simion asked. 'Have you come up with anything on Abu Hosseyn?'

'I asked a few questions. Nobody seems to know the name.'

'Here's his picture,' Garrett said. He put the photofit of Nidal Faour on the table. Sayeed frowned at it.

'This man's name isn't Hosseyn,' Sayeed said. 'It's . . . Fouad. No, Faour. That's it. Nidal Faour. I know him: he lives up near the place Stendhal.'

'What else do you know about him?'

'You want a lot for a bottle of cheap Scotch.'

'Here.' Simion pulled out his wallet, and put two five-hundred franc notes on the table. 'Talk.'

Sayeed's hand closed on the notes. 'He's a *hachoir*. You know what that is, English?'

'We call them hit men,' Garrett said. 'You're sure it's the same man?'

'You don't believe me? Why would I make it up?'

'We heard he was a *chameau*. Handling false papers, that sort of thing.'

'Those two he shares his place with, they're the camels,' Sayeed said. 'Tamraz and Ali Dakhleh. They're both PLO.'

'And Faour?'

Sayeed shrugged. He took the top off the whisky bottle and sloshed some into a dirty glass. 'Ah,' he said, wiping his mouth with the back of his hand. 'That's good stuff.'

'I'll buy you a crate,' Garrett said. 'Which section of the PLO does Faour work for?'

Sayeed shrugged again. 'Who knows?' he said. 'They've got more branches than a tree.'

'What about Al Iqab?' Simion said.

Sayeed scratched his chin. 'I asked a few questions. Enough to find out that you're not paying me enough to find out.'

Garrett looked at Simion; a message passed silently between them. Simion took out his wallet and put ten one-thousand-franc notes on the table. Neither he nor Garrett spoke. Sayeed stared at the money but made no move to touch it or pick it up.

'You must want them pretty badly,' he said hoarsely. 'Okay if I have another drink?'

They let the uncomfortable silence work on him; his hand shook slightly as he poured the whisky into the glass.

'We're in a hurry, Sayeed,' Garrett said. 'Tell us about Al Iqab.'

'Listen,' he said. 'The word is out. These are serious people. Anyone who talks about them, *zzzzck*.' He slit his throat with his finger.

'Who are they?' Simion demanded harshly. 'What are they?'

'Nobody knows. Something special. A punishment. That means a group set up to make a revenge attack. The rumours say, anything they want, they get. No questions asked.'

'What have they asked for?'

'I don't know. I don't know.'

'That's ten grand on the table, Sayeed. You could fly to Rio with that kind of money. Anywhere.'

'Make it fifteen,' Sayeed said. 'For Zufila. And the kid.'

'Talk first,' Simion said.

'I can't tell you much. Just what I heard. I was at Faour's place.'

'Address?'

'You know the fucking address.'

'Tell me, anyway.'

'Rue Franclis 29.'

'And?'

'We did some hash. That was why I went, they always have stuff. I was talking to Dakhleh. He was giving me all that Palestine shit. You know? "Give me the flag of Palestine, I am small but the victory is great" – all that stuff.'

'You don't believe in that any more?'

'I don't believe in anything any more. I asked him what he meant. He said something about this being the year, that they'd all remember this year.'

'What did he mean?'

Sayeed shrugged. 'He said it had begun.'

'He used those words?'

'It has begun. We have begun. Something like that.'

'And then?'

'I said, what? And he said, the punishment.'

'That was all?'

'Isn't that enough?'

'When was this?' Garrett asked.

'About a week ago. Last week.'

'You haven't seen Dakhleh since?'

'He said he was leaving town for a while. Tamraz, too.'

'Where were they going?'

'The coast. St Valery-sur-Somme.'

'Did they say why?'

'No. And I didn't ask.'

'Two camels,' Simion murmured, 'making a rendezvous at St Valery-sur-Somme. Sound interesting, Charles?'

'Some illegals coming in?' Garrett wondered. 'Some uninvited visitors needing papers?'

'I'd bet on it,' Simion said. Both men stood simultaneously. Sayeed stared up at them, frowning.

'Get your coat,' Simion said. 'We'll take you in. Protective custody. Just in case.'

'I thought you said you didn't have anybody on your back.'

'Doesn't hurt to play safe,' Simion said. 'Tell the woman.'

Sayeed went to the bedroom door and banged on it. The

woman opened it, her expression one of contemptuous disdain.

'What now?' she said, her tone that of someone who was not interested in the answer.

'They're taking me in for questioning,' Sayeed said.

'He won't be back tonight,' Simion said. He handed Zufila a card. 'You can call this number for information.'

'Keep the bastard, for all I care,' she spat, and slammed the door.

'Love,' Garrett said. 'Your magic spell is everywhere.'

Simion put the cuffs on Sayeed and led him out of the apartment and down the stairs to the street. 'We'll go back to the Piscine,' he said. 'Park our friend. Then I'll see if we can lay on a helicopter to take us down to St Valery.'

They went out into the street. The old crone was nowhere to be seen. They had gone about fifty yards when Sayeed stopped.

'The money!' he said.

'Zufila can look after it for you,' Simion said. 'Keep moving.'

'You crazy? She'll send it to her fucking relatives on the West Bank!'

'Go ahead,' Garrett said. 'I'll go back and get it.'

He turned and went back into the house, taking the stairs two at a time. The woman was sitting in front of the TV, with the little girl curled up asleep in her lap. There was no sign of the money.

'Come on, Zufila,' Garrett said. 'Hand it over.'

The woman ignored him. The tinny soundtrack music was familiar. Gene Kelly and Debbie Reynolds, *Singin' in the Rain*.

'The money, Zufila.'

She put the sleeping child down on the sofa and stood up to face him, arms akimbo, eyes shining with defiance.

'I never saw any money,' she hissed. 'So fuck off, *crapaud*.'

In the same moment, Garrett heard the explosion. He thrust the woman aside and threw the door open, bounding down the stairs to the street in long leaps. Outside, it was like a battlefield. The air stank of burning plastic and brickdust, mixed with the sharp sour tang of high explosive. He could hear hoarse shouts, the sound of running feet, a woman screaming. A burglar alarm had gone off somewhere. The explosion had hurled the car several feet in the air and sideways, smashing it against the wall of a building, flattening the passenger side of the vehicle like a stamped-on beer can, exploding the petrol tank and setting fire to the rear of the car. Smoke hung like an oily rag above the street.

Garrett ran to the car, glass scrunching under his feet. A man with blood on his hands sat hunched over on the edge of the kerb; another was propped against the wall, eyes vacant, clothing torn. Somewhere, the woman was still screaming. Garrett took off his leather jacket. Using it to protect his hands and arms, he wrenched open the door of the car. Burning heat rushed at him. Simion lolled into his arms. The side of his face was cooked crisp, like pork coming out of an oven.

Garrett lifted him out and dragged him clear of the burning vehicle. His hands slid on something slick, and he realized Simion's left arm was a tattered pulp of bloody flesh and bone. A quick check of the throat pulse showed he was still alive. Garrett laid the man flat on the pavement and got a tourniquet on the shattered arm, halfway between shoulder and elbow. He looked up to see people standing nearby gawping at him.

'Get an ambulance!' he yelled. '*Vite, vite! Une ambulance!*'

They stared at him as if he was a Martian. Garrett opened his mouth to yell at them again, then shut it as he heard the sound of police sirens approaching. Simion was very pale, and breathing stertorously. Come on, for Christ's sake, Garrett thought. Come *on*! The first police van came down the street and skidded to a stop, spilling gendarmes. The *pompiers* in their silver helmets and belted jackets were right behind them. Shouted commands bounced off the scarred walls. Two firemen ran to the burning car, spraying it with extinguishers that sounded like roaring beasts. A gendarme ran across to where Garrett was kneeling.

'*Secours est en route*,' he said. '*Est-il toujours vivant?*'

'*Juste,*' Garrett told him.

The other policemen fanned out into a cordon, herding the crowd back. A detective in a raincoat and trilby hat pulled back the door and leaned into the car.

'*Bon Dieu,*' Garrett heard him say.

9

Garrett reached St Valery-sur-Somme at around five in the afternoon. DGSE put a powerful Peugeot 405 Mil6 at his disposal; he pushed it hard, north up the autoroute to Amiens and on to Abbeville. There he turned towards Cambron and picked up the D204, a country lane that skirted the *marais* stretching down to the ruler-straight line of the wide Abbeville-Somme canal on its way into the little fishing port.

The town lay on a curving headland on the southern side of the river. He passed the railway station, a salt warehouse on his left, then a children's playground in a small riverside park. Dinghies and larger sailing boats were moored along the canal bank. The tide was a long way out, and the whole estuary was a succession of sandbanks and channels. Here and there on the shining sand, Garrett could see people walking; way out, boats bobbed on the water. Old men smoking pipes leaned on the railings along the embankment facing the sea. It looked like an Edwardian painting.

As the road curved sharply to the left, Garrett saw a restaurant on the seafront with a newsagent's shop next to it. Pulling in to the kerb, he parked, and walked back the way he had come. He went into the newsagent's shop, bought an evening paper and asked directions to the old town.

St Valery spread up both sides of two hills between the road to Cayeux and the seafront. On the hill to the west was the old town; to the east the more modern area called Le Tivoli. The DST safe house was an old *demeure* on the rue de Ponthieu, close to the abbey; it had once been a centre for Oriental studies, before that a girls' school. The streets were cobbled and narrow, with high anonymous limestone walls surrounding the houses; the one-way system was arbitrary, but the old newsagent's directions led Garrett right to where he wanted to go. The rue de Ponthieu was empty and silent. A sign on one wall advertised a furnished house to let. He parked the car with the offside wheels on the pavement and walked up the slope until he found number 89. He rang the bell and the door half-opened.

'*Oui?*'

The man looked like a garage mechanic, a short, squat, dark-haired fellow of perhaps forty, dressed in blue overalls, a cigarette hanging from his mouth.

'Garrett.'

'Rabier,' the man said. There was no greeting; he merely opened the door wider. Garrett stepped inside. Rabier led the way into a cobbled courtyard. To the right was a badly overgrown patch of grass; to the left a double door, beside which stood an old iron water pump. A heavy farmyard smell hung on the still air.

'You keep goats,' Garrett observed.

Rabier grunted, and gestured towards the entrance. They went along a marble-tiled hall. To the right, Garrett saw a dilapidated conservatory.

'*Voilà,*' Rabier said.

They went through a kitchen into a dining room. A man and woman sat at the table in the centre of the room. The woman was casually dressed, everything in neutral colours, Prisunic rather than Printemps. She was in her mid-twenties, brunette, neither beautiful nor plain. The man was older, nearer fifty; there were grey streaks in his wiry brindle hair. He wore the waistcoat and trousers of a dark blue woollen suit; the jacket hung on the chair behind him. A 1:25000 scale IGN map of the town and river estuary was spread out in front of them, held down at the corners by coffee cups.

'*L'anglais,*' said the man who had brought Garrett in.

'You're Garrett?' the man at the table said. There was no welcome in his voice. Unit leader, Garrett decided. And pissed off at being stuck with me. 'I'm Christian Germain. They told me to put my people at your disposal.'

In spite of what happened to Simion. Garrett could hear the words as clearly as if they had been spoken, and knew that

91

Germain knew he had. Enough resentment to shift a table, Garrett thought. Not a good start.

'Irène Level,' said the thin-faced brunette on Rabier's left. 'Welcome.' She smiled, showing unexpected dimples, and shifted on her seat, body language to tell Garrett *I'm not his.*

'Thanks,' Garrett said. 'Any news of Simion?'

Germain shook his head. 'He's still in *intensif*,' he said. 'Bad burns. Shock. They amputated his arm.'

'Do they think he'll pull through?'

The man shrugged. 'You want to tell us what happened?'

'We went to see a worm. While the meet was on, someone plastiqued the car.'

'You were lucky.' Meaning, *how come you're still alive?*

This was going to be hard work. Germain was the type that took every suggestion as a challenge to his authority. Ambitious, vain and very territorial, truculence came off him like a vapour. He clearly viewed Garrett's presence as a personal criticism levelled at him by Paris. Well, he'd met the type before. There were a lot of them.

'I'm glad to have the chance to sit in on this,' he said tactfully. 'What's the situation?'

'We located the two camels, Tamraz and Dakhleh; they're in a *pension* near the harbour,' Germain told him. He was a big, solidly built man with a large head, the grey-flecked hair thinning at the crown. 'We tried laser bugs. No use. Too much traffic on the quay. So I've got two operatives in the room next to them. Video surveillance. RDF on their car. We didn't try to bug the phones: they won't use them.'

'What have they been up to?'

'Nothing covert. A walk around the town. A meal at the restaurant. They hired a powerboat.'

'Interesting,' Garrett said. 'Have they been out in it?'

'Not yet.'

'Where is it?'

'On a mooring at La Ferté, between the casino and the station.'

'You've got watchers on it?'

Germain looked nonplussed; he displaced his confusion with surliness. 'I haven't got an army up here, you know,' he said. 'I can't watch everything.'

'I understand that,' Garrett said. 'But the fact remains that those two may have hired the boat for someone else to use.'

'I suppose you're right,' Germain said reluctantly. 'I'll get someone over there.'

'Good,' Garrett said. 'What else have you got for me?'

He said it without thinking; Germain glared at him for a moment, then said, 'We've listed every visitor in town. Thank God there aren't that many. There are twenty-eight to choose from. Eight Germans, four Italians, four English, two Japanese, two Americans, eight French. Of course, there may be others, in private homes.'

'We'll have to take our chances.'

They took the French first. A tailor and his wife, from Nantes. A family from Avallon, mother, father, daughter, son-in-law. Two young couples from Paris, one pair working in a publishing house, the other a photographer and his model. They all looked harmless enough.

The Germans next. Four from Frankfurt, travelling together in a VW bus. All in their fifties. Unlikely. Two from Stuttgart, also middle-aged. Likewise. Two students, one from Garmisch, one from Mittenwald.

'Where are they staying?'

'*Chambres d'hôte*. Bed and breakfast. A house on the Quai Lejoille.'

'What are they, backpackers?'

'Bicyclists.'

'Scratch them,' Garrett said.

The four Italians were a family from Turin, mother, father, eighteen-year-old son and sixteen-year-old daughter. *No.* Two Yamamotos from Osaka. *Forget it.* The Americans were a middle-aged New York couple travelling with English friends. They looked harmless enough.

'What about the English?'

'Two men. One is called Taunton, the other Johnson.'

'Together?'

'They're staying at the Relais.'

'Relais?'

'Guillaume de Normandy. On the Quai du Romerel.'

'How long have they been here?'

'Three or four days.'

'Doing what?'

'Nothing much. Fishing.'

'Are they covered?'

'No.'

'Don't you think we'd better put someone on them?' Garrett said. Germain looked up quickly, ready to take offence. Garrett kept his expression neutral, as if he didn't mind what Germain did. The Frenchman frowned, then shrugged.

'Irène,' he said to the woman. 'You go too, Alain.'

Rabier nodded and went out of the room. He came back after a few minutes, wearing a sports jacket and light brown trousers. The thin-faced woman already had her coat on.

'We'll take the Renault,' she said. 'Can we eat at the Relais?' The dimples changed her expression completely: she looked ten years younger when she smiled.

'Get a receipt if you do,' Germain said, humourlessly. When they were gone he turned to face Garrett.

'You think these English are involved in some way?'

'It won't hurt to be sure. Can your people get photographs?'

'Of course,' Germain said stiffly.

'Better do it, then, no?'

Germain shrugged again. 'Have you got any idea what these people are up to, Garrett?' he said.

'I've been asking myself that question ever since I left Paris,' Garrett replied. *Except when I was thinking about Simion lying in a puddle of his own blood, and the pulped mess in the car that had once been Sayeed.* 'These two camels are connected in some way to a terrorist group called Al Iquab, the Punishment. My guess is there's a rendezvous here. The fact they've hired a boat means that either illegals or weapons – or both – are coming in. The camels have been sent down with false papers for the team. How long have they been here?'

'Three days. Two nights.'

'And no contacts made, nothing?'

Germain shook his head. 'I like to know what I'm getting into. Those big shots in Paris must think we're mind-readers, they just throw these things at us, not a word about who these people are, or what they're up to.'

'I know the feeling,' Garrett said, feigning sympathy. 'I can't be sure what's going on, but it's something they think is worth killing to protect.'

'I've got a lot of people tied up here doing nothing,' Germain said. 'I tell you, if they don't make a show of it soon, my inclination is to call the whole thing off.'

'They'll move,' Garrett said. 'What are the tide times?'

'Full tide at oh-three-oh-four and nine-fourteen.'

'They might go out with the *chalutiers*,' Garrett mused. 'But I doubt it. They'd be too conspicuous coming in, unloading in the middle of the night.'

'If they bring in guns, I think we ought to take them.'

'That won't get us anywhere. We want to know who they are, where they're going and what they plan to do when they get there. We want photographs of every one of them to go into the TREVI computer. We've got to find out what they're planning.'

'I don't agree. If we take them now, it won't make any difference what they're planning,' Germain said, stolidly ignoring what he must know: that if they arrested this group, another they did not know about would take its place. Garrett decided not to argue the point immediately.

'How many agents have you got in St Valery?'

'More than I can spare. My section is understaffed as it is. Those at the Piscine, they think we can make miracles.'

'How many?' Garrett persisted.

'Eight here. Six more on standby at Abbeville.'

'So, we wait. Is there anything to eat?'

'In the kitchen.'

From a well-stocked larder with slate shelves, Garrett brought out two white baguettes, unsalted Normandy

95

butter, a wedge of Reblochon, another of Brie, and some goat cheese that looked as if it was ready to make a run for it. He found a packet of Jacques Vabre coffee and set up the *filtre*, making it good and strong. While it was brewing he put some apples, pears and a bunch of black grapes into a heavy stoneware dish. There were even a couple of bottles of decent Burgundy: Jadot Nuits-St-Georges '85, Garrett noted with approval. He uncorked one and put it on the table, aware that Germain was watching him speculatively.

It looked to Garrett as if he had little choice between a thick ear and a hiding. Germain's commitment was minimal because there was nothing in it for him. If the operation was a success, Garrett would get the laurels and he would go back to looking out of an office window in Abbeville. Unless he pulled a stroke. That was what was going around in that simmering Gallic brain. He's calculating the odds, Garrett thought. Whether to drag his feet and leave me to take the stick, or whether to take a chance and go for glory. Damn.

This was going to be tough going.

The night passed without incident. They put the watchers on alert at dawn as the local trawlers trundled along the lighted line of the Somme channel and out into the mist, but as Garrett had anticipated, the subjects made no move. Garrett and Germain snatched a few hours' sleep, taking turns to man the transceiver. The first action came a little after seven-thirty, when the radio crackled into life. Germain put on the headphones and listened.

'Okay,' he said and hung up. He turned to Garrett. 'The camels have made a move. They're at the Porte Guillaume. It's an old gate, a monument. The British brought Joan of Arc through it in 1430, on the way to Rouen. It's not far from here. Bad for us. A residential street on one side, a narrow lane on the other. They'd spot a stakeout in ten seconds.'

'You think they're making a drop?'

Germain spread his hands. 'Possibly.'

'Show me on the map.'

Germain pointed. The rue de Ponthieu ran almost north-south. At its north end was the place St Martin with its church. From the church, around the hill on which the abbey stood, a series of streets led westwards to the old stone gate. From there, the rue de L'Abbaye ran straight as a die towards the old mariners' chapel on the Mont de la Chapelle.

'We've got to move fast,' Garrett said. 'Contact the local electricity authority. Tell them we want a blackout. Every house on that street, as soon as they can fix it. The minute the power is off, move your people in. Use public utility vans; not too many: we don't want to scare them off.'

'I'll do it, I'll do it,' Germain said grumpily. Garrett recalled Irène Level's body language: perhaps Germain was heavy-handed with his female operatives as well. He made some coffee, and set myrtle jam and butter and fresh bread on the table. Germain put down the phone.

'Lights out in ten minutes,' he said. 'Did I smell coffee?'

'Help yourself.'

'They ate in silence, watching the clock. At seven-fifty-five, the transceiver came to life again. Germain put the cans on.

'Okay,' he said, after a few moments. 'Out.'

He put the headphones down and came back to the table.

'That was Irène,' he said. 'Your Englishmen, Taunton and the other one, have visitors. Two men, driving a Range Rover. It's hired. Paris plates. They've all gone down to the harbour.'

Garrett frowned. 'Have they checked the registration of the Range Rover?'

'Hired to a Robert Harwood, British passport. Born Manchester, age thirty-five. Red hair, blue eyes.'

'Doesn't tell us a thing,' Garrett said. 'What about Tamraz and his friend?'

'They went straight back to the *pension*.'

The transceiver crackled again. Germain had the headphones on. Garrett reached across him and snapped on the speakers, ignoring Germain's scowl. Philippe Savry's voice filled the room.

'. . . happening all at once, chief.' The agent's voice was tense, edgy.

'Say again, Savry,' Garrett said.

'Tamraz and Dakhleh. They've checked out. Luggage in the car. They're on the move.'

'Direction?'

'East.'

Germain stared at the transceiver. Its papery crackle seemed very loud. The sound surged, hissed.

'There's a *siffleur* on board?'

'Affirmative.'

'Go with them as far as Abbeville,' Germain told him. 'Then return here. I'll get a B-team to pick them up.'

'*Compris.* Out.'

The transceiver hissed emptily. Germain called the support-team leader in Abbeville and gave instructions in rapid-fire French. An interchangeable handover tail would pick up the terrorist car there and shadow it to wherever it was going. While he was speaking, the doorbell jangled, making Germain jump. Garrett opened the door and took a flat package from the motorcycle policeman standing there.

'Garrett?'

'Surveillance photos of the Englishmen,' Garrett said, sliding the prints on to the table. Germain spread them out and stared at them with pursed lips.

'You know any of them?' he said.

Garrett nodded. 'The one who calls himself Harwood. His real name is Hennessy.'

I'll find you one day, you bastard! One day we'll settle this, Garrett!

'Who's Hennessy?' Germain asked.

'He's an IRA armourer.'

'IRA?' Germain said. 'What the hell are IRA doing here?'

'I don't know,' Garrett said. 'All we can do is watch them and find out what they're up to.'

'I don't get it,' Germain said. 'A PLO group and an IRA unit working together?'

'They can't be,' Garrett said.

'They're here, man!'

'At the same time, maybe,' Garrett said doggedly. 'But not together.'

'Maybe it's just coincidence.'

Garrett shook his head. 'In our business there's no such thing as a coincidence,' he said.

A little before eight o'clock that fine, bright, sunny morning, a red Renault 21 slid into the car park near the *port de plaisance* of St Valery-sur-Somme, a large, open gravelled area fringed by pollarded plane trees, looking out across the river and the estuary beyond. The woman who got out of the car was strikingly beautiful. Perhaps thirty, she was dressed in a Lacoste windcheater, a white cotton roll-necked jersey and baggy Rohan trousers. The cool morning breeze lifted her jet black hair as she walked to the wall overlooking the river and leaned against it, lighting a cigarette with a cheap lighter.

A few minutes after eight, the two camels, Tamraz and Dakhleh, came along the Quai du Romerl in a Renault 7, heading across the place des Pilotes and into the rue de la Ferté towards Abbeville; as the car passed the car park, the driver flashed his headlights.

'*Bon,*' the woman said softly, smiling. The drop was made. The camels were on their way home.

The car hissed past, followed after a few seconds by an anonymous-looking Peugeot 309. A frown replaced the woman's smile. Could they have picked up a shadow? Was there any way. . . ? She shook her head. No, it wasn't possible. Just the old enemy again, the paranoia of the hunted. Think it through. The door had been closed in Paris. Every possible precaution had been taken. The operation could not have been penetrated. Another car went by. The driver was a young girl of about twenty, alone. You see? Normal traffic. People going to work. Relax. Relax. She lit another cigarette, inhaled deeply, sighed out the smoke. Easier said than done.

Four or five minutes later a blue Mercedes estate came up the road from Abbeville and turned into the car park. Two men got out and walked across to where the woman stood waiting. They were swarthy, dark-eyed, heavily built men, dressed in dark trousers and khaki military-style jerseys. They watched silently as another car, an old Citroën DS estate rolled in and slid to a stop alongside the Mercedes.

Four men got out of the Citroën and joined the group, like mourners assembling for the funeral of someone they do not know well. The breeze soughed in the knuckled trees and across the shimmering surface of the Somme. In the near distance, a boat engine rumbled. Then another. Voices called out: local sailors getting ready to catch the tide. One or two slid past the place where the woman was standing, on their way down the river towards the estuary.

'*On y va, chef?*' one of the men standing beside her asked the woman. She looked at her watch.

'Yes,' she said. 'Get the boat, Hatem.'

The man called Hatem jerked his head, and another of the group hurried with him towards the harbour. The woman turned and stared across the estuary, as though she was trying to hear something far away. After a few minutes, a powerful engine throbbed below on the water. Two of the men who had remained with the woman went down the stone steps to the jetty. A big powerboat slid alongside. One of them caught the painter tossed from the boat and looped it round an iron bollard, while a second took another line from the stern and held it.

'Khussah!' the woman said. 'As-Sahli!'

Two to the men stepped forward and stood in front of her at a kind of attention.

'You know what you have to do,' she said. 'We rendezvous here at eleven-thirty precisely. Hassan and Abu-Salem will cover you.'

The two men moved off, walking rapidly along the Quai Blavet towards the centre of town. The second pair waited perhaps five minutes and then moved off in their wake, crossing over so that their course paralleled that of the first two.

The woman went down the stone steps and got into the launch. The man at the stern unhitched his line and jumped in. He took the helm, calling out softly to the man holding the bowline. With a deft flick, the man slipped the line off the bollard and stepped on to the deck of the boat. At the helm, Hatem put the engines ahead and the powerful cruiser moved purposefully forwards.

The woman in the cockpit was smiling again. Soon, she thought. It was going well. A little while longer, and then the punishment. Death to the hated.

10

Eight-fifteen.

The old *demeure* on the hill, the transceiver hissed, crackled.

'Bonnetain to Leader.'

Bonnetain was the agent watching the boat the camels had hired. 'Go ahead,' Germain said.

'Two men. They're moving the boat downriver.'

'You're on the north quay?'

'Affirmative.'

'How long can you keep her in view?'

'All the way to the semaphore.'

'Do it.'

'Understood. Out.'

'Looks as if you were right, Garrett. Two parallel pickups,' Germain said. 'It's weird.'

'Weird's the word,' Garrett said. 'Get on to the coast-guard. Ask them if there's a ship hove to in the estuary.' The phone shrilled again. He pounced on it.

'Savry? Where are you? *Bon.* No, we need you back here. Call in when you get to the bridge. Out.'

The transceiver came to life again. 'Bonnetain to Leader.'

'What have you got?'

'The boat is making a stop. A woman getting on board. Tall, slim, dark hair, good-looking. Four men leaving the area. Going towards town. Two this side, two across the road.'

'What about the boat?'

'Heading out into the estuary. Two men and the woman aboard.'

'You've got pictures?'

'Affirmative.'

'All right,' Germain said. 'Stay in place. Out.'

He swivelled round to face Garrett. 'This is going to be

102

difficult to orchestrate, Garrett. I just haven't got the man-power. I think I'd better close them down as soon as they come in.'

He wants to go for glory, Garrett thought, his heart sink-ing. 'It would be risky,' he said, playing on Germain's uncertainty. 'It could blow up in your face.'

Germain scowled, and Garrett knew what he was think-ing: if it blows up in anybody's face, it won't be mine.

'Anything on the camels?'

'Savry said they took the Amiens road,' Garrett told him. 'Looks as if they're heading for Paris. Did you get the coastguard?'

'Yes. You were right: there's a freighter out there. Heading into the tide, staying pretty much in the same place. They gave me a bearing.'

'Have we got charts of the estuary?'

'Here,' Germain said. He spread a multicoloured map on the table. The beautifully engraved Service Hydrographi-que de la Marine charts were much superior to the Admiralty maps Garrett had on board *Sunday Girl*. Germain handed him the bearing he had scribbled down, and Garrett scanned the chart expertly.

'I thought so,' he said. 'She'll be moving up the Channel with just enough way on her to make it easy for another boat to come alongside. They can drop the stuff over the side with cork floats or in a net. The whole operation shouldn't take more than fifteen minutes.'

'I can get the coastguard to watch them on radar.'

'Not worth it. The coastguard will probably have a dozen bips on their screen, any one of which could be our boys. Besides which, we don't need to watch them. They've got to come back here.'

'I suppose so,' Germain said.

'Lemaitre to Leader,' a voice said on the transceiver. Lemaitre was one of the agents hidden in the public utility vans. 'We've got visitors.'

'How many?'

'Two I can see.'

'We made it four coming your way, two acting as backup,' Garrett said. 'Don't move till you spot them.'

'Check.'

The transceiver hissed emptily; the room was fiilled with tension.

'Lemaitre to Leader.'

'Go ahead.'

'Two men making the pick-up. Two others covering.'

'All right. Leader to Team. Here we go. Don't scare them off.'

A complex series of movements was now set in train as Germain's surveillance team went into action. As the workmen from the electricity authority began testing equipment on the street, one of the electricity authority vans would drive past the two men, photographing both, then park at the lower end of rue Porte Guillaume. As their quarry passed them, the two agents would 'hand them on' to another pair of agents, who would take turns to shadow the target duo on foot. Lemaitre would then pick up the second pair, with another backup team standing by for the handover.

'Lemaitre to Leader. Passing them now. No sign of panic. Okay. In position . . . now. Out.'

'Leader to Lorain. Got them?'

'We've got them,' the hand-on agent replied. 'No problem.'

'Which way are they going?'

'Porte Nevers, Quai du Romerel.'

'Okay. Stay with them. Out. Leader to Chabron. What have you got?'

'Our two are going the same way.'

'We'll tell him. Out. Leader to Lemaitre.'

'Here.'

'Two more pigeons coming your way.'

'Got them,' Lemaitre said. Garrett pictured him in the little van, the second agent crouched in the back with the camera and the other surveillance equipment. Lemaitre would go back up the hill in the van this time; his partner would take photographs as they passed the two men coming down.

'Rostang, this is Leader, come in,' Germain said.

'Here.'

'Two pigeons coming down. Pick them up at the church.'

'*D'accord.* Out.'

Staring at the map, the men in the house on the rue de Ponthieu visualized the movements of the men they were controlling. The first two terrorists walking east towards the *port de plaisance*, the agents alternating in pursuit, peeling off after every couple of hundred yards. Behind the first two pigeons, the second two, their invisible tail stretched out behind them. Five minutes went by; ten.

'Lorain to Leader. Come in.'

'Go ahead.'

'They're in the car park. They got into a car. A Citroën, I think. I can't get close enough to see.'

'Don't try,' Garrett said urgently. 'Keep your distance. Backup on the way.'

'Okay. Out.'

'Leader to Lemaitre.'

'Lemaitre.'

'Relocate. Place St Pierre, opposite the boat slip. Don't use the main road. Confirm when in place.'

'Affirmative. Out.'

'You've been right so far, Garrett,' Germain said. There was no admiration in the remark.

'It's a distribution meet, all right,' Garrett said. 'The camels dropped false IDs. Our pigeons picked them up. Now they're waiting to hand them on. At the same time they'll distribute whatever the boat has gone out for.'

'What about your Irishman, Hennessy? Where does he fit into this?'

Garrett scratched his ear. 'Would you feel better if I said I don't know?'

Germain opened his mouth to speak, but before he could say whatever it was he intended, the transceiver barked into life again.

'Savry to Leader. Come in.'

'Where are you, Philippe?' Germain said.

'By the turning bridge. Shall I come in?'

'What equipment have you got on board?'

'Still and video. Parabolic mike. Reel to reel tape. That's about it.'

'All right. Drive to the car park opposite place St Pierre. As you turn in you'll see twor or three cars parked on the left: a blue Merc, a red Renault. Park in the corner furthest from them.'

'And then?'

There are four men in a parked car, possibly a Citroën. They're waiting for something. We want to know what it is.'

'Okay. I'll move in.'

'Savry,' Garrett said urgently. 'Don't take any chances.'

'*Compris,*' the agent said. 'Out.'

'Garrett moved away from the transceiver and Germain slid into the chair. The set gave its preliminary hiss and crackle.

'Lemaitre to Centre. I'm in position.'

'Got your mikes set up?'

'Affirmative.'

'Are you getting anything?'

'Indistinct stuff. We need to be closer.'

'Scan the car park. Tell me what you see.'

'Moment,' Lemaitre said.

'What have you got?'

'Red Renault 21. A Citroën estate, the old DS model. Another one. Blue. No, not a Citroën. Mercedes, is it? I can't see properly, they're all parked alongside each other, facing west. One other car just came in, a Peugeot 309.'

'Philippe and Cécile, ' Germain said. 'All right. Leader to Team: hear me. Lorain is on the promenade, under the trees, about fifty metres west of the target zone. Chabron is fifty metres east. Bonnetain is on the north bank, opposite. Rostang is at the corner of the rue de le Ferté, near the tourist bureau. Lemaitre is in the place St Pierre. Leader will now transfer to mobile unit. Over and out.'

He must have pushed a buzzer somewhere; two men came in from the hall. Both were young, alert-looking. He assumed they were DST agents not yet assigned to field work. They nodded at Garrett but no attempt was made to make introductions.

'Take over,' Germain said to one of them. 'Let's go, Garrett. Time to move out.'

Parked outside the house was a spectacularly filthy VW Kombi with local plates. It looked as if it might belong to a badly run plumbing firm; in fact, the vehicle was packed with hi-tech surveillance and communications equipment. Germain took the van down through the old town and along the Quai du Romerel. At the end of the rue de la Ferté he turned left into the Place Guillaume le Conquerant and coasted into a parking space near the monument to the Norman king.

Garrett looked at his watch: nine-twenty. It was an hour since the boat had gone out. How far out was the steamer? He mentally checked the chart again: a couple of miles. With a big powerful boat like that they could be out there in ten or fifteen minutes, no trouble at all. Twenty, thirty minutes to transfer the cargo. Less to come in, running with the slackening tide. He flicked the transceiver on.

'Rabier, this is Mobile, come in.'

'Rabier.'

'Any sign of the Englishmen?'

'Nothing yet.'

'Keep your eyes peeled.'

'Will do. Out.'

Garrett frowned at the silent set. Did Hennessy know the Arab unit was in St Valery? Did they know he was? What was he picking up? Guns, explosives, all were grist to the terrorist mill. The presence of the IRA's top armourer in France was an indication that Hennessy was planning to arm an IRA assault unit with a target somewhere on the mainland of Europe. The likeliest candidates were British Army bases or personnel in northern Germany. But what had that to do with the men waiting in the boat slip car

107

park? Was there a connection? What was their boat bringing in, and what was their target? He shook his head; some things you just didn't know and had to guess at.

'Rabier to Mobile.'

'Go ahead, Rabier,' Germain said.

'English boat in sight.'

'How far away?'

'Three, four hundred metres.'

'Where's Irène?'

'In the van.'

'Get back there.'

'*Volontiers*,' Rabier said. They could almost see the grin. Garrett thought about Irène Level's unexpected dimples and was surprised to experience a twinge of envy.

The trouble with you, Garrett, is you'd rather chase some bloody terrorist than chase me around a bedroom. I know grandmothers who have a better sex life than I do.

'Mobile, this is Rabier. Subjects have landed. They're bringing boxes off the boat. They look heavy.'

'Get as many pictures as you can. Advise if they start to move.'

He had hardly finished speaking when Lorain, the agent on the promenade, called in.

'Target boat coming up the channel.'

'Where is she now?'

'A good way out. Maybe two kilometres,' Lobain said.

'How many on board, can you see?'

'Negative. They're all under cover.'

'Stand by,' Germain said. 'Lemaitre, what can you see?'

'We've got a traffic jam here,' Lemaitre reported. 'A Volkswagen Golf just drove in. Two men getting out. Now the ones in the Citroën. Six of them altogether. They're going down to the slip.'

'Mobile, this is Chabron. I see them. They're waiting for the boat. She's coming up the channel now.'

'Get some pictures.'

'Will do.'

'Mobile to Savry. Can you see anything?'

'Affirmative. They're taking boxes out. About two

metres long. Rope handles. Bulky. One to each man.
They're bringing them to the cars.'

'Any markings?'

'FFVO. Then a name I can't read. Something-t-u-n-a.'

'You filming?'

'Still and video.'

'Keep at it. Cécile can give us the vehicle details.'

'White Volkswagen Golf, 194 BJG 17, Charente-Mar
registration,' the woman said. 'Blue Mercedes estate, 1814
ZL 17, same again. Black Citroën DS, 1854 BF13,
Marseilles. Red Renault 21, 388 CFF 75, Paris. That's the
woman's car.'

'Is she in it?'

'No. She's giving each of the men something. Envelopes.'

'Documents,' Garrett said. 'Tell your men to stand by,
Germain. They'll be moving out any time now.'

'Rabier to Mobile, the Englishmen have loaded up.
They're moving.'

'All in the same vehicle?'

'Affirmative.'

'Which way?'

'East, by the look of it. Through town. Shall I follow?'

'Affirmative,' Germain said. He was sweating, breathing
hard as if he had run upstairs.

'Lemaitre to Mobile.'

'Go ahead.'

'Our pigeons are moving, too.'

'This isn't going to work, Garrett!' Germain said. His
voice was trembling and he was sweating profusely. 'If we
go after them there'll be twelve, fourteen cars on the road
– it's going to look like the Monte Carlo Rally! They'll spot
us in thirty seconds.'

'They'll split up outside town,' Garrett said. 'They can't
all go the same way. Give it a chance!'

Germain shook his head, his eyes blank. 'East or west,
there's only the one road, and I can't get past them. I'm
going in.'

'Don't be a damned fool, Germain!' Garrett snapped.
'We want them alive, not dead!'

'Keep out of this, Garrett,' Germain said flatly. 'I'm making a pre-emptive field decision.'

'You're making the worst blunder of your life!' Garrett said. It was a mistake: Germain's eyes narrowed and he hit the dashboard with his fist.

'We'll see,' he snapped. 'We'll see about that!' He snatched up the mike. 'Leader to Team: all hear. We are closing down the car park. Repeat: we are closing down the car park. On my command, Lemaitre will block the eastern exit with his van. I will take the western exit. All operatives then move in to apprehend opposition personnel, eight men and one woman. Mobile moving now. Out.'

He started the truck up and roared out on to the road, tyres screaming as he accelerated towards the tree-ringed car park at about sixty miles an hour.

'Germain!' Garrett yelled, hanging on to the handle above the door. 'Call it off! You're going to get everybody killed!'

'Shut up, shut up!' Germain screeched. 'I'm relieving you, you hear me?'

'I hear you,' Garrett said flatly. 'You're crazy!'

'Leader to Team, Leader to Team, we are go, move in now! Repeat, now!'

His men emerged from concealment as he threw the clumsy Kombi into a skidding bootlegger's turn that swung the vehicle across the highway to block the exit of the car park. At the same time, Lemaitre raced across the road in the blue and white electricity authority van, headlights on full, to block the exit at the Abbeville end. Even as the other DST agents ran towards the car park, their guns drawn, the big blue Mercedes came roaring out, smashing the van aside like a child's toy, headlight glass spraying in a glittering arc into the air as it fishtailed on to the road, swerving left and then right, burning rubber before it straightened up and roared off towards Abbeville. Right behind the Merc, pursued by a fusillade of shots, came the old Citroën DS, leaping three feet into the air as it hit the ramped pavement. It came down with a massive metal sound, slewed across the road, sideswiping a parked Fiat, then roared off after the Mercedes.

Germain leaped out of the Kombi and ran in a crouch into the car park. Garrett heard the hard spiteful sound of small-arms fire, and then a harder, deeper bang. Black smoke rose above the trees. He slid the Smith and Wesson ASP from its shoulder holster and ran around the back of the Kombi, using the trees for cover. He had gone no more than five yards when a red Renault 21 burst straight through the fence surrounding the car park, smashing aside a litter bin, wheels spinning on the dusty gravel as the driver fought to control the car.

As if it was all happening in some strange slow motion, Garrett's eyes met those of the woman behind the wheel. She was dark and beautiful, with high cheekbones and full, sensuous lips. He saw the dark eyes narrow, watched her swing the wheel to aim the car at him. In that endless fraction of time, he was already firing his gun, emptying the magazine as he dived desperately out of its path. He heard the tight bang of the windscreen disintegrating, and thought he heard a scream as the Renault went past him like a juggernaut, hit the road, bucked against the kerb-stones on the far side, tyres shrieking as it straightened out again and disappeared round the bend in the road by the restaurant.

Garrett got to his feet and ran through the screen of trees into the open space. On the far side of the car park, a smashed red Peugeot 3409 was burning furiously. The Volkswagen Golf stood with its door open and its engine running, two dead bodies sprawled on the gravel nearby. A DST agent, pistol cocked, stood over two men who knelt beside the vehicle, their hands behind their heads. Germain was standing slackmouthed in the centre of the car park, his unfired Beretta still in his hand, staring at the burning Peugeot. There was no sign of anyone else. Jesus, Garrett thought. They got away. All this, and they got away.

He turned to see a DST agent coming up warily, gun trained on him. Garrett realized he still had his own empty weapon in his hand. He spread his arms.

'I'm Garrett,' he said. 'Who are you?'

'Paul Lorain,' the man said. 'What a mess, uh? What a pile of shit!'

'Who's hurt?'

'Who isn't hurt, you mean. Lemaitre has got a broken hip. Chabron took a bullet in the leg. And that!' He jerked a thumb angrily at the burning car on the far side of the lot. 'Look at that! Look at it!'

'Who was in it?' Garrett asked.

'Savry,' the man replied, angrily. 'And Cécile Laurent. They never had a chance. Rockets, for Christ's sake! Those bastards had rockets!'

Germain turned towards the sound of their voices.

'I didn't know,' he said, his voice a querulous whine. He stretched his hand out, took hold of Garrett's forearm. 'Garrett, you can see that, can't you? I acted for the best. There was no choice, I had to do it. How could I have known they'd have rockets? Oh, Jesus, what a fucking mess.'

Garrett thrust him aside. 'Get this bastard out of here,' he said to Lorain. 'Get him out of here before I kill him.'

Then he ran to the Kombi to summon help.

11

'Stop the car,' Hennessy said. 'Pull over!'

Gallagher, driving, checked the mirror and pulled in to the kerb outside the Syndicat d'Initiative on the rue de la Ferté.

'What is it?' he said.

'Listen!' Hennessy hissed, winding down his window.

They all heard it now; none of them needed telling it was the flat *rip-rap* of small-arms fire. Ahead they saw a dark pillar of smoke rising into the sky, vehicles slewed in the middle of the road, police lights flashing.

'What d'ye reckon's going on?' Gallagher said. He was young, only about thirty, a good-looking fellow with clear blue eyes and a dark beard. 'There's all sorts of fuzz down the road, d'ye see them?'

'Going to wait till they come and get us, then, are you?' Hennessy snapped. 'Shift this bloody heap!'

Gallagher threw the Range Rover into gear, roaring around the corner, then left again on the Quai Blavet, brows knitted with concentration as he straightened up the vehicle.

'Up the hill, there, lad!' Hennessy said. 'Drive!'

The younger man turned across the rue de la Ferté and opened up the big engine. The Range Rover swept smoothly up the rue des Moulins. Nobody spoke. As they approached a crossroads, Hennessy told the driver to turn right and stop. They were on the top of the hill now, overlooking the town and the shimmering estuary beyond it.

'What was it, Sean?' Gallagher said. 'What the hell's happened down there??'

Hennessy did not reply for a moment, but sat looking thoughtfully out of the window. The sound of police sirens cut loudly through the everyday morning sounds. He shook his head.

'It must have been them others,' he muttered.

'Others?' Taunton said. 'What others?'

'There was another boat out there this morning,' Hennessy said. 'Another pick-up. It looks as if whoever made it has run into trouble. Which means the bogeys had them under surveillance.'

'I don't believe what I'm hearing,' Taunton said. 'Are you seriously telling us we weren't the only boat out there this morning?'

'That's what I said.'

'And you took us into it, knowing that?'

'I didn't have any choice.' Hennessy replied savagely. 'I knew it was risky, but we needed the stuff and there was no other way to get it.'

'And now we're up shit creek,' the thin man in the rear seat said venomously. 'Without a paddle.'

Although his passport gave his name as Bartholomew Johnson of Maida Vale in London, the thin man was in fact Seamus McQueen, born in the year after the end of World War Two at Newtownards in Northern Ireland. The man sitting beside him, Frank Taunton, was also Ulster-born. His real name was Peter Egan and, like Gallagher, he was a son of Derry.

'Why?' Gallagher asked. 'What difference does it make to us?'

'Eejut,' Hennessy said, without heat. 'Don't you see, if the bastards were watching anybody, they were watching everybody.'

'There was no sign of surveillance, Sean,' Gallagher protested hotly. 'I swear it. I checked. Peter double-checked. We didn't see anything anywhere.'

'This isn't the bloody RUC you're dealing with here, Tony,' Hennessy said. 'These people are pros.'

'You're saying you think they'll be on to us, then?'

'It's always wise to act as if they are,' Hennessy said. 'Don't be fright, it's not the end of the world, just a change of plan. All right, Tony, let's go. I'll give you directions as we go.'

'Right,' Gallagher said, and moved off slowly into

the morning traffic. Hennessy let him pass the first street on the right then watched their rear carefully. A green Mazda 626 slid out of the side street and moved up behind them.

'We're coming to a junction,' he told Gallagher. 'It's called the Place de la Croix l'Abbé. Go left, and then take the first left when you hit the crossroads.'

Gallagher did as he was bidden. The narrow road led downhill. There was a defeated-looking farm off on the right. The Mazda turned follow to them.

'You know where we're going, Sean?'

'I know.'

He unfailingly observed the same routine in every strange town he visited, poring over maps and then walking for hours until he had completely familiarized himself with its streets and traffic system. They made a sharp turn left, doubling back to the wooded slopes around the Château d'Eau above Le Tivoli. Hennessy checked behind him. The tail car was following at a respectful distance. The big question was: did whoever was tailing them have back-up? And the answer was always the same: act as if they have. It made things a bit trickier, but still not impossible. We'll have to move soon, Hennessy thought. The roadblocks will be going up before long.

'All right,' he said, 'this is what we're going to do.' He told them slowly and carefully what he had in mind. Gallagher was no genius, but he could drive. When he was sure the younger man knew exactly what he meant, Hennessy made his move. 'Next left, Tony. Then turn up the wick.'

They turned left into the rue de Neuville and roared down the hill, putting a distance of several hundred yards between the Range Rover and the pursuing Mazda, emerging in the Place Maréchal Foch and swinging left past the cemetery.

'This'll do,' Hennessy said. 'Slow down. Pull in as close as you can to that van on the right. As soon as I'm out, drive halfway up the next block. Stop for thirty seconds, then go again. You're sure you've got the route straight?'

'Top of the hill, take the right fork, straight down to the main road,' Gallagher said. 'Don't worry, Sean.'

Hennessy scowled at Gallagher's insouciance. 'Get it right,' he said. 'You won't get a second chance.'

Gallagher put the Range Rover close enough to the van parked on the right-hand side of the road to make it impossible for the pursuers to see Hennessy slide out and duck behind the vehicle. He watched as Gallagher roared up the hill, pulling in at the next junction; the Mazda accelerated past and then braked as the driver saw the Range Rover stop, double-parking alongside a white Opel.

From behind the van, Hennessy checked back down the hill. If there was a backup car, he couldn't see it. He eased around behind the Mazda, and all in one movement he opened the rear door and slid inside, clamping his arm around the passenger's neck and jamming the barrel of his Heckler and Koch P7 M13 against the man's temple.

'Not one word, boyo,' he hissed. 'If you understand, you just nod. Got it?'

The man nodded. To Hennessy's surprise, the driver was a woman. So much the better, he thought grimly.

'You, girlie, you so much as hiccup and I'll blow your friend all over the roof of this car, you hear me?'

'I hea—'

'I said *nod*!'

Irène Level nodded, her face white and still.

'Right, then,' Hennessy said. Up ahead of them the Range Rover was pulling away from the kerb. 'Follow the leader.'

Irène put the car into gear and moved off up the hill after the big vehicle. Hennessy risked a quick look back. There was no backup. As they reached the crest of the gentle hill, the Range Rover speeded up. They left the town behind, running down a long gentle slope, the sky ahead bright with the reflection of the nearby sea. Here and there sand dunes broke the flat surface.

'See those woods ahead,' Hennessy said. 'Stop when I tell you.'

The copse was called Bois Houdane. A track ran

diagonally through it on their right; Gallagher would be parked there. Hennessy checked their rear: nothing behind them.

'Slow down,' Hennessy told the woman. 'Stop just before you get to that track going into the woods.'

As they came to a stop, Seamus McQueen ran out of the side track and around the car, wrenching open the door and hustling the woman out. Hennessy pushed Rabier in front of him, shoving both the DST agents ahead of him off the road and down into the ditch, standing above them and well to one side.

'Oh, please!' the woman said, as Hennessy shot her. A moment later McQueen turned his gun on Alain Rabier. The Frenchman spat contemptuously at McQueen's shoes as the Irishman shot him in the head. Hennessy walked away from the two bodies lying in the ditch and went over to where Tony Gallagher was standing in front of the Range Rover, staring in disbelief at what he had just seen.

'Don't stand there like a bloody stuffed dummy!' Hennessy yelled at him. 'Get the stuff into the Mazda! Quick, now!'

Gallagher, Taunton and Johnson hastened away and began unloading the suitcases from the Range Rover parked on the track under the trees. They lugged them over to the other car, heaved them into the boot, and stood back, panting.

'All right, let's go,' Hennessy said. 'At the interchange, take the right fork to Cayeux. Move it!'

They roared off. No one looked back at the bodies sprawled half in, half out of the shallow ditch at the side of the narrow road.

They joined the main road a few hundred yards further on, turning west towards Cayeux. It ran parallel to the bay formed by the headlands of Cap Hornu and le Hourdel. Fingers of fine white sand lay drifted across the road, which swung south between copses of pine. At Brighton they could see the stark white finger of the lighthouse fronting the beach. Cayeux was quiet as they drove through; on the south side of town the road looped back towards the main highway to Le Tréport. Gallagher pushed the revs up to four thousand.

'Take it easy, Tony,' Hennessy advised him. 'We don't want to get stopped for speeding. Keep your eyes skinned for police. There's bound to be a checkpoint up along here somewhere by now.'

They were coming into the village of Brutelles. Gallagher eased off the loud pedal, and gestured ahead with his chin.

'Talk of the divil,' he said, and now Hennessy saw the police cars parked at the crossroads, the gendarmes lugging striped sawhorse barriers into the road.

'What do we do, Sean?' Gallagher said, tensely.

'Nothing,' Hennessy said. 'Take it easy. They're looking for a Range Rover, not a Mazda.'

As they eased up to the barriers, a gendarme saw the local licence plates and waved them past, making an impatient hurry-up sign. Gallagher raised a hand in acknowledgement.

'If you insist,' he grinned. '*Au revoir*, dickhead.'

As soon as they were out of sight of the roadblock, he piled on the revs, heading south. On the outskirts of the little town of Eu, they turned east on the rue des Belges and picked up the D1015 to Beauvais. They covered the hundred miles to Paris in well under two hours. Within an hour of their arrival, the consignment of guns and explosive had been repacked in three separate vehicles for onward transmission to Germany.

Although Garrett had whistled a police helicopter into the air within three minutes of the shoot-out in the car park, the terrorists seemed to have vanished without trace. The problem was, as Garrett knew, there was a whole network of lanes connecting the small villages lying on the salt marshes surrounding St Valery; with even the most sophisticated roadblock system it would be impossible to stop every gap. Nevertheless, he did everything that could be done, masterminding the operation from inside the DST Kombi and calling in all the help he could get, from the local constabulary and the DST support team in Abbeville to 'head office' in Paris.

The immediate search-and-find priority was the red Renault 21 that had been driven by the woman leading the Arab team; running it a close second were the blue Mercedes and the Citroën. The computer had already confirmed what Garrett suspected, that each of the vehicles was stolen. There was also the matter of finding Hennessy's Range Rover: communication with the car shadowing it had broken down, but whether that had sinister implications or was simply due to faulty equipment had not yet been established.

One by one, Garrett carried out the housekeeping tasks that had to be done, alerting A8 in London and BfV in Cologne to watch out for Hennessy and his confederates, making sure copies of the surveillance photographs were faxed to DST and the TREVI computer, making a succinct telephone call to Bleke. By the time he had completed these routine tasks, the grisly work of extricating what was left of Philippe Savry and Cécile Laurent from the charred hulk of the Peugeot 309 was over, the ambulance men working behind a solid cordon of gendarmes thrown around the area by the local prefecture. In the car park, a tow truck with the legend 'Lefebvre et Tellier' painted on its doors was being hitched to the wrecked car. Garrett looked out at the estuary. Brilliance danced on the water. Gulls circled overhead. Although it was not yet eleven, he felt enormously tired. He went back into the van and sat at the console, waiting.

Twenty minutes after the confrontation, the helicopter pilot reported that he had located the red Renault, apparently abandoned, in a copse near a farm halfway between Estreboeuf and Boismont, a couple of kilometres out of St Valery. A posse of gendarmes hurtled out there to find not just the Renault 21, but all three of the missing cars abandoned beneath the trees.

The bad news was that there was no sign of the terrorists; since the farm stood on a junction of minor roads that led south to the main Abbeville-Dieppe highway and north to

119

Nouvion and the Boulogne road, with half a dozen alternative options in between, Garrett gave up hoping the roadblocks would net their quarry. They had no idea what the terrorist squad was driving, what kind of papers they were carrying, or in what formation they were travelling. For all anyone knew, they might very well by now be chugging out of Abbeville on a train bound for Paris.

The good news was that Garrett seemed to have wounded the woman terrorist who had driven the red Renault at him. The gendarmes reported that the windscreen of the car was shattered and that there was blood on the upholstery. Not for the first time, Garrett thanked the memory of the firearms instructor at Fort Monkton who had drummed into them the fact that ninety-nine out of a hundred bullets would not even go through the door of the standard saloon car, no matter what the weapon firing them; and that precious few handguns were powerful enough to punch a slug through a windscreen except at point-blank range. The only way to make sure your shots paid off was to load with the new THV – it stood for *très haute vitesse*, very high-speed – bullets, which travelled one hundred per cent faster than standard side-arm loads and delivered the same percentage extra in stopping power. Unlike other rounds, the THV bullet also delivered all its energy to the target, rather than passing right through it. In this instance it had clearly paid off.

He took stock of the situation he was left with. It wasn't terrific. Whatever its aims, Al Iqab was now armed with some very sophisticated weaponry. He knew, because satellite reconnaissance had quickly provided an identification of the ship which had hove to in the estuary, that the weapons had come from Bulgaria. A computer check of the markings on the crates that had been brought ashore indicated that the weapons were manufactured by FFV Ordnance in Eskilstuna, Sweden, who made mortar bombs, assault rifles, heat-seeking antitank weapons. From the way they had taken out the DST car, Garrett concluded it was probably the latter. He knew the cell consisted of about ten, and that the leader was – unusually in an Arab organization — a sensuously beautiful woman of perhaps thirty, probably, but not definitely Arab. It wasn't much.

I ought to be angry, he thought. He wasn't; if anything, he was sad. Germain had really screwed it up. Nobody minded a man making a mistake. Going berserk was something else. Counter-terrorism was a *reactive* discipline. You waited, you watched, until your enemy gave you a lead you could exploit. A high body count told you nothing and led you nowhere. He saw in his mind's eye a picture of Germain being taken back to the safe house in the rue de Ponthieu to await orders, shoulders slumped, head down. He wondered what would happen to him. If DST worked anything like the British, he would be taken quietly out of service and put somewhere he could never imperil anything more important than a lupin. He looked up as a local officer came hurrying across to him.

'You're Garrett? Sergeant wants you. Urgent.'

He went across to the police car. A beefy sergeant, perspiring freely, told him that some local people had seen what looked like a large bundle of clothes lying half in and half out of a ditch beside the road from the town, and got out of their car to investigate. When the woman who had been driving saw what was in the ditch she went into hysterics and had to be rushed to the St Valery hospital.

A squad car was sent out to the scene; it was a mess. In the ditch were the bodies of Alain Rabier and Irène Level. She was the one with the dimples, Garrett thought, remembering the quick flash of envy he had felt. He sighed: DST was taking a hell of a beating today. He called one of the DST agents across. It was Rostang: he looked edgy and pale, like a man on a boat who has had his first intimation that he's going to be seasick.

'*Ça va?*' Garrett said.

'I've had better days than this,' Rostang said bitterly. 'What's the word?'

'I'm closing down,' Garrett said. 'The birds have flown.'

'*Merde!*' said the agent.

'That's one word for it,' Garrett replied. 'Take over here, will you? I've got some things to do.'

'*D'accord,*' Rostang said, and slid into the chair by the console. Garrett walked back across the road to the sergeant in the local police car.

'Can one of your boys give me a lift to the gendarmerie, sergeant?' he asked.

'Take you myself,' the Frenchman said. 'Get in.'

The car was a Citroën. It smelled of Gauloises and stale coffee. The sergeant drove like a Parisian, carelessly but well. He said his name was Legros, and that he had lived in St Valery since he was a child; his father was a local baker.

'Used to go round with him, every morning before school, delivering the bread in an old Renault van,' he said, as they sped along the Quai du Romerel. 'Old ladies used to give me things to eat. Dried apple rings. A peach. I had breakfast from six till nine. Those were the days. You mind if I ask you something?'

'Go ahead.'

'What was this business today? Suh-deck, no?'

Before Mitterand rechristened them in 1981, DGSE had been known by the initials SDECE, 'suh-deck' for short. Garrett was surprised that a policeman in a small coastal town would know the nickname, and said so.

'We're not all *rustres*, you know,' Legros said grumpily, wheeling the big car expertly through the narrow, cobblestoned streets of the old town. 'What's an English doing mixed up in it?'

'Special duties,' Garrett said. It was one of those phrases that meant everything and nothing. The sergeant seemed to find it answered his question.

'You going to question those two we brought up here?'

'That's the idea.'

'I'll give you a tip. Try the young one. The older one, *le grêlé*, that's a tough little bastard.'

He wheeled the Citroën around in front of the big limestone building in the place St Martin and they went inside.

'Wait here. I'll check with the inspector.'

'Thanks.'

Garrett waited in the grubby reception area with its comfortless wooden bench. Police stations were the same all over the world. A sliding hatch and a bell with a sign that said 'Ring for attention'. Posters that told you to watch out for burglars, flattened cigarette butts littering the floor. Passers-by stared in through the glass swing doors, wondering if you were a thief or a criminal. Duty officers with clipboards under their arms glanced at you as they went by: do I know him?

'Can you come with me, sir?'

The desk sergeant was holding the inner swing door open. Garrett went through into a hall with an open-plan staircase and a large notice board with notices pinned to it. The sergeant led him down a corridor to a locked door, on which he knocked. A judas window slid open, locks rattled.

'To see the prisoners,' the sergeant said. The phlegmatic-looking jailer nodded and led Garrett down a stone staircase to a cool, stone-floored basement. There were two cells, side by side.

'Which one first?' the jailer said. 'Sir?'

'Let me take a quick look,' Garrett replied. The jailer shrugged and slid aside a judas window so Garrett could look in. A man of about thirty sat on the bunk, hands clasped between his knees. He was thin and dark, his face badly pockmarked. *Le grêlé*, Garrett thought, the tough one. In the second cell was a younger man, paler skinned than the pockmarked one. He lay on his back, hands clasped behind his head, staring at the ceiling.

'I'll take this one first,' Garrett said. 'Anyone else talked to them?'

'Not yet,' the jailer said. 'They're sending someone up. From Paris, I'm told.'

He opened the door of the cell. The young man inside looked up as Garrett came in, putting a defiant look on his face, like a child persisting with a lie; but his dark eyes were liquid with apprehension. Garrett felt a quick pulse of excitement. This one was scared; maybe he could break him fast. He heard the voice of the psychologist who had taught them interrogation techniques at Borough High Street. First scare them utterly shitless. Then all you have to be is polite, and they'll kiss your arse. Garrett gave the jailer the nod and the man went out, locking the door behind him.

'All right,' Garrett said, 'let's start with your name.'

'Donald Duck,' was the defiant reply. Garrett looked at the man for a moment, and then slapped him off the bunk into the corner of the cell. The man sprawled on the floor, a trickle of blood coursing down his chin from a split lip.

'*Toujours la politesse*,' Garrett reminded him. 'Let's try again, shall we?'

The Arab scrabbled into a sitting position, wiping his mouth with the back of his hand. There was a sort of fearful wonder in his eyes now. Garrett knew what the look meant.

'Name!' he snapped.

'Ahmad Khussah,' the man said.

'Where are you from, Khussah?'

'Originally, you mean?'

'You can start with that.'

'Beit Hanoun.'

'West Bank?'

Khussah nodded.

'You know who I am?'

Khussah shrugged, trying for nonchalance. 'Another cop, I expect.'

'You're not in the hands of the cops any more, sonny,' Garrett said, putting contempt into his voice. 'You're a prisoner without a name in a cell without a number. You've already ceased to exist.'

'What you talking about?' Khussah said, trying unsuccessfully for a sneer. 'Who are you, anyway?'

'Office of Executive Action,' Garrett said, making it up as he went along. 'We don't use names.'

Khussah frowned. 'Office of what?'

Garrett smiled forgivingly. 'They didn't tell you about

this part, did they?' he said. 'They didn't tell you what would happen to you when you were handed over to us.'

'What—'

'Want to know what we do?' Garrett said. 'I'll tell you. We get rid of unwanted vermin. No questions asked.'

The Arab tried again for a sneer and again it didn't quite stick. The apprehension in his dark eyes deepened; he was starting to believe it. Garrett put the pressure on.

'Your friend has told us everything,' Garrett said, taking his Smith and Wesson ASP out of his shoulder holster. 'So we don't need you any more. Anything you want before. . . ?'

'Wh – whu – what do you mean?'

'I mean I'm going to kill you,' Garrett said, as if he was surprised he had to explain it.

'You're bluffing,' the man said. 'You can't just—'

Garrett slammed the slide noisily back to put a round into the barrel of the pistol. The Arab blanched and stretched out his arms with his hands up in front of his face.

'No!' he said hoarsely. 'Wait, don't! In the name of God, don't!'

'Too late for all that,' Garrett said. 'On your knees, facing the wall.'

'No, please!' the man said. 'Wait, please, wait.'

'What for? We know all we need to know. The name of your group is Al Iqab. You were working with two men called Tamraz and Dahkleh. They dropped your false papers at the Jeanne d'Arc gate. While you made the pickup, the woman went out in the boat to get the weapons. Let's get this over with.' He raised the gun.

'No!' Khussah screeched. 'God, no!'

'Then talk to me, Khussah! Tell me something I don't know.'

'She is going to America,' Khussah said. 'Leila Jarhoun.'

'Tell me about Jarhoun.'

'She is the leader.'

'I know that. What else?'

'She will go to America. On the appointed day, she will send the signal from there.'

'America's a big place,' Garrett said.

'New York!' Khussah said frantically, 'New York!'

'When?'

'Soon. I don't know exactly.'

'And what will the signal be?'

'I don't know.'

'What happens when it comes?'

'We were to be told.'

'Who is we?'

'I didn't know any of them. Ibrahim, Tamraz, Dakhleh, yes. But not the others.'

'Full names, Khussah!'

'Ibrahim as-Sahli. Nafez Tamraz. Ali Dakhleh.'

'What about the others?'

'I don't know their names. One is called Hatem. That's all I heard, his first name.'

'You expect me to believe you, Khussah? You think you can palm me off with shit like this?'

Khussah groaned, and fell to the floor, prostrating himself in front of Garrett.

'I swear to you, on my mother's grave, I don't know any more. If I did, I'd tell you. I'd tell you, I swear it?'

Garrett put the muzzle of the gun behind the man's ear. Khussah screamed. He heard the jailer's keys jangling, and the door swung open. A thickset man in civilian clothes stood outside, an angry look on his face.

'What the hell is going on in here?' he shouted.

Garrett stepped aside. 'What you see,' he said. 'I'm interrogating this prisoner.'

'You're Garrett?' he snapped.

'I'm Garrett. Who are you?'

'Claude Desmesnil,' the man said. 'Section D8, DST. As of now I'm taking over this investigation.' D8 was counterespionage. It looked as if Desmesnil was off his territory and maybe out of his league.

'You got here fast,' Garrett observed.

'I hurried,' Desmesnil said, giving him a drop-dead stare. He was one of those well-upholstered types, not overweight enough to be called fat, rosy-cheeked and pale-eyed, with receding hair that had not quite gone back far enough to say he was balding. 'Who gave you authority to question these prisoners?'

Garrett flipped open his ID wallet and let Desmesnil see it. The man shrugged.

'All right, Garrett. You've had your suck of the tit. From here on in you leave this to us.'

'I made that mistake already,' Garrett replied. 'I'm not about to do it again.'

'You don't have a lot of choice,' Desmesnil sneered. 'You're relieved. General Izbot wants to hear your version of what happened here. It had better be good. The word is this operation was a complete fuck-up.'

'Is that why they sent you up here, Desmesnil?' Garrett said harshly. 'Are you another of those DST cover-up merchants, sent down here to sweep this whole thing under the carpet so the President doesn't have another *Rainbow Warrior* on his hands?'

'What I'm here for doesn't concern you, Garrett.' He turned to the jailer. 'This man is not to be admitted in here again under any pretext whatsoever. Understand?'

The jailer shrugged. 'Anything you say,' he replied. He looked at Garrett without interest. People came, people went. Next week it would be back to the old routine again.

'I am going to have five minutes with the other prisoner,' Garrett said. 'And I'm going to have them now. And you'd better not try to stop me.'

'You threaten me?' Desmesnil said, flexing his hands.

'Don't fool yourself,' Garrett said. 'You're fat and you're out of condition. Get in my way and I'll tear your face off.'

Desmesnil's eyes flickered uneasily, and Garrett knew he had him: the man was big, but that was all.

'I'll come in with you,' Desmesnil said, gesturing to the jailer to open the door. Garrett put a hand on his chest and effortlessly stopped him.

'You. Will. Not,' Garrett said.

Desmesnil's rosy cheeks flushed crimson; for one joyous moment Garrett thought he might still have a fight on his hands, but Desmesnil didn't follow through. Pity, Garrett thought; there were some people in the world it was a pleasure to teach the rough facts of life.

He went into the cell. Ibrahim as-Sahli was sitting in the same place on the bunk, his head in his hands. He did not look up as Garrett came in. He was about twenty-five, with high, bony cheekbones and deep, dark eyes. His skin was pitted with smallpox scars.

'Is this the first time you've been arrested?' Garrett asked. He waited while Ibrahim thought about it, decided there was nothing to lose by admitting it, then nodded.

'I see,' Garrett said, thoughtfully. 'So you haven't really got any idea of what is going to happen to you?'

'What do you mean?' as-Sahli said, looking up. There was an unease in the dark eyes that had not been there before.

'You won't be staying here,' Garrett said. 'They'll be taking you to Paris.'

The man shrugged. 'So what?'

'You don't get it, do you? Listen: DST has got six dead agents and a lot of egg on its face. They want some answers out of you, and they'll get them. They've got a place down in the basement of La Piscine – the games room, they call it. They'll take you down there and connect you up to some machines they've got. You can say goodbye to your sex life once you've had the treatment. The eardrums usually go, as well, and sometimes the bones of the legs never quite knit the way they're supposed to. But I expect your people told you all this when they recruited you, didn't they?'

'You expect me to believe all this crap?' as-Sahli said scornfully. 'You think you can frighten me?'

Garrett shrugged. 'I thought you were halfway smart. But you're stupid. Well, if you want to spend the rest of your life peeing into a plastic bag, it's not my problem.'

This time he was rewarded by a stream of filth, street argot mixed with some Arabic words that were spoken too fast for him to catch them. It wasn't difficult to work out that they were not complimentary. Garrett shook his head, as might someone impatient with a wilful child. He hauled the man to his feet and hit him in the belly. The man folded over, retching, his forehead to the floor.

'I haven't got a lot of time,' Garrett said conversationally. 'So don't waste the little I have.'

He hauled the man upright again and sat him on the bunk that hung from the wall by two chains. The man sat with his head hanging, his breath whistling hoarsely through his open mouth. Garrett moved and he flinched violently. The big man smiled; psychological advantage was important.

'Now,' he said, turning the prisoner's chair round and straddling it with his arms folded along the top of the back rest. 'Let's begin again, shall we? Your name is. . . ?'

'Ibrahim as-Sahli.'

'Where are you from?'

'Paris.'

'Before that.'

'Khan Yunis.'

'Israel?'

'Palestine.'

'Of course. And why are you here in St Valery?'

'You know.'

'Don't make me angry again, Ibrahim. Just answer the question.'

'Identification papers.'

'What for?'

'I don't know.'

'I'll ask you again: what for?'

'I don't know, I tell you. You think they tell us?'

'What is the name of the woman?'

'I don't know.'

'What came in on the boat?'

'Boxes.'

'Yes, but what was in them?'

'I don't know.'

'What kind of weapons were in the boxes?'

'I tell you I don't know.'

'You were there when they fired one at the car in the car park, weren't you?'

'I saw nothing. I heard an explosion, turned round. The

129

car was on fire. Then there was shooting everywhere, cars crashing. Someone shouted at me to get down or they'd kill me. That's all I know.'

'How many members does Al Iqab have?'

'What's Al Iqab?'

'You're pretty good, Ibrahim,' Garrett said. 'For a kid. But you're not in my league. Tell me about the woman.'

'What woman?'

'Leila Jarhoun,' Garrett said. The man's head came up, and he regarded Garrett with glittering hatred. Then he spat on the floor.

'That's right, Ibrahim,' Garrett said. 'Your fat friend told me everything.'

'That gutless tub of lard!' as-Sahli hissed. 'I knew he wouldn't—' He silenced himself, black eyes burning with suppressed anger.

'Tell me about Jarhoun,' Garrett said. 'Where is she from?'

'I thought you said Khussah had told you everything,' he sneered.

Garrett was across the cell in one tigerlike bound. He bunched as-Sahli's shirt in his fist and drove the man back hard against the wall of the cell. The breath whooshed out of the man's lungs and his head made a light noise, like a coconut shell, as it hit the wall. Garrett let him go and he slid down into a sitting position on the floor, eyes glazed.

'Answer me, you worthless piece of shit,' Garrett said, letting all his hostility out. 'Or I'll really hurt you. Now, who is Leila Jarhoun?'

Ibrahim as-Sahli shook his head. 'No,' he said. 'I tell you nothing. Nothing!' He spat blood. 'You kill me if you like.'

Garrett took out his ASP and held it down by his side.

'Go ahead!' the Arab shouted. 'Go ahead! I have no fear! I am nothing. The Struggle is all!'

'You're not worth a bullet,' Garrett spat. 'I'll save that for your lady friend.'

'You talk big!' as-Sahli sneered. 'But first you have to find her.'

'I'll find her, Ibrahim,' Garrett said. 'You can be sure of

that. Wherever she is, whatever she plans to do, I'm going to find her.'

The Arab smiled. He had his courage back now, and this time the contempt was real.

'I hope you do,' he said. 'Every night at sunset I will pray you find her. And that she kills you!'

He thought of Jessica, wondered if she would ever understand.

You see it all in black and white, don't you? Does that make it easier?

Nothing ever makes it easier, Jess.

You're not interested in their causes, their reasons for doing what they are doing?'

I'm not a psychologist, Jess. My job is fighting terrorism. Killing.

If necessary, yes. That's part of it.

Why, Charles, Why do you do it?

Someone has to. Someone has to make the stand, someone has to say, no, you will not.

He believed that. There had been a time when he had his doubts about the rights and wrongs of it, but that had been before he saw the bright bloody flayed strips of meat hanging on the trees at the site of a crashed plane brought down by a terrorist bomb, the charred carbonized remnants of what had been children in the wreckage of a church at Enniskillen, the spastic stumbling wrecks of women tortured with cattle prods and broken bottles, the jellied bodies of babies used to shield assassins from return fire. No cause, no belief, justified inflicting such suffering.

You have to believe that. You have to believe it, or you couldn't do what you do.

She was right. You had to carry inside you the conviction that what you were doing was for the greater good. He understood, of course, that many terrorists believed implicitly that what they were doing was also for the greater good, but he knew that they were wrong. If history had taught men anything, it was that nobody ever won wars, that killing – one man or a million – did not make your cause more just, your claims more believable, your demands more persuasive.

Ordinary people had a right to expect to live a decent life, to watch their children grow up and get married and have children of their own, to succeed or fail or win or lose. The madman who wanted to take that right away with gun or bomb forfeited his own rights the moment he took that path. This was Garrett's credo: he had to live by it, and maybe one day he would die by it. That fact alone freed him from the need to justify or apologize. In his jungle all the animals were feral.

12

Since the assassination of Abu Jihad, few of the fourteen members of the Executive Committee of the Palestine Liberation Organization risk travelling abroad. When for political or other good and sufficient reasons one of them is required to do so, he travels in one of the PLO's private jets, thus avoiding the dangers of hijacking and airport assassination. Such was the case when Ibrahim Ali Kutayfan, Deputy Director of the Operational Planning Department, travelled to Zürich for a conference deemed by the Executive Committee to be 'of imperative necessity'.

Arrangements for the flight were made with the utmost secrecy; the aircraft's itinerary and destination were released to the pilot only a few minutes before takeoff. Kutayfan himself arrived for embarkation accompanied by his personal assistant and bodyguards, as well as two armed officers of the 'Public Relations Department' – as Al Mukharabat, the Iraqi secret service, is known – and the plane left immediately. Kutayfan landed at Kloten airport in the middle morning hours of a bright October day. A stretch Mercedes limousine was waiting on the tarmac to whisk him through diplomatic and security clearance, and directly from there to the suite awaiting him at the Dolder Grand Hotel in the Zürichberg's Kurhausstrasse.

Apart from the black and white keffiyeh headscarf of the Palestinian fedayeen fighter draped around his shoulders, Kutayfan wore western clothes. A man of medium height who thought of himself as stocky and strong built, he was in fact vastly out of condition and at least twenty pounds overweight. He was something of a gourmand and, unusually in an Arab, a connoisseur of fine wine. He inspected the suite that had been reserved and pronounced it satisfactory. The undermanager assigned to see to the

133

honoured guest's every whim bowed his way out backwards.

'Has the woman been heard from?' Kutayfan asked, turning to his amanuensis, Abder Sowan, a slim, dapper young man seconded to the Deputy Director from the Social Affairs Department.

'The rendezvous is confirmed,' Sowan told him.

Kutayfan looked at his watch; slightly less than an hour. He took out the dossier assembled by the Information Department and riffled through the wad of cuttings about the incidents in France. It was hard to know who to be angrier with: the woman, for such clumsy mayhem, or his chief, Ali Ahmed Zaid, Director of Operational Planning and Kutayfan's direct superior, who had right from the start cleverly distanced himself from the Al Iqab group.

'It's a brilliant concept, Ibrahim, brilliant,' he had said. 'Worthy of the cause for which it was conceived. But so complex, so many things to go wrong.'

'Nothing will go wrong,' Kutayfan assured him. 'The leader is quite exceptional.'

'She may well be all you say, my friend.' Zaid nodded. 'And more. But. . . .' He held out his hands, palm up, and shrugged.

'You won't take it to the Executive meeting.'

'You know how things are right now. The moderate faction is very strong. I can't support you, Ibrahim. It's too risky. I like it very much, but it's just too risky.'

'I will take full responsibility,' Kutayfan said impatiently. Damn the moderates! They were all fools. Did they really believe they could reclaim the homeland by *talking*? As long as there was an America, there would be an Israel. And as along as there was an Israel, there would be no Palestine. Talk would not change it. Only terror. The trouble was, Zaid was getting old. Ten years ago he had been a fire-eater. Now, he always wanted everything guaranteed, tied up with a blue ribbon. That wasn't the way things worked. You had to take chances.

'You realize I would not be able to . . . protect you in the event of a failure, Ibrahim,' Zaid pointed out. 'The Central Committee. . . .'

'To hell with the Central Committee!' Kutayfan snapped. 'Do they plan executive actions – or do we?'

'We, of course,' Zaid replied smoothly. 'But the Committee has to sanction it. And if – I say, if – they do. . . .'

'The jackals must have their meat,' Kutayfan said disgustedly.

Zaid shrugged. 'As I said, if it were solely my decision, I would sanction your project. But there are other considerations, Ibrahim. World opinion is important to us. We must at least appear to conform.'

'So be it,' Kutayfan said. 'I will assume sole responsibility.'

'I will inform them of your courageous decision,' Zaid said, closing the dossier Kutayfan had placed before him. Only as he walked out of the office did Kutayfan realize how beautifully Zaid had manipulated him into putting his own life on the line if Leila Jarhoun's punitive action went awry. Well, there was a positive side even to that: if Al Iqab's strike was successful, the Chairman might well be encouraged to believe that Zaid was past his prime. Which would leave the door wide open for Ibrahim Kutayfan.

Now, as he gazed out of his bedroom window at the tranquil gardens below, he realized just how dangerously he had allowed Zaid to put him right in the firing line. Bad enough that the Executive committee had censured him for allowing the Al Iqab operation to burst open like a festering wound, first in the French tabloids, and then in news media around the world. On top of that he had been sent, like some village errand boy, to review the entire operation with its leader and to report back to the committee on the steps he had taken. This was serious criticism of his planning, and while he resented it, he knew that if he did not take back convincing evidence that the operation was not compromised, the committee would pull the plug on it. And on him.

Leila Jarhoun arrived promptly at eight. She was wearing

a heavy woollen coat, a fur hat and high leather boots; it had begun to rain, and a wind coming down from the north had scoured the streets clean of all but the most dedicated pedestrians. She handed the coat and hat to the security man and shook her long black hair free. She was wearing a lemon yellow silk blouse and a long black woollen skirt with a silver belt. They embraced and kissed in comradely fashion, and as they did Kutayfan experienced a moment of intense physical awareness. She sat in an armchair opposite his.

'You are fully recovered?' he asked.

She made an impatient gesture. 'Must we speak of it?'

'I merely wished to say you . . . look fine.'

'They did what they could,' she said. It was apparent she wanted no sympathy, so Kutayfan abandoned the topic. He had as little time as she for small talk. He tossed the dossier of press cuttings on to the table. One of them fluttered to the carpeted floor: PALESTINIAN TERROR GANG IN SEASIDE OUTRAGES.

'You know why you have been summoned here,' he said. It was not a question. He watched Leila's reaction closely. She did not appear to be apprehensive. If anything, her mood was defiant.

'I know why,' she said. 'And it was completely unnecessary.'

'Unnecessary!' Kutayfan snapped. 'The Central Committee decides what is necessary! You are merely the instrument of its will, and you would be well advised not to forget it!'

'I apologize to the deputy director for the sin of my vanity,' Leila said, head bowed, Kutayfan nodded, mollified.

'We will speak no more of that,' he said. 'Now, what went wrong?'

'A few things did not go according to plan,' she said. Her voice was low, controlled, throaty. In spite of himself, he imagined her naked, sated with lovemaking; it was that kind of voice.

'You have a talent for the understatement,' he said,

putting all the sarcasm he could muster into the words. 'A car bomb in Paris, a gunfight like some Hollywood western, and you observe that a few things did not go according to plan.'

'You are angry, comrade,' she said. 'So am I. But what happened is incidental to our plans.'

'I am grateful for your reassurance,' he said, maintaining a scornful attitude. It made him more comfortable; he liked to be in control of all situations involving women, and there was something about this woman that made him constantly uneasy, physically as well as mentally aware of her.

'It was not meant to be reassurance,' she said, and for the first time he saw what might be anger, or impatience, kindling in the dark eyes. 'You have entrusted me with a task. In carrying out that task I have encountered difficulties. I have dealt with them in the manner I felt appropriate.'

'I see,' Kutayfan said, leaning on it. 'You feel it *appropriate* to wipe out half of the French secret service when you encounter difficulties?'

'Comrade Deputy, you are unfair. I am on the ground. I have to make executive decisions.'

Kutayfan gestured towards the dossier of cuttings. 'Has it occurred to you that other executive decisions may be made if you cannot satisfactorily explain yours?' he said. 'Remember: if I cannot protect myself, Leila, I can hardly protect you.'

She frowned, catching the import of his words. 'I had not realized your position was so . . . delicate.'

'I trust you will convince me that it is not,' he said smoothly. 'Begin whenever you are ready.'

Subsequent to Faour's departure, she told him, one of the acquaintances of his two friends Tamraz and Dakhleh was identified as a DST spy. Tamraz and Dakhleh were already briefed for the St Valery drop. Disposing of them would have imperilled the landing operation; there was not time to make a substitution. Instead she put a watch on the spy, Fuad Ismail, code name Sayeed; the old woman spotted the DST case officer as soon as he showed his face.

'I decided immediately to effect a protective sanction,'

Leila said. 'The only alternative would have been to abort the entire operation.'

'I appreciate your predicament,' Kutayfan said. 'But your sanction did not in fact protect the operation at all. You were under surveillance from the moment you arrived at St Valery.'

'Bear with me a moment, Comrade Deputy,' the woman said, holding up an impeccably manicured hand; Kutayfan noticed that she did not wear any of the heavy jewellery favoured by so many Arab women. Even her perfume was light and delicate. 'What we did not know, could not have known, was that another operative was involved. He escaped the car bomb quite by chance; we did not know until the old woman telephoned, by which time he was gone. Ismail must have known where Tamraz and Dakhleh were going; the agent who survived set up the surveillance.'

'Sloppy intelligence work, Leila,' Kutayfan said. 'You were unforgivably careless.'

'We were completely unaware of the man's existence,' she protested angrily. 'To the best of our knowledge the spy had been eliminated, the door closed.'

'In the circumstances, then, you were fortunate that you were not made to pay more dearly for your carelessness.'

'We paid enough,' she said, her hand touching her cheek. 'If it had not been for the fact that the DST unit leader panicked, it could have been much worse. Even so, we were forced to improvise.'

'Improvise,' Kutayfan echoed ironically. 'That's one way of describing it. Very well, you improvised, and by Allah's good grace you evaded capture. Now, more importantly, how badly are you compromised?'

'They know we are called Al Iqab, The Punishment. But I want them to know that. They know we have the weapons. I want them to know that, too. They have two of my people. As-Sahli and Khussah. They are *rifa'at*, bullets. They are not important.'

'What do these two men know?'

'Only what I wanted them to know.'

'What is that?'

138

'That I, Leila Jarhoun, am the leader of Al Iqab. That The Punishment will commence with a signal from New York. As-Sahli and Khussah can only tell them that they were to go to Frankfurt and wait. You see, they will know everything, and yet they will know absolutely nothing. The cars we used in France were all untraceable. Neither I nor any of my unit is on any computer, in any terrorist dossier. If they have photographs they will be useless; they will not be able to identify any of us, because none of us has any kind of police or criminal record. We are unknown.'

Kutayfan thought carefully. Perhaps the project was still viable. How sweet a victory over Zaid, over all of them, it would be!

'You are saying that we can proceed?'

She hesitated before speaking, and he sensed her reluctance to admit any further impediment to the plan they had drawn up together after the assassination of Abu Jihad.

'The answer is yes,' she said. 'Providing—'

'Ah,' he said. 'Another proviso.'

'We must effect another protective sanction,' she said.

He frowned. 'Another?'

'The man I spoke of, the one who escaped the Paris action. Our DST contact has identified him: his name is Charles Garrett, and he is British.'

'British Intelligence?' Kutayfan said, surprised. 'How are they involved.'

She shook her head. 'I don't know. It may not even be British Intelligence. Desmesnil said Garrett is attached to a secret organization called PACT. Our Information Department specialists have no knowledge of it, nor can they identify Garrett from the photofit picture I made for them.'

'And this is the man you wish to terminate?' Kutayfan pursed his lips and leaned back in his chair. 'I am not convinced of the wisdom of antagonizing British security. Our relations with them are currently in useful equilibrium. And anyway, if what you say is true, and Garrett is a member of their secret service, his assessments will already have been computerized.'

'I realize that, of course,' Leila said. 'And in other circumstances I would agree with you that the sanction would achieve nothing. In this instance, however, Garrett's involvement is critical.'

'What is it you are not telling me, Leila?'

'I keep nothing from you, Comrade Deputy. I have had some of our best people in London trying to obtain information on the organization Garrett works for. They have been unsuccessful. I have therefore assumed that this organization is both ultrasecret and inimical to our interests. That is why I suggest a protective sanction. I do not want to take any further chances.'

'In that I concur completely,' Kutayfan said, urbanely. 'I merely wish to be certain that no . . . personal motivation is involved in your request.'

'You mean this?' Her hand touched her face again. 'It is of no moment. I must endure it only for a short time.'

'Very well, you have your sanction. I will arrange it through the embassy tomorrow.'

Leila Jarhoun smiled. 'I knew I could rely on you, Comrade Deputy. I wish there was some way I could demonstrate my gratitude for your confidence in me.'

Her voice was earnest, fervent. Was there invitation in those damned unreadable dark eyes, or merely admiration? Were not the two bedfellows, anyway? The word echoed in his mind: *bedfellows*.

'In the present circumstances,' he said tentatively, 'it is acceptable that you address me as Ibrahim.'

'I am honoured.'

'I ordered wine,' he said. 'Will you have some?'

'A small glass,' she said. He had taken the trouble of studying the hotel wine list carefully; it was not a great one, but there were one or two decent vintages. He chose a 1982 Billecart-Salmon, insisting it be left unopened in the ice bucket; he would open it himself when he was ready to drink it, and be damned to the sommelier's hurt feelings. Kutayfan went across the room and touched the bottle. Most of the ice had melted; the wine would be cold, but not frozen. He made a little performance of removing the gold foil and the wire cage, turning cork against bottle in the approved champagne manner so that the cork eased rather than popped out. He poured two glasses and handed one to Leila Jarhoun.

She leaned back on the sofa and put one arm along its back. Her movement drew his attention to her breasts beneath the fine silk blouse. There was nothing wrong with that lithe, tigerish body. He didn't have to look at her face. He swallowed, and hoped it had not sounded as loud to her as it did to him.

'Is there . . . is there anything else you would like?' he asked her.

Leila Jarhoun smiled a crooked smile, this time delicately touching the tip of her pink tongue against her upper lip. She held out her hand to him.

'Yes,' she said, as if she had read his thoughts. 'Turn off the lights.'

By the time Garrett got to Paris, DST had run the surveillance photographs of Leila Jarhoun and her accomplices through the computers. Apart from establishing that Jarhoun had been among known terrorists who stayed at or frequented the Hotel Liban, the net result was a big fat zero. None of the men who had accompanied her to St Valery was 'known'.

Even so, Garrett sat down with an identifications expert and put together a photofit impression of Leila Jarhoun. It caught her dark beauty well: the liquid eyes above high cheekbones, the heart-shaped face, the full, sensual lips. A copy was faxed to the State Department in Washington for onward transmission to the Task Force to Combat Terrorism and all Bureau of Immigration examiners. Another was fed into the TREVI computer. It came up empty yet again.

Now it was October and the backroom boys still weren't having a lot of luck, Garrett thought. Although they had the names of four of the ten men who had been in St Valery, neither they nor the computer banks of any of the European security agencies – BfV in Cologne, DI5 in London, and the rest – could come up with any hard information. Even the Israeli Mossad said it was unable to help. It looked as if each one of Leila Jarhoun's squad had been picked fresh; that was to say, none of them had any track record, none of them was known to TREVI, nor any of the major counter-terrorist organizations.

All the elementary precautions that could be taken were taken anyway; copies of all the photographs were distributed to security offices, immigration, passport control and customs officials at every major European airport and embarkation point. It was long odds against anyone spotting the quarry; but you had to give it the chance to happen.

The two captured terrorists, as-Sahli and Khussah, were taken away for what was euphemistically referred to as deep interrogation. Garrett was not invited to sit in, and had no desire to do so. The salient facts were straightforward: the men had been recruited and assigned to Al Iqab specifically because they had no record of any kind. Their assignation was to proceed from St Valery with one of the weapons to Frankfurt. They would be contacted there by others who knew the rest of the plan. Together they would await the signal from Leila Jarhoun. Garrett doubted the DST dredgers would get much more than that out of the captives for the simple reason that it was all they knew. The whole plan hinged on a cutout system, with each party knowing only what he needed to know, thus making it impossible for him to betray the next link in the chain.

Garrett's own debriefing session at La Piscine was mercifully short; some of the tabloid coverage of the events at St Valery had been pretty sensational, and Garrett got the impression that the senior officers who discussed the matter with him were more concerned with quietening things down than stirring them up. He sensed also their reluctance to further embroil an 'outsider' and was perfectly content that they did not do so. It did not escape his attention that they asked him a lot of questions about Germain and not a few about Claude Desmesnil. He answered all of them as honestly as he knew how. From the tone of the questions, he concluded that if Germain was in trouble, Desmesnil was not exactly flavour of the month, either.

Before he left France in late July, Garrett called the service hospital in Paris where Eugene Simion was being treated. The prognosis was still the same: 'grave'. Simion was holding on; that, at least, was something. A DGSE driver took him to Charles de Gaulle airport, which looked just as much like a space station as ever, and wished him a good journey.

'Tell me something,' he asked the man as he got out of the car. 'Do you know a man called Germain? Christian Germain?'

The driver nodded. *'À la Piscine ils l'appellent Monsieur Hulot,'* he told Garrett. *'Vous comprenez?'*

'I do indeed,' Garrett said. If Germain was known at DGSE headquarters as Jacques Tati's well-meaning blunderer, it was anything but a compliment. Somehow, however, the more he thought about it, the funnier it got. Finally, halfway across the English Channel in the British Airways Boeing 757, Garrett burst out laughing. Monsieur Hulot, for Christ's sake! The man sitting next to him, neat in pinstripes, portable computer on his knee, raised a questioning eyebrow. Well, Garrett thought, he had probably never seen the films.

A waiting Granada Ghia took him straight to Lonsdale House, where he reported to Nicholas Bleke. The older man listened gravely, without interrupting, as Garrett related the events of the preceding days.

'This thing has come a long way, Charles,' he observed, when Garrett finished speaking. 'Yet we still don't have any clear idea of what the connection is between our murders and this terrorist group.'

'Whatever it is they're planning, it's international,' Garrett said. 'That woman Jarhoun in the States, the others in Europe.'

'Yes, yes, but *what?*'

'I've got a few ideas.'

'Want to try them out on me?'

143

'Not now,' Garrett said. 'I haven't quite got a handle on them yet.'

'What about Hennessy?'

'I've briefed Derek Warren at the MoD. And just in case, I've sent a dossier to Special Branch. They'll pass word along to the RUC in case our boy has something else up his sleeve.'

'This is something new, the IRA buying behind the Iron Curtain. What do you make of it?'

'They must have had something very special on offer for Hennessy to agree to accept a split shipment.'

'You think they're up to something in Germany?'

'No reason for them to take delivery in France otherwise.'

'I suppose you're right. Anything else?'

'I've put the flopsters on overtime.'

'What are you looking for?'

'A PLO safe house, somewhere in England, probably London. Somewhere they can hide a team: maybe as many as four men, with heavyweight weaponry.'

'There must be more than a few.'

'It's just a hunch. We've got some names now: Hosseyn, or Faour. The two camels, Tamraz and Ali Dakhleh. Khussah and as-Sahli and the two men who covered them, Hassan and Abu-Salem. Then there was someone called Hatem and the woman, Jarhoun. I'm trying for a match, anything.'

'Worth a try,' Bleke agreed. 'All right. Get some rest. You look as if you need it.'

My day for compliments, Garrett thought; he went out into Berkeley Square and took a taxi to his flat at Whitehall Court. It was a grace-and-favour residence, provided as part of his job; a study, a sitting room, a dining room with a bay window that looked out across the river, two bedrooms and the usual offices. It was more than enough for his needs. It pleased him to be living in the very building in which the British secret service had been born. Here, in 1909, Mansfield Cumming, the original 'C', had set up the Secret Service Bureau foreign department in his flat on the top floor, a maze of passages and steps and oddly-shaped rooms reached only by private lift. The building's other residents – George Bernard Shaw among them – apparently never realized what was going on above their heads.

It was good to be back. A note on the table from his daily help, Mrs Phillips, told him that she had done the shopping he had asked for, and that everything was in the fridge. Garrett poured himself a large Glenfarclas and opened a few windows, letting in the late afternoon sunshine and the sound of traffic on the Embankment. A train rattled out of Charing Cross station and over Hungerford Bridge. He picked up the phone and dialled Jessica's number. It rang five times, then the answering machine cut in.

'This is Jessica Goldman. I'm sorry I'm not available at the moment. Please leave your name and number after the tone, and I'll get back to you as soon as I can.'

'I hate talking to machines,' Garrett said. 'Even when they sound like you.'

There was a click and the metallic hiss on the line disappeared.

'Garrett?'

'Well, now, ain't you the sneaky one.'

'I was in the shower. When did you get back?'

'Just. It's been a hard day's night. How do you feel about a late dinner?'

'Oh, I'm tired of all these overpriced Chelsea restaurants. Why don't you come over and I'll cook something.'

'That's funny, I was going to say exactly the same thing to you.'

'You cook?'

'Renaissance man.'

'What have you got in mind?'

'That's an interesting question. But let's stick to food.'

'I'll eat anything. Except meat.'

'How about *truite au bleu*, new potatoes, green salad with my own dressing, a bottle of elderflower wine, some Pont l'Évêque and a pot of this Jacque Vabre coffee I brought back with me.'

'Elderflower wine?'

145

'You know the address. Knock a da door, ring a da bell. Whenever you're ready.'

'I have to get dressed.'

'Hell,' Garrett said. 'Come as you are.'

He put Lady Day on the turntable, and as she took a chance on love he washed some new potatoes and put them into a small saucepan with an inch of water in it. When the potatoes were cooking he soaked a couple of chicory heads in warm water to take away the bitterness before slicing them finely. He put two tablespoons of oil and one of vinegar into a jar, added a dab of Colman's mustard, ground fresh black pepper into it, capped the jar and shook it vigorously until it emulsified.

He laid the table, using the bone-handled knives and forks he'd bought off a stall in Camden Passage, Waterford glasses: no matter what anybody said, they always made the wine taste better. He looked at the old brass candlesticks on the bookcase then shook his head. Too corny. The intercom buzzed. It was George, the doorman, letting him know Jessica had arrived. He went back into the kitchen and uncorked a bottle of Rock's Elderflower. The doorbell rang.

'Ready or not, here I am,' Jessica said.

'Giz a kiss, then,' Garrett said. She was wearing a tan trenchcoat, a black beret, black leather boots. Beneath the raincoat she had on a sleeveless canary-yellow dress. He took her coat and hat and hung them in the hall cupboard.

'Like your frock,' he said. He handed her a glass of wine and beckoned her to follow him back to the kitchen.

'Thank you, kind sir,' she replied, sipping the wine. 'This is good.'

'Flowers hand-picked last June by an actor of my acquaintance,' Garrett said.

'Do you make all this up, Garrett?'

'He makes gooseberry champagne, too.'

Jessica leaned against the door jamb and watched as Garrett made a mixture one part vinegar and seven parts water, which he put in a wide flat dish to heat. The fish were already cleaned. He slid them into the simmering stock as Billie Holiday complained about that old devil called love.

'Another glass?'

'Elderflower wine,' Jessica mused. 'I feel I ought to be drinking this in a punt, at Henley.'

While the fish cooked, Garrett emptied the potatoes into a small tureen, shaking them to coat them with the melted dab of butter he had put in earlier, then sprinkling finely chopped parsley over them. He gave the trout seven minutes altogether, then lifted them gently on to a stainless-steel serving plate.

'Bring the salad,' he told Jessica. They sat opposite each other at the old oak table in the window bay and ate without talking. After they finished, they stacked the dishes and took their coffee over to the big sofa in front of the fireplace. Billy Holiday was wondering where her lover man could be; when she got through, the machine clicked off.

'More,' Jessica said. 'I like her.'

'Everybody likes Eleanora Fagan,' he said.

'You do that a lot, you know,' Jessica told him.

'Do what?'

She leaned back and held his gaze. 'Non sequiturs.'

'It's reflex,' he confessed. 'Sort of covers up what I'm really thinking.'

'Ah,' she said, smiling. 'I thought the silence was my magic spell working on you.'

'The silence was your magic spell working on me.'

'It was a nice dinner.' She kissed him. He put his arms around her and felt her body arch towards his own, soft, firm, perfumed, strong.

'That was nice, too,' she said.

'We could do it again, if you like.'

She came into his arms again and kissed him, and this time the kiss went on and on. Then she made a small sound, and he released her. She looked him straight in the eyes, as if seeking the answer to some unspoken question.

'I didn't expect this,' she said. 'Not so soon.'

'Me neither.'

'And I'm not sure I want to get this involved.' She got up off the sofa and stood in front of the fireplace.

'Is that why you keep calling me Garrett?'

'Who's the psychologist around here?'

'Tell me what's bothering you.'

'I don't know if I can. But I can tell you this: if there is going to be anything between us, I want to know what's going on in your head. I don't just want to be someone to help you forget the grim reality out there Charles.'

'You think that's how I see you?'

'I don't know,' Jessica said. 'You haven't said a single word about France. Just this Michael Caine number.'

'France wasn't particularly wonderful. I thought you might prefer Michael Caine.'

'Wrong. If we're going to share anything, we're going to share everything. Good times, bad times. Don't put me up on some stupid pedestal so I don't get mud splashed on my pretty frock.'

'I never thought about you that way.'

'Which way did you think about me?'

'I thought – I think you are the most attractive woman I know. I admire your sophistication, I like your sense of humour, I think you're very beautiful.'

'You don't know anything about me.'

'I was just about to get started on that when you interrupted me.'

'You remember Rita Hayworth?' she asked.

He frowned, surprised by the question. 'Yes.'

'Her real name was Margarita Cansino. She once said all men wanted was to take Rita Hayworth to bed; the trouble was they woke up the next morning with Margarita Cansino. Men forget that: they only commit themselves physically. Once she makes it, a woman's commitment is total: she brings all her other baggage along. Not just her body.'

'I think I was prepared for that.'

'I wonder,' Jessica said. 'You know I'm Jewish.' He nodded. Since their first meeting he had gone down to Registry at Curzon Street House and checked her file. Her parents, Albert and Hannah Goldman, lived in Finchley, north London. An older brother, Arthur, was in the rag trade; a sister, Leah, was married to a management consultant. Jessica had been married to Brian Golding, a practising orthopaedic surgeon, the Harley Street variety. The marriage had ended in divorce two years earlier, after seven years, and she had reverted to her maiden name. Garrett found it hard to imagine Jessica married to someone called Brian.

'Go on.'

'My grandparents were German,' she said, hesitantly. 'He was a doctor. In Berlin, in 1936. The Nazis passed a law that said no Jew could be a doctor. They sold what they could, left everything else they owned behind, and got out. Just walked away from it. They were among the last ones to leave.'

'What has that got to do with us?'

'Wait,' she said, laying a gentle finger on his lips. 'I'm coming to that. All my life I've heard stories about what it was like in Germany in those days. People forced to look on helplessly while atrocities were committed, knowing they had no redress against the man who committed them, secret policemen who had traded unquestioning loyalty for unlimited protection. And that's what you're part of, isn't it, a secret police force?'

'I suppose you could call it that. But it's not the Gestapo. It exists within the constraints of a democracy, not a totalitarian state.'

'I know that, of course. And I believe instinctively that what you do is largely for good, not bad, but . . . something warns me to take care. I'm like someone standing on the edge of the cliff. I know if I take one more step I'm committed, and I'm just not sure whether I want to be.'

She sat down beside him, and he put his arm around her and stroked her thick black hair. 'I understand. At least, I think I do. I want to ask you to do something for me.'

'What?'

'Give me time. I've got some relearning to do.'

'We probably both have,' Jessica said.

He kissed her gently. 'Give me a chance, Jess. Give us a chance.'

'I want to.'

'And something else. Trust me.'

'Ah,' she said softly. 'That's much more difficult.'

He was awakened by the soft chirr of his alarm, and switched it off quickly before it woke Jessica. She lay on her side, her lips slightly parted, her hair spread across the pillow. He put on a towelling robe, went into the kitchen and filled the Krups coffeemaker with water. He put a paper filter into the cone and spooned in three measures of the French coffee. While it filtered, he toasted four wholemeal muffins, and put them in a warmed chafing dish. He put butter, honey and Hero black cherry jam on the table, set two places, then squeezed two glasses of fresh orange juice, which he carried into the bedroom on a wooden tray.

Jessica was already awake; she had heard him moving around in the kitchen. She sat up, tucking the sheets around her waist.

'Good morning,' she said, turning her face up to be kissed. 'Good morning, good morning, good morning.'

'Good morning, Margarita,' Garrett said and handed her the orange juice.

'What did you just call me?'

'Slip of the tongue,' Garrett said. 'What was your name again?'

She gave him a hoyden grin, then her face became serious.

'I'm sorry for all the doom and gloom last night.'

'I recall a number of interesting sensory experiences,' Garrett said. 'But doom and gloom were not among them.'

Jessica finished her orange juice and got out of bed, naked. He watched with undisguised pleasure as she walked across the room to pick up the bathrobe he had laid across a chair for her. She felt his scrutiny and coloured slightly.

'Stop that, Garrett!' she scolded.

'I wouldn't know how,' he confessed. 'Come and have some breakfast.'

'I want to have a bath first. Have you got any bubble bath?'

'A big tough fellow like me? Of course I have.'

She went into the bathroom and turned on the water. *You scrub my back and I'll scrub yours. Best offer you'll get today, me bucko!* Diana's ghost was never far away. He shook his head and she vanished. He could hear Jessica singing to herself, the splosh of moving water. He went into the bathroom, picked up the big sponge he had brought back from Mykonos, soaped it, and began washing her slim, tanned back, her neck, and then her firm, full breasts. She leaned back to be kissed. Her lips tasted of oranges.

'Come on in,' she said. 'The water's lovely.'

They were halfway through breakfast when the telephone rang. Jessica looked at it and stuck out her tongue. Garrett shrugged and picked it up.

'Go ahead,' he said.

'Duty officer, Lonsdale, sir,' a voice said. 'Urgent dossier here for you from R2.'

R2 was the DI5 computer. 'Classification?'

'VIPAR.' That meant it could not be discussed over the telephone. The high security classification meant Five must have come up with something solid.

'I'll be right there.'

'Very good, sir.'

The connection was broken. He put that phone down; when he turned around, Jessica was putting on her raincoat.

'Hey,' he said. 'We didn't finish breakfast.'

'No,' she said.

'Come on, sit down, talk to me.'

'You're not here any more. When the phone rang, you stopped being the nice man I made love to. You turned into somebody else.'

'Jess, I'm sorry.'

'It's all right,' she said, a shade too brightly. 'I guess if Margarita Cansino can get used to it, I can.'

'I told you I had some relearning to do,' he said. 'Let me call you later.'

'I'm going to be pretty busy,' she said. 'I was going to break it to you gently, maybe over our second cup of coffee. Now. . . .' She shrugged. 'I'm being sent on a course. America. I'll be away for about six months.'

'When?'

'I leave next Friday.'

'Friday? I'll see you before then, won't I?'

'I . . . don't know, Charles. I think maybe it would be better if we both took a little time to see how we feel about this. About us.'

'Let me drive you home.'

'I'll go straight to the office. I can change there.'

'We'll get a cab—'

'No,' she said firmly. She went over to the door, stopped, then came back and held his face in her cool, slim hands, and kissed him on the lips.

'Bear with me, Charles. You see, I know now that it would be very easy for me to fall in love with you. And it scares me.'

After Jessica left, Garrett stood for what seemed a long time, staring out of the window without actually seeing anything. Maybe she was right, he thought. The job would always come first; it always had. *You're never here when I need you, but you always expect me to be here when you need me. What kind of a bargain is that supposed to be?* He shook his head impatiently, as if by doing so he could rid himself of the unwelcome thoughts that were crowding in.

Fifteen minutes later, as he came out into the street and hailed a taxi to take him up to Hill Street – no one who worked at Lonsdale House ever alighted at its front door – a dark blue Ford Orion Ghia slid around the corner of Whitehall Place and tucked itself behind his cab. When the taxi stopped at the corner of Hill Street, the Orion shot past it and around the northern perimeter of the square, stopping at Conduit Street to let a thin-faced, swarthy man of

152

about thirty get out. He stood by the Follett car showroom window waiting for Garrett to come across the gardens, then crossed the street in the opposite direction to Garrett. He went into the gardens, turning to watch Garrett go into Lonsdale House. Then he continued across to the west side of the square, where the Orion was waiting outside Annabel's, engine running.

'It's him,' the man said as he got in.

13

The file being held by the Duty Officer for Garrett was from the DI5 Operations Division in Euston Tower. As well as the general functions of OD, the tower housed Five's twelfth-floor R2 computer facility and the special postal investigations department on the twenty-fifth floor, conveniently – but not accidentally – sandwiched between those of British Telecom and the DHSS, and just a few minutes' walk away from the Five/Six Liaison building at the top of Gower Street. Garrett signed the dossier out and took it to his office. It was a thick red manila folder carrying the usual DI5 covering slip with its printed Official Secrets Act caveat. He opened it and began to read.

Putting the computer searchers – internally referred to as flopsters – on overtime trawling had paid off. There were nearly a dozen known PLO safe houses in the UK. All were kept under electronic surveillance with a HUMINT top-up, usually on a 'twicer' basis, unless Five had specific reasons for stepping up the input. Trawling – you fed the words, phrases, or names you wanted the computers to look for and they 'trawled' everything in their vast memories for those key words – offered a wide variety of cross-referencing opportunities: from information contained in straightforward visual surveillance conducted by A3, based at Curzon; telephone and electronic surveillance by the Grove Park unit, working in conjunction with 'Tinkerbell', the telephone-tapping unit at Ebury Bridge Road; documentary overview by the St Martins Le Grand letter-opening section, cross-checked with the Department of Health and Social Security computers in Euston Tower, Driver and Vehicle Licensing in Swansea, the National TV Licence Records Office in Bristol, Post Office Girobank records and the aliens register at the Home Office in Croydon; and last, and probably most importantly, intercepts obtained by GCHQ, the signals intercept facility in Cheltenham.

It was the latter organization, listening to all embassy traffic as a matter of course, which had provided the initial lead. Three months earlier, GCHQ had detected a 'squirt' – a radio transmission of a tape message sent at perhaps five hundred times normal speed, lasting only a few milliseconds. This had emanated from one of the Middle Eastern embassies in Kensington Palace Gardens; it had been taped and passed to the decoders at Century House. The message could hardly have been briefer: *Abu-Salem is ready*.

Garrett's interest in Abu-Salem connected with an ongoing DI5 surveillance operation. It was Five's brief to watch the activities of covert organizations in Britain: the PLO safe house in Walker Road, Southall, had been under observation almost from the time it was set up. A trawl of A3 reports produced a dossier on Zaher Abu-Salem, twenty-two, a Palestinian research assistant born in Sawahiri ash-Sharqi, enrolled in the PLO while still at university. He had entered Britain via Manchester Airport, flying KLM from Athens under his own name and using a Jordanian passport; when checked, the airline's records revealed that Abu-Salem had in fact flown a circuit, originating in Cyprus. He had taken a plane from Nicosia to Belgrade, and then flown to Athens. When he reached the UK, he obtained work as a forecourt attendant in a Shell garage on the Uxbridge Road, and with two other 'Jordanian' immigrants, rented the Southall house.

An A1(A) team broke into the house as soon as feasible, and wired every room. An intercept was put on the phone, although the occupants of the house rarely used it for anything except ordering takeaway food. A team of watchers from A3 kept the place under surveillance until it became apparent that its occupants were sleepers. Until a signal activated one, or all of them, it was pointless to keep them under continuous surveillance.

The 'screech' intercepted by GCHQ alerted DI5 to the fact that Abu-Salem was on ready. Two weeks later, he booked a ticket to New York with TWA. Arrangements were made to cover his movements, but somehow Abu-Salem slipped his watchers and disappeared. A check with TWA revealed he had exchanged his New York ticket for a return to Frankfurt, and from there had flown to Paris. He had returned to England on the Boulogne-Folkestone ferry just two days earlier.

On the day preceding Salem's return, the other three residents of 28 Walker Road, Southall, drove in separate cars to various ports on the south coast (the A3 watchers reported). All used one-day passports obtained at a nearby post office. Abdul Rahim, 28, drove to Dover in a Ford Cortina estate JPL 345V, taking the two p.m. Seaspeed Hovercraft to Boulogne. Waheed Huwayhi, 23, in a Rover 2000 TTP 529X, took the Sealink ferry from Newhaven to Dieppe. Hassan Abu Zaid, 25, in a VW Beetle RMP 628W, travelled Dover-Calais by Townsend-Thoresen. All were back in Southall the same night. Each brought in duty-free spirits, cigarettes and various packages. Subsequent electronic surveillance indicates that among these were some kind of weapon or weapons. Abu-Salem returned to Southall the following day. He came through Immigration on his own passport, and declared nothing at Customs. He had only a small suitcase.

Garrett put the report down. Now they had something.

One: Abu-Salem was one of the Al Iqab group who had been at St Valery for the document and arms meet. Therefore he was probably one of the 'donkeys' who, like Khussah and as-Sahli, were to go to specific locations with the stolen weapons and await the mysterious signal sent by Leila Jarhoun from New York. Unlike all the others, however, Abu-Salem had a problem: getting the weapon through British Customs. To get around that difficulty, his confederates had met him in France, each smuggling in one or more disassembled parts. Two: the cell at Southall was probably the executive team. Three: whatever Al Iqab was planning, it had moved to an active stage. He passed word to DI5 to put the house in Southall under intensive scrutiny: if any of the men living there left 'carrying' – anything that could be part or all of an anti-tank launcher – he was to be informed instantly. To be doubly sure – there was always a chance the men at Southall were not the shooters – Abu-Salem was to be shadowed around the clock. Garrett also made a mental note to ask the Department of Justice in Washington to step up surveillance at all American gateway cities: Leila Jarhoun must be found.

The second part of the dossier was the result of a different kind of trawl. Garrett had reasoned that if the PLO had sent a hit man to London to obtain Special Branch warrant cards, there was a halfway decent likelihood they had done the same in whatever other locations they were planning to strike. Acting on that hunch, he asked R2 to contact police forces throughout Europe for details of any murder or murders, solved or unsolved, in which the modus operandi included dismemberment of head and hands, the burning of identifying scars, or the theft of clothing and identification. He had suggested it as nothing more than a long, long shot. To his surprise, the gambit paid off with a jackpot.

In Germany, two policemen had been found dead, killed within days of each other, one near Rüdesheim, the other at Boppard; in Italy, the headless bodies of two tourists, one Austrian, the other Swedish, were found in shallow graves not far from the beach at Ostia, the seaside resort near Rome. It was like some bizarre summer epidemic that had swept through the capitals of western Europe: the apparently motiveless murder of a caterer's driver and his mate near Zürich; of a press photographer and a kiosk attendant in Stockholm; other double killings at a small town near Oslo in Norway, in Brussels and Amsterdam, each corpse apparently mutilated to prevent or delay identification.

In Belgium the victims were an airport baggage handler and a heavy goods vehicle relief driver; in Amsterdam, a foreman of the State Waterways Department and a civil engineer. There seemed to be no pattern to the killings. If there was one, it was not immediately apparent: the flopsters had fed all the known facts about the victims into the mainframe, but apart from the manner of their deaths, they appeared to have nothing whatsoever in common.

Garrett paced up and down his office like a caged tiger.

'Dammit, there must be something!' he said, slamming the R2 dossier down on his desk. 'There has to be!'

He was reasonably confident that all these murders had been committed for the same reason as those which he had investigated with Tony Dodgson: for the personal or business IDs of the dead men. But what would a terrorist want with the accreditation of a foreman of the Dutch State Waterways Department or a Swedish kiosk attendant?

He picked up the phone and dialled the eight-figure number that connected him directly with Neal McCaskill, Deputy Director of Analysis at Euston Tower. It rang three times, and then McCaskill answered.

'Aye.' No one gave names or numbers at the Glass House, but Garrett recognized 'Mac' McCaskill's Scottish burr immediately.

'Mac, this is Charles Garrett. Today's clearance is Alphabet.'

'Confirmed,' McCaskill said. 'How are you, Charles?'

'I wanted to thank you for all the hard work your boys have done for me.'

'Aye, and well ye might,' McCaskill said. 'Ye've had more than your share of mainframe time lately, Garrett.'

'Sorry to hear you say that, Mac.'

'Oh-oh,' the Scot said. 'Do I hear another priority request coming up?'

'Something like that.'

'I might have known.'

'Mac, did you get a chance to look at the dossier you sent down to me?'

'Fat bloody chance of that!' McCaskill exploded. 'Do you people have any idea how understaffed we are up here?' Garrett grinned; it didn't take much to get Mac's Glaswegian dander up.

'Take a look at it now, Mac, will you? The access code is PACT-388-49291/F for Freddie.'

'Garrett, I can't just stop what I'm doing to look at some bloody dossier—'

'Punch it in, Mac. It won't take a minute.'

'Aye, well, all right, then,' the Scot said, and Garrett heard him muttering under his breath as he tapped the access code into his personal desk computer.

'Got it?'

'Aye,' McCaskill said. He whistled softly. 'Stone the crows, ye've got a few horizontals here, Garrett.'

A 'horizontal', in the trade's grimly humorous jargon, was a dead man. 'That's what I want to talk to you about, Mac,' Garrett said. 'Your boys have done a hell of a fine job getting this information together, but there's something missing.'

'Oh aye?' McCaskill said heavily. He didn't like having his hackers criticized by people he contended didn't know shit from silicon. 'And what might that be?'

'I need a common denominator, Mac,' Garrett said. 'Something to tie all these people together.'

'Something like what?'

'Our thinking on this is that these men were all killed for their personal or business identifications,' Garrett said. 'If we're right, then each of them has something in common with the others. I want your boys to put the dossiers of every one of them through the mangle. The works, Mac. Right down to their collar sizes. And I want it yesterday.'

'Is that all?' the Scot said sarcastically. 'Well, that's no problem at all. We'll just drop everything else we're doing and devote ourselves exclusively to your little job. Would that be in order, Your Wonderfulness?'

'Be nice to me, Mac,' Garrett said. 'Or I'll set Bleke on to you.'

'Och, ye're a hard man, Garrett, if you'd do such a terrible thing to a friend. All right, I'll get on to it. But Garrett. . . .'

'Yes, Mac?'

'Don't hang upside down from the chandelier waiting for the results, will you?'

'Of course not,' Garrett said. 'Tomorrow will be fine.'

He hung up while McCaskill was still in the middle of saying something inelegant. Garrett smiled. If the problem could be cracked, McCaskill's boys would crack it. He picked up the phone again; this time he dialled Jessica's number at Kelvin House.

'Doctor Goldman.'

'Jess?'

'I'm sorry, Charles, I can't talk now.'

'Wait, Jess, this is business, not pleasure.'

'You're supposed to give the clearance code.'

'Alphabet, dammit! Jess, I need some advice.'

'You can say that again.'

'One question. Well, two, anyway.'

'Two and no more. I really am busy.'

'First question. Who's the behavioural science expert over there at Kelvin?'

'That would be Pat Miller.'

'Can you give me his number?'

'Chauvinist pig,' she said, and he could almost see her smiling. 'Patricia Miller. She's American. Learned her business with the FBI Mind Hunters. She's on . . . let me see . . . 9856. Question two?'

'When can I see you?'

'I'm sorr-ee. We are not allowed to give out that information.'

'I know you're hard to get,' he growled. 'Stop proving it. I need to talk to you.'

'Call me at home,' she said. 'I have to go now.'

'I don't want to talk to your damned answering machine!' he said, but she had already hung up. Well, if Jessica Goldman thought he was going to chase after her all over London like some lovesick adolescent, he had news for her: she was absolutely right. He grinned and dialled the number she had given him.

'Dr Miller.'

'Dr Miller, my name is Charles Garrett. I work for the research department of the Foreign Office.'

'What can I do for you, Mr Garrett?' said the woman at the other end. The voice was authentic Middle West.

'Omaha, Nebraska?' Garrett guessed.

'Not bad,' she replied. 'Wichita, Kansas, actually. You were about to tell my why you called.'

'I'm in the middle of an investigation, and I need some advice. I'd like to see you, if that's possible.'

'Let me look at my book,' Dr Miller said. 'How long do you need? If an hour or so will do, I'm free at about four today.'

'That'll do nicely,' Garrett said.

'May I ask who gave you my number?'

'The department I work for does not divulge its sources, Dr Miller.'

'That answers my question,' she said. 'You're a spook.'

'Could be,' Garrett said. 'See you at four.'

He looked out of the window. It was one of those winter days that look inviting from the inside of a centrally heated office, sunny and bright, the sky an empty blue. But the tops of the trees in the square were moving, and he knew that by four o'clock, when the pale sun had waned, there would be a biting north wind blowing on the street.

He set the alarm on his desk clock for three, then went across the room to his PC console. He punched his personal password into the interrogator unit, a resin block about the thickness of a floppy disk which contained a radio receiver, transmitter and microprocessor. This would interactively log his usage, making an indelible record of whatever information he accessed.

The first of the European dossiers he called up were those of the German murder victims. Herbert Lichtenfeld, twenty-five, civil policeman, *Polizeirevier* No. 3, Nordend, Frankfurt. Home address in Seckbach. Secondary school education, joined the police at the age of nineteen. Married, three children. General duties, no security work. Nothing there. Next, Peter Heim, forty-eight, police sergeant, *Polizeirevier* No. 6, Bornheim. Home address Walter Kolb Siedlung, half a mile from the station. Married (second wife) with four children, one grandchild. Secondary school education, apprenticeship in a leather factory. Joined the police at thirty. General duties, including desk sergeant at the station.

Two Special Branch officers in London. Two ordinary policemen in Frankfurt, which was known to be one of the

Al Iqab targets. Was there a connection? If so, what was it? Garrett shook his head. This was getting him nowhere. Try another, at random: how about Frederick Harmsen, civil engineer, whose headless body had been found in a derelict barge in the Zuideramstelkanal in Amsterdam, or Johan Somerwil, foreman of the State Waterways Department, likewise dead in a tulip grower's barn at Aalsmeer, south of the capital? What curious tie bound all these strangers together? What about Ragnar Berglund, photographer for the Stockholm newspaper *Aftenbladet*, or twenty-three-year-old caterer's driver Hans-Peter Kaderli of Hombrechtikon, near Zürich? What was so special about them?

The alarm buzzed; it was three o'clock. Garrett sighed and turned away from the computer. The way things were going, it looked as if he was going to have to take this one to the Brains Trust, the weekly meeting of PACT executive officers, chaired by Nicholas Bleke, at which everyone got a chance to add their input to their fellow officers' cases. Garrett did not think highly of the procedure, which he considered bad for security, but Bleke claimed it got results.

He closed down the PC and got his overcoat from the cupboard. He handed the Cryptag security unit to the duty officer, signed out and went down to the street in the lift. It was already getting dark and the street lights were on. He walked briskly over to Bond Street and up Conduit Street, crossing over Regent Street and heading east along Great Marlborough Street, passing the anonymous building on the left-hand side that houses the press department of the security services. When he got to Berwick Street he turned south, loitering through the market for ten minutes or so before turning back north, across Oxford Street. It took him about another ten minutes to get to Kelvin House. If he was aware of the two men who were following him, he gave no visible sign of it.

Patricia Miller's office was neat, bright and functional. An uncluttered desk with a bookshelf unit behind it, some standard MoD armchairs for visitors, a sofa next to the high window, an Apricot PC on a console with the usual software boxes and continuous stationery, a set of framed reproductions of Picasso's bullfight sketches, not so much paintings as Rorschach tests.

Dr Miller was about forty, small and well-upholstered, with blonde hair and startlingly blue eyes. She wore a loose-fitting, open-necked cobalt blue cossack-style blouse and a dark blue skirt, a man's wrist watch on her right wrist, a thin gold chain around her neck. No wedding ring, Garrett noticed.

'Well,' she drawled. 'Do I pass muster?'

'Sorry, doctor,' Garrett smiled. 'Force of habit.'

'It's okay,' she said. 'Us women are funny. We get mad if you give us the once-over and we get mad if you don't.'

'You won't take it amiss if I say you're somewhat different to what I anticipated.'

'I'm used to it,' she said, waving him to a chair. 'People hear behavioural science and they expect someone who looks like Golda Meir. I was a big disappointment to my mom, too. She wanted me to be a beauty queen.'

'In Wichita, Kansas?'

'Don't make cracks about Wichita, mister. It's a great place.'

'I know. Wyatt Earp. McConnell Air Force Base. Cessna Aircraft.'

'My God, that's amazing!' she said. 'Most Englishmen don't even know where Kansas is, let alone Wichita.'

'I read a lot,' Garrett told her. 'How long have you been in Britain?'

'Nearly four years,' she said. 'My husband and I split up in 1985. I thought it would be a good idea to put a lot of miles between us. That, however, is another story. Now, what can I do for you?'

'You were on the FBI's "mind hunter" programme, weren't you?'

'That's right. I was a profiler for about two years.'

'How did you get into it?'

'I'd been working on VICAP – that's an acronym for Violent Criminal Apprehension Program – as a liaison officer between the bureau and the police. Somehow or

163

other I got into hostage-negotiation techniques, and from there it was a natural progression to the Behavioral Science Unit.'

'I've heard a lot about mind hunting, but I don't have the remotest idea what the technique is.'

'The idea is to try to formulate a psychological, sometimes even a physical profile of a fugitive from a variety of types of information: genetic fingerprinting, surveillance reports, statistic profile guidance, psycholinguistics—'

'Sorry,' Garrett said. 'Could we backtrack a little, there?'

'Sorry,' Patricia Miller smiled. ' 'kay, let's say we have a serial killer, known only as X. His victims are all women, nothing in common between them except their sex. No eyewitnesses, no photographs, nothing. 'kay, this is what we try to do. Forensics can maybe give us a blood sample, or a saliva or semen smear. That will give us a genetic fingerprint: you know about them?'

'Something to do with genetic make-up. DNA cells. No two persons have identical sets.'

'Ten out of ten. 'kay, so if the guy kills again, we will be able to show genetically that it was he and no other who was involved. In the process we will have established his blood type, race, possibly even hair and eye colour. Another technique involves finger- and footprinting; the height at which prints are left is often a clear indication of the height of the man involved, and the size of the hand or foot prints gives us some physical parameters. A big husky guy usually has big hands and feet, a thin, weedy man small ones. It's not infallible, but it's a pointer.'

'What about personality?'

'I'm coming to that. 'kay, let's say what we have so far is a very blurred snapshot. We know the guy is a male Caucasian, height somewhere between five-eight and six feet, brown hair, brown or green eyes, well-built – say a hundred and eighty pounds. We can feed that into the computer and see whether any of the suspects come close to that description. Conversely, we can countermatch our snapshot against the statistical profile created by the computer from hard information already fed to it – manner in which the wounds were inflicted, force used, and so on. A little guy using a knife won't cut anything like as deep as a big guy.'

'You talk like a cop,' Garrett said.

She smiled. 'That's what I was. Do you want some tea?'

'I'd rather listen.'

' 'kay, now the hard part. A profiler's job is to create a psychological portrait of the criminal. It's nothing like enough to know he's probably six feet two and built like a Mack truck. What we need to know is what will he do in a given situation – trapped in a house with a hostage, or pursued in a car by officers. If we have voice recordings, we can call in a psycholinguist – the one at the FBI when I was there was a professor of psychology at Syracuse University – who tries to tell us, from the voice, something about the background and mind of the man. Where he comes from, what kind of education he had, what hang-ups he has. If we have a ransom note or something the guy wrote we can work out with that, although it's not usually as helpful as a voice recording. We take everything we know about the guy into account: what kind of locations he kills in, whether he stalks his victims or picks them at random, the actual killing itself, what kind of sex if sex is involved, mutilations – everything the guy does tells us something about him. That's what we used to call mind hunting.'

'I'm impressed,' Garrett said. 'And surprised.'

'Why surprised?'

'You're not snowed under with requests for assistance.'

'I've got a caseload,' she said. 'But it isn't breaking my back. You British seem to prefer the traditional to the experimental.'

'Not all of us,' Garrett said. 'And certainly not me.'

' 'kay, how can I help you?'

'I'm hunting a terrorist,' Garrett told her. 'A young woman. I wondered whether your unit could come up with a profile.'

She grinned. 'I like being called a unit,' she said. 'But I don't have any staff, Mr Garrett. There are just the three of us here: my echo, my shadow and me. But we'll be glad to help, if we can.'

'Her name is Leila Jarhoun,' Garrett said.

It was nearer six than five by the time he got through telling her about Leila Jarhoun. Dr Miller checked Jessica's office for him and reported that she had already left. He thanked her and they shook hands.

'Something special going on between you and Mrs Goldman?'

'Why do you ask?'

'She's an interesting lady,' Dr Miller replied.

'They only come in the one variety,' Garrett said.

'Can I give you some advice, Mr Garrett?'

'Of course, although I don't promise to take it.'

'In my line of business you get to know when someone has papered over the cracks in their life. If you two are involved. . . . Hell, what I'm trying to say is, go easy with her. She's . . . fragile.'

'Would you like to tell me what that means, doctor?'

'Let me ask you this: do you know anything about her? Or is that a dumb question?'

'She's thirty-two. Formerly married, now divorced. And yes, I know a little about her.'

'Has she talked about her husband?'

'Not at all.'

'Would you happen to know why they divorced?'

'Only that it was a no-fault decree.'

'Was it?' Dr Miller said. 'That's interesting. I would have bet. . . .' She shook her head. 'Sorry. I'm always doing that, and I shouldn't. Just . . . I had some experience in that department myself. It takes a while to get through it. So give her time, Mr Garrett. I don't know what it is, but that girl is carrying a heavy load.'

There are days when I feel I'm carrying quite a load myself, doctor. I could tell you all about it if you've got a couple of weeks to spare.

'I'll keep it in mind,' Garrett said. 'You'll get back to me about Jarhoun?'

'Soon as I can. If you come across anything else you think might be helpful, shoot it over here. If I'm not around, leave a message on the tape.'

'Thanks again.'

'Any time.'

Garrett went down to the tiled entrance hall and signed out at the desk. The commissionaire was watching the news on a portable TV. A card in a slot on the wall said 'Alert State Amber'. Six o'clock and all's well, Garrett thought. He stepped through the swing doors and out into the street. And the world blew up in his face.

14

Two chance factors saved Charles Garrett's life. The first was that as he saw the car roar into life and swerve over to the right-hand side of the street, he reacted instinctively, throwing himself backwards towards the shelter of the doorway he had just left. The second was that the assassins overthrew the grenade, which rolled right across the pavement and hit the wall of the CME building as it exploded. As a result, at least half of the 3,500 three-millimetre steel balls packed into the plastic shell wasted their kinetic energy against the solid brick wall; there were more than enough left, however, to scythe outwards in a killing arc that mowed down five pedestrians, smashing in the windows and riddling the bodywork of two cars parked at the kerb.

In that same millisecond, as he scrabbled backwards on to the stone steps of Kelvin House, trying desperately for the cover of the entrance, Garrett's unprotected right leg was directly in the lethal line of flight of the fragmentation devices. Moving at about sixteen hundred metres a second, four of them ripped through the soft flesh of his calf, pulling an agonized shout of pain from the big man that blended with those of the wounded passers-by lying askew on the bloody pavement.

Garrett blacked out; when he opened his eyes, strobe lights were flashing, men shouting. His entire right side felt numb; someone was kneeling by his side, but he could not properly focus his eyes. Pain swam up his body and he passed out again.

He was in a room. High windows, the noise of traffic. Where? Paris? A woman stood facing him, her back to the window. He could not see her face. Then she turned, and recognition rushed through him like water. She was dark and beautiful, with high cheekbones and full, sensuous lips. She smiled.

'Leila Jarhoun,' he said. He tried to go to her, but his feet would not move. He looked down and saw that he was bound to an upright chair. Naked. He looked up. She was naked too. Her body was supple and slender. She put her hands beneath her hair at the nape of her neck and lifted the long dark hair over her head. Her breasts rose, the nipples pink and raised. She came closer, closer still. Her face descended upon his and he raised his yearning mouth to hers, his whole body throbbing with desire.

'No,' she said. 'It can never be. Never . . . never . . . never.' She dissolved and was gone. He fell back into emptiness. Darkness came back.

'Charles?' someone was saying. The voice reminded him of someone. He opened his eyes, and it was Jessica.

'Can you hear me, Charles?' she said. Her face was drawn and white as if she had received a terrible shock. He wondered what it could have been. He looked past her at the white roof above him. He felt the bed beneath his back. Hospital? Then he remembered.

'Jess?' he said, or thought he did.

'Charles, can you hear me?' she said again, her face close to his. She was so lovely. He tried to nod; pain throbbed inside his body.

'Yes,' he said. Then more strongly, 'Yes.'

'Oh, Charles,' Jessica said, 'Charles.' She started to cry and he tried to reach for her but he could not move his arms. He remembered the dream, the dark hot eyes.

'What—'

'No, you mustn't talk,' she said. 'You've been hurt.'

'I remember,' he said. 'There was a bomb.'

'They said it was a grenade.'

'When?'

'Yesterday.'

Cold fear touched him. 'I was hurt. My leg.'

'It's all right.'

'How bad?'

'They'll tell you. Later.'

'You tell me. Now.'

'It was a mess. They thought they might have to . . . well, your leg was all chewed up. The tibia was cracked. They've fixed all that. You just need time to heal.'

'You're sure?'

'I'm sure. I wouldn't lie to you, Charles.'

'No,' he said, and the fear receded. 'You wouldn't.'

'Charles, I have to go,' Jessica whispered. 'You remember America?'

'America,' he said. What was he supposed to remember about America? His brain felt like a suet pudding. Pumped me full of drugs, he thought. The darkness beckoned, making his eyelids droop. There was something he wanted to say to Jessica, but he could not remember what it was. He slid back into the soft warm welcoming darkness. Jessica stood up and turned away from the bed, to find Nicholas Bleke watching her silently.

'Hello, Jessica,' he said.

'Hello, General Bleke,' she said, without warmth.

'Just Mr these days. You used to call me Nicholas.'

'I no longer think of you as a friend.'

'I'm sorry to hear that,' Bleke said imperturbably. 'How is Charles?'

'You mean, all things considered? All things considered, he seems fine. Of course, we don't know for sure yet whether he'll ever walk properly again, but I doubt that so small a matter would cause you any loss of sleep. Mr Bleke.'

'You blame me . . . for this?'

'Who else would I blame?'

'Charles works in a dangerous business, Jessica. He knows it and accepts the risks. If you are his friend, you must know that.'

'I do know it. It's the motives of those for whom he accepts the risks that I question.'

'We can hardly debate them here,' Bleke said. 'But you must believe we are all working in the best interests of our country.'

'Who was it who said that patriotism was the last refuge of a scoundrel?'

'Samuel Johnson. But I don't think he meant to imply that patriots are scoundrels.'

'Why have you told the newspapers that Charles was killed in the explosion?'

'We would like whoever threw the bomb to believe they succeeded; that way they may betray themselves.'

'In other words, you have no idea who did it.'

'On the contrary.'

'Why don't you arrest them, then? End this thing?'

'That's not how we work,' Bleke said. 'If our enemies present us with an advantage, we must accept it gratefully.'

'You'll send him out there again, won't you?'

'As often as he'll go.'

'And there'll never be any end to it, never any time he won't be in this kind of danger.'

'I can't answer that.'

'During our brief acquaintance, Mr Bleke,' Jessica said impatiently, 'the one consistent thing I've noticed about you is your remarkable gift for talking without saying anything.'

Bleke smiled, and did not reply. Somehow his silence angered her even more. 'I have to go,' she said.

'You leave for America tomorrow, I understand.'

'How did you know that?'

Bleke shrugged. 'I hope you find it rewarding,' he said, and the way he said it seemed to her to convey a meaning other than the words. The astonishing thought occurred to her suddenly that this man might well have arranged her secondment to New York, everything, to take her neatly out of Garrett's life at a time of particular difficulty. Would he, could he, be so ruthless? She looked into Bleke's level grey eyes and decided yes, he could. It was a chilling realization of her own – of anyone's – helplessness in the face of such power.

'If Charles wakes up, please tell him I'll see him tomorrow before I leave,' she said.

'Of course. Goodbye, Jessica.'

She met his eyes and held them. 'I do not love thee, Dr Fell,' she said. She turned on her heel and left the ward.

Bleke watched her go, his eyes reflective. That was quite a girl, he thought. The Spanish said it best: *muy mujer*, much woman.

He went over to the bed in which Garrett lay sleeping, took the clipboard holding his medical charts off the end of the bed, and read the notes. It was a bad wound, but not grave; four of the wicked three-millimetre fragmentation pellets had torn through Garrett's leg, ripping apart the extensor and soleus muscles, cracking the tibia but not breaking it. The wounds, although serious, had been relatively clean. The general prognosis was that there would be no major permanent damage. Garrett would have to be strapped up and stay off his feet for a week or ten days; it would be perhaps another three weeks before he properly regained the use of the leg and foot.

As he replaced the charts on the bedrail, Garrett's eyes flickered open. Bleke reached for a chair and pulled it over to the side of the bed.

'How are you feeling?' he said.

'Bloody awful,' Garrett mumbled. 'Is there anything to drink?'

Jessica Goldman had brought in a bottle of Perrier water; Bleke poured some and gave it to Garrett, who drank it greedily, then put down the glass with a sigh.

'They must have given me every drug known to medical science,' he said. 'I'm as dry as a temperance meeting.'

'You sound cheerful enough.'

'Cheerful is one word for it. Tell me, did I dream it, or was Jessica here?'

'She was here. She gave me quite a hard time. She thinks I exploit you ruthlessly. I suspect she's right.'

'She's sensitive to our line of work,' Garrett said. 'Her grandparents—'

'I know,' Bleke said. 'You're a fortunate fellow, Charles. If I knew a lady like that, I'd cultivate her diligently.'

'She wouldn't like being cultivated,' Garrett said, with a grin. 'Or wooed. She has a mind of her own.'

'I rather got that impression,' Bleke said. *I do not love thee, Dr Fell. Why is it I cannot tell. But this I know and know*

172

full well. I do not love thee, Dr Fell. 'I'm to tell you she'll come in to see you tomorrow before she leaves for America.'

'Tomorrow?'

'She's on BA 177 from Heathrow. Two o'clock takeoff.'

'Damn,' Garrett said. 'We needed more time.'

'It will come,' Bleke said. 'It always does.'

Garrett struggled to a sitting position and looked around. 'Where am I, anyway?'

'Kelvin House. You're a fool for luck, Charles. They had you on an operating table twelve minutes after that bomb went off.'

'The moral of the story is, if you have to get blown up by a bomb, do it outside Central Medical, is that it?'

'It wasn't a bomb,' Bleke said. 'It was a fragmentation grenade, military definition Arges HdGrO 72; they're made in Schwanenstadt, Austria. Used by the Austrian army, not to mention one or two Middle and Far Eastern ones I could name.'

'What about the bombers?'

Bleke unfolded a newspaper and laid it in front of Garrett. Garrett picked it up and began to read.

BOMB OUTRAGE IN WEST END
FOUR DEAD IN SOHO STREET CARNAGE

A few minutes after six o'clock yesterday evening, in a street crowded with home-going workers, terrorists unleashed random violence upon the population of London. Moments after a blue car with two men in it drove at speed up Cleveland Street in Soho, a bomb exploded on the pavement, killing three men and a woman and severely injuring four others. Emergency services at the scene said it was 'like a butcher's shop'.

At about six-twenty, just minutes after the bombing, a blue Ford saloon driven by two men of Middle Eastern appearance crashed while attempting to evade a police roadblock in Chalk Farm Road, Hampstead. When officers approached the vehicle, two shots were heard; both occupants of the car were found to be dead on arrival at hospital. No warning of the bomb attack was given. No terrorist organization has as yet claimed responsibility. Police named the dead as James Herbert, a copywriter; Clive Barker, a carpet salesman; Charles Garrett, a civil servant, and Gillian Cooper, a journalist. A police spokesman said that the identity of the terrorists was unknown; investigations were continuing.

'I'm dead?' Garrett asked.

'I think we can assume that it was Leila Jarhoun's people who tried to take you out, Charles,' Bleke said. 'So let them think you're out. It will give you time. Space to move around in.'

'What I'd like to know is how they isolated me.'

'Jarhoun got as good a look at you in St Valery as you did at her. She would have given her people a photofit. The PLO isn't exclusively made up of mad bombers, you know. They have a perfectly good intelligence service.'

'Even so,' Garrett said. 'They would have needed more than a photofit.'

'What kind of more?'

'Location, for one. How did they know I was in London?'

'You suspect an inside job?'

'Not our people. Someone in DST perhaps?'

'It's a possibility,' Bleke said. 'I'll have a word with René Izbot.'

'Anything on the two that threw the grenade?'

'Not much. They flew in from Cairo on tourist visas. They were carrying Jordanian passports, but I'm willing to bet my pension they were no more from Jordan than we are.'

'The car was hired, I suppose?'

'Of course,' Bleke said. 'The grenade probably came in separately in a diplomatic bag, and they picked it up after they got here.'

'I'll say one thing for these people,' Garrett said. 'They're very good at leaving us with dead ends.'

'How did you spot them, anyway?'

'They were pretty clumsy. I should have realized why. They weren't on a surveillance mission. They were just waiting for a chance to take me out.'

'At least you'd put footmen on them, or they'd have got completely clear.'

'I doubt they would have told us much even if we'd taken them alive. They were just a hit team,' Garrett said. 'Has anything new come in?'

'Two things you had on the wire. You asked the

Europolice to check for an Abdul lookalike. They had one in Frankfurt.

'The Frankfurt killings were the last in the sequence. So whoever killed the two policemen was also taken out. Which means we finally found Nidal Faour. What was the second thing?'

'Your request to the FBI paid off. They took longer to come up with something because they have rather more killings to check. It was your stipulation that the murders be motiveless but not random that made it easier, they said. They came up with a couple of lookalike killings in New York. The two that came closest to your specifications were a Polish woman who works for a contract office-cleaning firm and a United Nations tour guide.'

'No link? No common denominators?'

'Nothing in the report.'

'How about McCaskill's boys? Have they come up with anything?'

'Nothing yet.'

'How long am I going to be stuck in here?'

'I've had a word. The medics say that on present indications, you'll be walking in a few days. You'll probably need crutches, though.'

'The hell I will,' Garrett said, Bleke smiled his non-committal smile and said nothing. 'Can I get some equipment in here – a phone, a computer terminal?'

'I'll see to it,' Bleke said. 'In the meantime, get some rest.'

Garrett yawned hugely; 'Now you mention it, I am tired,' he said wonderingly. He closed his eyes and in a moment was fast asleep. Bleke got up and put the chair back against the wall. He looked down at Garrett and then, after a moment, touched his shoulder gently.

'Take care, lad,' he said, then turned away and left.

Hennessy sat by the window, staring out at the street below. What lay ahead of him now – what lay ahead of all of them – was the hardest part of what they did: going to ground. Their first priority was finding a place or places to live, fairly close to each other and not too far from the killing ground. The next hurdle was to find work, any kind of work. Only then could they finalize the plan they had come here to execute.

He did not like Germany, never had. He had been twice before: once in March 1987, when he was a member of the hit team that put a three-hundred-pound bomb outside British Army headquarters in Rheindahlen, and once fifteen months later, when the target was Glamorgan Barracks in Duisburg. On both trips it had rained the whole bloody time, and it looked as if this one was going to be no improvement. It had never stopped for one minute since their arrival. Trolley cars, headlights glaring in the murk, clanged along the Graf Adolfstrasse towards the Hauptbahnhof; a policeman in a glistening waterproof cape directed traffic from his podium in the centre of the junction of the Königsallee, or Kö, as the locals preferred to call it. Bloody Germany, he thought, what a bloody miserable country.

It had taken them three days to cross France and Belguim. In accordance with standard procedure, they split up into two teams soon after their flight from St Valery, abandoning the DST Mazda in a car park on the Place Clemenceau at Abbeville, each pair stealing another vehicle to take them on to Amiens, where the procedure was repeated.

The next stop was Antwerp, where the cars were again abandoned, this time in favour of the train, which brought them to their rendezvous: the Holiday Inn on Graf Adolfplatz in Düsseldorf. The day following their evening arrival, McQueen and Egan, now using British passports in the names of Rickards and Gregory, hired a Hertz VW Kombi and set off on their reconnaissance trip to look for accommodation somewhere in the Mönchen-Gladbach area. In the meantime, there was nothing for Hennessy and Tony Gallagher to do but sit and wait.

The target itself had already been selected; as soon as they got their base organized and found cover jobs, the work of making the assessments could begin. Hennessy didn't envy the men who were with him the task of crawling around in the undergrowth near a top-security installation in freezing rain, but that was their speciality. His turn would come. As he watched, he saw Tony Gallagher, head down against the rain, come across the road from the Königsallee and hurry over towards the hotel. A few minutes later the lift whined in the corridor outside and he heard Gallagher's discreet coded knock on the door.

'You get the papers?' he said, as Gallagher took off his soaked raincoat.

'They only had the *Telegraph* and *The Times*,' Gallagher told him. 'All the rest were sold out.' He tossed the papers on to the bed and went into the bathroom. Hennessy opened the *Telegraph* flat on the bed. He stared at it in disbelief.

'Will you look at that!' he breathed.

Gallagher came out of the bathroom, drying his hair with a face towel. He leaned over Hennessy's shoulder and read the headlines aloud.

' "Terrorist bomb attack in London street. Four killed, eight injured in Soho horror." ' He frowned and looked at Hennessy. 'That's not our lads, is it?'

Hennessy shook his head. 'Read on, read on,' he said impatiently.

' "Three men and a woman were killed, and seven others injured yesterday when a terrorist threw a hand grenade from a car in Cleveland Street, Soho. Police said most of the injured were cut by flying glass and shrapnel and all but one – including a pregnant woman – were released from hospital after treatment—" '

'Look, look!' Hennessy said impatiently, and stabbed a finger lower down the column. 'Bloody hell, are you blind? It's Garrett! Charles Garrett!'

'Who's he?'

'Sweet-scented Jesus, Tony, how long have you been on active service?'

'Two years. Why?'

'You've never heard of Garrett?'

Gallagher shook his head. 'It says he was a civil servant.'

'Aye, and he was that,' Hennessy said. 'A bloody British spy, that's what he was. All right, now let me ask you

177

something else: do you know the name Patrick McCaffery?'

'I've heard of it,' Gallagher said. 'But I don't know much about him.'

Hennessy shook his head disgustedly. These kids today, they had no idea of what it had been like in the old days. Half of them didn't even know who Michael Collins was.

'He was a lad, was Pat McCaffery,' he said. 'Mad Pat, they called him. A big, tall, thin drink of water of a fellow with a shock of black hair, and eyes as green as Wicklow. Hard as nails, but brainy with it.'

Mad Pat McCaffery, born in Drogheda in 1942, graduated early from stone-throwing and joy-riding; first employed to ditch and burn cars used in bank robberies or sectarian killings, he became a fighting member of the IRA on his eighteenth birthday. By the time he was twenty he was a veteran of the streets; by twenty-five an officer, and a year later interned at Long Kesh on criminal charges.

Being Mad Pat, already something of a legend, he made a legendary escape: his brother Peter, a priest, smuggled a clerical suit into the prison; McCaffery walked out under the noses of the security forces and went on the run to Eire, where he became active in ambush activities on the border. He killed his share, and never had an own goal, but they were losing more fights than they won: Mad Pat soon perceived that the IRA could never effectively counter the combined British intelligence services in Stormont and Lisburn unless they created an equivalent organization as good, if not better, than the one opposing them. To do this, they needed finance. NORAID, the North American funding unit, would provide some of the money, but if the job was to be done properly, it would take more than that.

McCaffery began by outlawing the thick-ear type of 'protection' practised in the province. No more gangs demanding money with menaces from shopkeepers or publicans, no more beatings or smashed-up premises for those who didn't pay. Apart from being against the law, it was bad PR. Why do it illegally when it was just as easy — and enormously more profitable — to do it on the up and up?

'We went legit,' Hennessy said. 'Security firms, with boards of directors, profit-and-loss statements, taxes. In ten years, we started up fifty, sixty, each of them turning over two hundred thousand, a quarter of a million a year. On top of that, they were used to buy surveillance equipment, monitors, armoured cars.'

McCaffery's next stroke was to introduce London-style taxis in the province. The operation began in June 1972, when five cabs arrived in Belfast. At the same time an orchestrated campaign of violence against municipal transport systems was launched; city buses were systematically stoned and firebombed. Within three months, three hundred corporation buses had been taken off the streets and the IRA, with more than six hundred cabs, had a virtual monopoly in transport. Within a year both its taxi companies were worth a million pounds, providing a perfect means of laundering illegal funds through investments and overseas bank accounts – all strictly legal. Another valuable by-product of the taxi service was, of course, that no one could go anywhere without the knowledge of the IRA intelligence network.

'It was just bloody brilliant,' Hennessy said. 'Bloody brilliant. There we were, generating enough legitimate money to buy all the guns and ammunition we wanted. The Brits were going berserk. So, of course, they made a priority of finding out who was the brain behind all this, and once they found out, they fitted McCaffery up.'

'Ah, the bastards,' Gallagher said automatically. 'Did they kill him, Sean?'

'Not right then. We have a good man in New York, Brian McGuinness,' Hennessy told him. 'Now up to that time, we'd been buying only rifles, pistols, explosives and detonators. But the troops were using helicopters more and more, and we needed something with more firepower, rockets or surface-to-air missiles. McGuinness was given the job of getting some.

McGuinness agreed to buy a five-hundred-thousand-dollar package of weapons that included Redeye missiles, grenade launchers, and Heckler and Koch sub-machine-guns. The money was flown to Switzerland and paid into a specified numbered account and the shipment left Charleston, South Carolina, ostensibly bound for Lisbon.

'The boat was to heave to off Rossan Point in Donegal, transfer the stuff to a trawler that would bring it in to Portnoo. McCaffery took a team up there to collect it. But the whole thing was a bloody fit-up.'

'How did you find out?'

'By accident,' Hennessy said. 'One of our people in New York happened to see someone with McGuinness, and recognized him. He'd known him in Germany as an Army intelligence officer. His real name was—'

'Garrett,' Gallagher said.

'You have it. By the time we found out he was a plant it was too late,' Hennessy said. 'McCaffery was already on his way to Portnoo to pick up the consignment: the Army was waiting for him. The lads never had a chance: four of them killed, McCaffery and five more arrested.'

'And what about this Garrett?'

'After that, we put him right at the top of our Seek and Silence list, but he'd dropped out of sight. We had other things to worry about. The biggest priority was springing Pat McCaffery: the bastard Brits would put him into deep interrogation and he knew too much. We also knew if he went to trial, they'd put him away for life.'

'You'll have another, Sean?'

'Aye, why not?' Hennessy said, lighting another cigarette. It was getting dark outside. He wished they had some crisps. He waited till Gallagher sat down again before continuing the story.

'We were still trying to come up with an idea when we got a lucky break,' he said. 'Caitlin McBride, the mother of one of the lads killed at Portnoo, was working as a cleaner in a big house at Lisburn. She heard some talk about McCaffery and reported it to us. We put watchmen on the couple she was working for. It turned out to be Garrett and his wife. They weren't using their own name, of course, but it was them, right enough. So there all at once was our handle for springing Mad Pat.'

'The wife?'

'Aye, the wife. Diana was her name.'

'You snatched her, then, did you?'

'That we did. We lifted her, neat as a trout, on the A30, coming back to Lisburn from visiting a friend in Glenavy. Took her to a house we had, halfway between Fintona and the border.'

How long are you going to keep me here?

Until your husband does what we want him to do, Mrs Garrett.

You think he'll bargain with men like you?

If he doesn't, Mrs Garrett, you will.

'Then what?'

'Garrett was running E4 teams out of the Rathole in Lisburn. We got word to him: his wife in exchange for Mad Pat. He said he needed a few days. We knew what he was up to, of course: he thought the security forces would find us.'

You think I'm frightened of you? You think you can scare me, you pathetic-looking cretin?

If you don't shut your mouth, I'll shut it for you.

'But they didn't.'

'No chance. We were hid away like mice in a cornfield. All we had to do was wait it out. The lads went to work every day. I stayed at the house guarding the woman.'

What do you think you're going to do, you shitty little creep? Rape me? Is that what's on your moronic little mind?

Is that what's on yours, Mrs Garrett?

'They stalled for a week, but they never had a chance of finding us. So we set it up, picked out a place. They wanted to change it as soon as I said where it was. I told Garrett if he didn't make the meet, I'd start sending him pieces of his wife in the post. That took care of that, and the meet was on.'

This place, this place, this place! I must be going mad. Even you are starting to look halfway human.

I'm human, Mrs Garrett.

Diana. My name is Diana.

'What happened then?'

'I set it up. Just the four of us: me and the woman on this side, Garrett and Pat McCaffery on the other. Of course, I was going to kill Garrett as soon as the handover was made.'

Your husband has agreed.

I never thought he would. I thought—

It doesn't matter what you thought. You're going back tomorrow.

Don't waste tonight, then.

'Where did you make the handover?'

'A crossroads between Fintona and Trillick. It was a perfect spot. No chance of an ambush, or so I thought. But I was wrong: the bastards had an SAS sniper there. As soon as the woman was over the line they took McCaffery out, a THV bullet through the head.'

'THV?' Gallagher hissed.

'It's a new French bullet they use now,' Hennessy said. 'Blew Mad Pat's head off his shoulders. I went mad, blind fucking mad. All I could think of was killing Garrett. I ran out from behind the car and fired a burst at him, and I saw it knock the woman over. There were bullets everywhere, the sniper firing, Garrett on one knee shooting at me. It was as if it was all in slow motion, but I knew I only had a few seconds to get to the switch car before the helicopters came, so I got the hell out of there.'

'So McCaffery was dead. And the woman?'

Will I ever see you again?

No. Never.

'She was dead, too.' His voice was flat and toneless, his eyes empty. Gallagher felt a thin chill of unease. A ghost walked over my grave, he thought.

'Well,' he said, gesturing towards the newspaper, 'now Garrett's dead as well.'

'I know it,' Hennessy said.

'You sound sad, Sean. I thought you hated him.'

Hennessy nodded. 'Aye, I'm sad,' he said. 'I wanted to kill the bastard myself.'

15

Using a passport and visa which identified her as Noor
Ibrahim, a citizen of Egypt, Leila Jarhoun flew to Boston
on a direct Swissair flight from Zürich. Clearing customs
and immigration without difficulty, she caught a shuttle to
New York, arriving in Manhattan on a Tuesday morning.
Ignoring the insistent limo touts, she took a bus to 42nd
Street and picked up a cab for the short journey to the
Hilton on Sixth Avenue. The streets were crowded with
trucks and vans. New York was never the same, but some
things never changed. Sirens. Wisps of steam coming out
of manholes in the road. The closing-down sale notices on
Fifth Avenue.

The room on the fortieth floor of the Hilton had a picture
window that looked north past the Essex House to Central
Park. It was furnished in the unexceptionable hotel-
modern style found in every major city in the world. Since
she would be in it only a few hours, it was more than
suitable for her purpose. She had told no one she was in the
city. Not until she had completed her preliminary recon-
naissances did she intend to telephone the contact number
she had been given. The PLO cover organization in New
York was a fund-raising operation called the American
League for the Liberation of Palestine. She had no inten-
tion of apprizing them of either her presence or her intentions until she was quite ready to do so.

After she unpacked her case, she looked at her watch:
eleven o'clock. It was sunny outside; the streets were
crowded with people already wearing lighter-weight
clothes. There was only a short interval between winter and
summer in New York. She put on a blouse, skirt, short
cotton jacket, flat shoes and a narrow-brimmed rain hat.
She got in a cab in front of the hotel and told the driver to
take her to United Nations Plaza; at her request, he

dropped her at the General Assembly building, between 45th and 46th Streets.

The visitors' entrance to UN Plaza was at the north end of the General Assembly building. In the crowded lobby, with its cantilevered balconies and soft lighting and its signs in English and French, was an information desk and a booth where tickets were issued when the General Assembly was in session; visitors lunching in the Delegates' Dining Room on the fourth floor also obtained their passes here. Beyond the lobby and to the right was the Meditation Room, its focal point a massive block of iron ore dimly spotlighted from above. Next to its entrance was a Chagall glass panel symbolizing the struggle for peace. Facing the Meditation Room, a facsimile of the original UN charter was on permanent display. Suspended from the ceiling above the stair landing connecting the lobby with the second-floor ceremonial entrance to the General Assembly hall was the Foucault pendulum, a gift of the Dutch people. In the basement there was a book and gift shop and a post office where you could mail cards bearing UN stamps. Even peace was an industry these days.

Leila Jarhoun watched as one of the frequent tours set off, a uniformed guide leading it like a school party on its forty-five minute journey. Each of those participating received a little tin clip-on badge with the UN logo in blue and white and the words 'United Nations Guided Tour'. Leila Jarhoun paid for a ticket, chose an English-speaking guide – more than thirty languages were available – and attached herself to one group, listening as dutifully as any student researching a project. The eighteen-acre site on which the complex was built had once been known as Dutch Hill and later Turtle Bay, the guide said. There had been an abattoir nearby. The first building, the thirty-nine-storey Secretariat, all green glass and aluminium grid, was where the day-to-day work of UN staff was performed; it had been completed in 1950. The neighbouring Conference Building, where UN councils met, and the domed General Assembly, were opened two years later. Little by little the surroundings had been improved and enlarged, and promenade, plazas and gardens created. The fourth building in the complex was the Dag Hammarskjöld Library, open only to graduate students working on special projects.

The whole city within a city belonged to the United Nations, the guide continued; it was invisibly fenced off from the city of New York, which had no jurisdiction here. In the three basements of the Secretariat building, which in turn connected with those of the Conference building, were maintenance shops, a fire-fighting unit, security officers, a three-level garage, receiving and dispatch bays, an automobile service station and a refrigeration plant. One hundred and fifty-nine Member States sent more than three thousand representatives to New York for the annual sessions of the General Assembly; the secretariat numbered over seven thousand employees. Visitors averaged around fifteen hundred a day, every day of the year. Four hundred and fifty journalists were permanently accredited, working out of specially designed offices on the third and fourth floors of the Secretariat building.

'Now we enter the General Assembly Hall,' the woman said, waving a languid arm like a magician doing a very simple trick. There before them was a blue, green and gold hall with its leather-covered tables and speaker's rostrum and podium, familiar from a thousand newsreels, Khruschev banging his shoe, Adlai Stevenson in the Cuban missile crisis.

'The Assembly Hall was remodelled in 1979 to accommodate a maximum of one hundred eighty-two delegations,' the guide told them. 'Each delegation has six seats. Behind these one thousand ninety-two places are a further four hundred seventy-six alternates, and at the sides are one hundred eighty-seven seats for alternates, observers and others. In the balcony, there are fifty-three places for news media and two hundred eighty seats in five rows for members of the public. All two thousand one hundred and three seats are equipped with earphones providing simultaneous translation into the six official languages of the Assembly: Arabic, Chinese, English, French, Russian and Spanish. . . .'

She even lists the languages in alphabetical order, Leila Jarhoun thought. 'Where does the Secretary General work?' she asked.

'When the General Assembly is in session he sits in the chair to the right of the President's podium,' the woman replied. She was short and pigeon-breasted, with wide hips and well-muscled legs which were no doubt the result of tramping the carpeted corridors of the UN complex every day of her life. 'He has a small reception room for his personal use. He also has an office in the Security Council Chamber on the second floor of the Conference building, next to the President's office.'

'Do all his staff work there?'

'No, no,' the guide said patiently. 'The executive offices of the Secretary General are on the thirty-eighth floor of the Secretariat building.'

'Thank you,' Leila said, making notes. She made many more as they toured the complex, asking questions which the guide answered carefully, like a smiling, talking encyclopedia.

When the tour was finished, and they returned to the cathedral-like lobby, Leila Jarhoun smiled in satisfaction; nothing had changed since she had made her preliminary reconnaissance. The first part of the plan could go ahead immediately. It was already quite warm on the street as she came out of the UN complex, but she decided to walk down to the New York Public Library, her next stop. When she got there, she took the lift to the reference section and settled down to complete her researches.

There was a great deal more material than she could have hoped for: pamphlets, illustrated books, diagramatic renderings, interior views, exterior views, technical details, architectural sketches, lighting charts, aerial photographs. She read them all avidly, paying particular attention to Eiffel's sketches and calculations for the armatures: there was no such thing as too much information. The hours sped past; she made pages and pages of notes on the yellow legal pad she had bought in a drugstore on 42nd Street.

As she worked, another part of her mind took her

back to the centenary celebrations of Frédéric-Auguste Bartholdi's creation. She had been watching them on televison in Abu Jihad's villa, hating the effrontery and vulgar profligacy of the Americans, when all at once the idea had come to her, fully realized, as if it had always been in her mind. Here, she saw, was a way all at once to avenge the death of her beloved father, strike the unforgettable blow for her homeland, become immortal in one earth-shattering moment.

That was in 1986. She had already become prominent in PLO circles as a firebrand former student leader, a revolutionary whose every waking moment was devoted to the liberation of the homeland. She rose through the echelons of the Information Department to the rank of lieutenant on the staff of Khalil al-Wazir, Abu Jihad, the father of the holy war; he discreetly smoothed the way for her to participate in the executive decisions of the organization. He had become her mentor, her avatar and, in time, assumed in her consciousness the role of surrogate father, a quiet, unemotional man in his early fifties whose mild manners concealed an iron determination to reclaim the land from which his parents had been expelled in 1948. In this ambition Leila Jarhoun had been closer to the murdered man than anyone else on his personal staff; she, too, burned to avenge her family's dispossession of its ancestral home following the creation of the State of Israel.

Leila's father, Talal Ahmed Jarhoun, had spent most of his lifetime nurturing and improving the orange groves at Bet She'an which had belonged to his family for three generations. He was prosperous, highly respected, active in community affairs. He was not one of the hotheads who wanted war with the Jews, but neither was he a well-intentioned fool who could not see the danger of Jewish aspirations. In the final analysis, it made no difference; in the bitter year of 1948, following the expiry of the British Mandate in Palestine, the Israelis expropriated the farm, rendering Talal Jarhoun and his family homeless. He fled south with his wife and children to the trans-Jordan village of Baqura, where he opened a small shop and tried to rebuild his life.

He worked hard, he earned the respect of his neighbours, and over the years he began again to prosper. It was all in vain; in the Six Day War of June 1967, during the massive bombardments of the Israeli Army, most of the village of Baqura was razed, and Talal Jarhoun was killed. Almost from that day, Leila had become dedicated to the cause of Palestine. She had revealed to no one the determination to avenge her father that smouldered within her. The time would come, she knew.

She was under no misapprehension: she realized it would be more than just difficult to persuade the leadership that a woman – even one respected for her abilities – could successfully mount an operation such as she had in mind, and even more difficult to convince them she should lead it. So she waited, for a time, for a reason, for an opportunity of sufficient importance to present itself; the assassination of Abu Jihad was that opportunity. She knew there would never be any better time than this.

The man to whom she took her plan was Ibrahim Kutayfan, Deputy Director of Operational Planning. During her years with Abu Jihad, she had sensed in Kutayfan the same frustrations she herself felt: the same angers, the same hatreds, the same impatience with talking. He was ambitious, and it took him only a few minutes of listening to realize that her plan might be a vehicle on which he could propel himself to the highest echelons of the PLO, perhaps even into the place of Abu Jihad himself. Leila was wise, wise beyond her years: she saw the greedy hunger for power that he kept hidden, and something else that flickered behind his eyes when he looked at her. He wanted her; one day, if it became necessary, she would use that weapon, as well.

It was after four when she came out of the Bryant Square side of the building. The Hilton was just twelve blocks away up Sixth Avenue. She decided to walk, calling at the Duane Read drug store between 44th and 45th to pick up a toothbrush and some shampoo. On the corner opposite Radio City a man was selling bagels: they smelled steamy and strong. When she got back to the Hilton she went straight up to her room and drew the shades. She was more than satisfied with her day's work. She was hungry, too, but the jet lag was beginning to bite now, and she knew better than to fight it. She could do the important field reconniassance tomorrow: there was no hurry. She took off her clothes and got into bed, falling asleep almost immediately.

The guns were pounding, flat dark hard sounds. Her father's voice. Wake up, child, wake up. Help your sisters. We must go, we must go. The sound of her mother crying. Hurrying down the stony street. The guns again, crump, crump, crump. The shells made a strange long thin sound: wutter-wutter-wutter. Then the explosion. Blood red flames. Screams, screams. Father! Father!

She awoke abruptly, bathed in perspiration and disorientated by the nightmare, her own scream strangled by a reflex trained for years to kill it before it was uttered. The memories of the razing of Baqura evaporated; she remembered where she was. She sat up in bed and looked at her watch: five-forty a.m. It was still dark outside, only a few lights on in the buildings visible from the window.

She shivered, and put on a long-sleeved towelling robe. At seven-thirty she called the contact number she had been given. The phone rang four times and then an answering machine cut in.

'You have reached the offices of the American League for the Liberation of Palestine,' it said. 'We are closed at present, but if you would like to leave you name and number, someone will contact you as soon as possible.'

'This is Leila,' she said. 'Call everyone together. Four o'clock this afternoon.'

That would spoil Asaad's morning, she thought, with a feline smile. Then she called down for breakfast: juice, coffee, toast, scrambled eggs, and a copy of the *New York Times*. She flicked on the TV and watched *Good Morning, America* until a knock at the door signalled the arrival of room service. She tipped the waiter and locked the door after him, then sat down at the circular table to eat a leisurely breakfast and plan her day.

189

No matter how many books you pored over in the public library, she thought, there were some things you could only check out on the ground. How long did a taxi take to get to Battery Park on a Sunday morning? How frequently did the boats leave, and how long did the journey take? Had there been any changes? Were there security guards now? Had the route been altered? The reconnaissance would take her until after lunch. After that, what? Lord and Taylor or Bergdorf Goodman? Bloomingdales or Macy's? She threw back her head and laughed out loud; she had a much better idea than that.

At three o'clock that afternoon, she came out of the Japanese Shiatsu massage parlour on upper Fifth Avenue, where she had spent the last hour, her entire body glowing with satisfaction. She got in a taxi and told the driver to take her to Fifth Avenue at 21st Street. She could still feel the gentle hands of the Japanese girl on her body. What was her name? Mishima, something like that. By the time the cab bounced past Scribner's, she had forgotten her; only the warm postcoital glow remained.

When she got out of the cab, a fresh warm wind was whirling between the buildings, lifting scraps of paper into the air. In Madison Square, bums swigged from bottles covered with brown paper bags. A black youth went by on roller skates, carrying a package, the tinny beat of his Walkman audible a yard away. Leila looked at her watch: she had half an hour. She went into a coffee shop. Red plastic-topped tables, booths at the front windows, a long counter with newspapers in Italian. A long room full of tables and booths at the back. A sign on the wall 'Occupancy by more than 151 persons is dangerous and unlawful'. Everything in dispensers.

She sat at the bar and ordered coffee. The man behind the counter was short and ugly, his fat gut covered by a soiled white apron. He cocked a speculative eye at her and she could almost hear his thought: nice piece of ass. One of the waitresses shouted something.

'Awrighta'ready, faChrissake,' the man said. He smiled at Leila Jarhoun. 'Great waitress – in a shoeshine shop,' he said. Another moron who thought that making other people look small was a way of making himself look big. Like Kutayfan, with his lardy skin and bad breath. She thought of Mishima's eagerness to please, her budlike breasts damp with perspiration. How easy it was to loathe men. She paid for her coffee and went out on to Fifth Avenue. The Empire State Building shone silver and slim to the north.

The offices of the American League for the Liberation of Palestine were on the top floor of a ten-storey building between 18th and 19th Streets. Ostensibly financed by public subscription, the organization in fact operated in tandem with a front travel agency in Brooklyn, where false billings and bogus refunds for purported airline travel undertaken by Palestinian students annually generated seven-figure funding for undercover operations, demonstrations, and transporting sympathetic journalists and activists to the West Bank on 'fact-finding' trips.

When Leila Jarhoun reached the top floor she found herself in a dead-end corridor in which a plain wooden door faced the lifts. The baleful electronic eye of a CCTV camera surveyed her. She pushed the buzzer; after a moment the security locks in the door clacked open. The doors opened into a small foyer. An armed security guard sat behind a desk with a seven-inch TV screen on it. He stared at her as she came in.

'Yes?'

'Tell Asaad that Leila is here,' she said.

The man spoke into an intercom; he glanced furtively at her when he thought she was not looking at him. It was a minor irritant: she was getting used to it. After a few minutes a tall, middle-aged man wearing a short-sleeved white shirt and powder blue trousers came out of a door to Leila Jarhoun's right. His hair was thick and wavy, streaked with grey; he wore heavy horn-rimmed glasses that gave him a studious look. When she turned to face him she saw his revulsion, although it was instantly masked.

'So you are the one,' he said, without the slightest hint of enthusiasm. 'I am Hamil Asaad. Come with me, please.

191

The others are waiting. Can I get you anything before we begin?'

'Nothing.' She had not expected a warm welcome. Kutayfan had warned her that the American organization had got itself into a nice comfortable velvet-lined rut, and did not want to put it at risk. For years, they had successfully maintained that terrorist acts in the United States would be counterproductive; the Executive Committee had acceded. When Leila's plan was sanctioned, the American organization protested strenuously that it would probably result in the ALLP being outlawed in America, and all its members deported to Palestine. As Kutayfan had cynically observed, none of those working in New York had any burning desire to return to the homeland. It was doubtful they would want to do so even if they achieved the liberation for which they were supposedly working, he added drily.

Asaad led the way into a conference room comfortably furnished with a teak table and leather armchairs; four men waited, already seated. Asaad introduced them one by one: Mahomed Nabhan, his brother Hassan, Khaled Abu-Takieh, Zaher Ali Dokr. They, too, were taken aback when she walked in, staring at her in stunned silence. Unsurprisingly, their greeting was less than effusive.

'We had expected more notice of your arrival,' Asaad said. 'When did you get here?'

'It is irrelevant,' Leila said. 'I am here.'

'If you had contacted us we would have met you at the airport. We have an apartment ready for you. It would be nice to know how long you propose to use it.'

The ALLP owned a two-bedroomed apartment in the Village; but it was not kindness which prompted Asaad to offer it to her. He wanted her somewhere he could monitor her every movement, every phone call. It did not matter. As soon as she was ready, she would drop out of sight. She was taking no chances of cold feet among the members of the ALLP council.

'I wish only to conduct the briefing,' she said.

'You could have left that in our hands.'

'When it concerns my mission, I leave nothing in the hands of others,' Leila said.

'It might be better if you were as efficient as you are vain,' Asaad said. 'But we have heard otherwise.'

'It is not vanity,' Leila said angrily. 'This is the way I have always worked.'

'Then you have only yourself to blame for . . . what has happened to you,' Hassan Nabhan said slyly.

'I wear my wounds like medals,' she said proudly. 'Do you?'

'We cannot all carry guns, Jarhoun!' Asaad snapped. 'Those who do, rely as much on us as we do on them.'

'I know that, and I am grateful to you for your support. I hope I may rely on it fully until my task is completed.'

Zaher Ali Dokr leaned forward, forearms on the table. He was a thickset man in his mid-fifties, with a bull neck and heavy jowls.

'Our information is that more than a few of the members of the Executive Committee had reservations about your plan,' he told her. 'Is that true?'

'No, it is not,' Leila snapped. 'The operation was sanctioned unanimously at the highest level.'

'I think you should know, if you do not already, that this council feels no enthusiasm for it,' Zaher told her. 'Such a deliberately hostile act is inimical to our best interests here. No earthly benefit can come to our people from what you have in mind.' The others nodded agreement.

'A people at war should have no desire for earthly benefits, Comrade Zaher,' Leila replied sweetly. 'As for your lack of enthusiasm, I will be happy, if you so desire, to inform Deputy Director Kutayfan that you find the tasks being set for you here in America too onerous. I am sure he will be happy to repatriate you to the homeland and send someone who does not to take your place.'

'You have no right to say that sort of thing to me, Jarhoun!' the fat man huffed, his face setting with suppressed anger. To be spoken to so cuttingly by any woman was bad enough; for it to be this one, with her arrogant whore's body and her disrespectful fishwife's tongue, was intolerable. 'I merely express our reservations. You may be sure that in spite of them, we will give you all the assistance you need.'

'I am glad to have your confirmation,' Leila said, piling it on. They had decided to give her a hard time. Very well, she would give them an even harder one. 'I will decide what I need and advise you accordingly. In the meantime, I wish to see the two women. Alone.'

'Alone?' Nabhar said angrily. 'These are our operatives, comrade. We do not permit—'

'Let me say this only once,' Leila said, letting the anger show now. 'I have been chosen to create a day of fire! A day to make the world aware of who we are and what we are! I intend to do it, but I am going to do it my way – and only my way! Is that understood?'

Asaad held up a hand to still the outburst that he saw coming. 'The council has expressed its reservations,' he said. 'Let that be the end of it.'

'I requested weapons. Explosives. Is everything I asked for ready?'

'Everything. The operatives are standing by, waiting to hear from you, comrade.'

She nodded. Abu-Takeih glared at her, across the table.

'Perhaps you will at least favour us with a rundown of your intentions,' he said, his voice heavy with irony. 'Especially since you expect us to provide you with the means of effecting them.'

He was a short man, running to fat, with a heavy beard. Chest hair sprouted out of the open necked Lacoste sports shirt he was wearing. Leila shook her head, refusing to let such childish hostility bother her. Let them go on thinking whatever they wanted to think. When the day of fire actually began, they would be as surprised as the rest of the world.

'You know my plan. A sleeper bomb planted in the office of the Secretary General of the United Nations, timed to detonate at precisely ten a.m. on an appointed day. The media will trumpet news of the explosion around the world within minutes. That news will be a signal to my organization, Al Iqab. The Punishment will commence!'

'What exactly is this Punishment? When will it take place? Upon whom is it to be inflicted, and why?'

'It is a cry of vengeance for the dispossession of our people. It is a warning to the world that the Struggle will never end. It is a punishment for the murder of our beloved leader, Abu Jihad. Exactly what it is, comrades, and upon whom it is to be inflicted, you will know soon enough.'

And sooner than you imagine, she thought, smiling to herself.

'The good news is, we think we've cracked your code,' McCaskill said, the dry Scots voice no more excited than it would have been had he been discussing the price of eggs. 'The bad news is, it doesn't get us anywhere.'

'Tell me anyway,' Garrett said.

'You know what our trouble was?' McCaskill said. 'We were being far too sophisticated. We tried everything – schools, childhood friends, holidays, hobbies, business acquaintances – and we got nothing. Then one of my bright young flopsters had a brilliant idea. It was not their jobs that were the common denominator, he said; it was what their jobs allowed them to do.'

'All right,' Garrett said. 'We've got a couple of German policemen, a Dutch civil engineer, two Austrian tourists, a caterer's driver – what have they got in common?'

'Airports,' McCaskill said.

'I don't get it.'

'You wouldn't,' the Scot said. 'That's why young Langford's stroke was so brilliant.'

'Langford is the flopster?'

'Aye. David Langford. One of our computer whizzes.'

'If he's cracked this, he's due a case of champagne,' Garrett said. 'Go on, Mac.'

'It all fits. Your Special Branch boys: their IDs give them go-anywhere rights at airports. The two German policemen were both from Frankfurt; both occasionally worked on security assignments at the airport there. The two Austrian

195

tourists? They both had return tickets Rome-Vienna. The tickets weren't on the bodies, which means someone could use them to get past security at Fiumicino. The caterer's driver killed in Zürich worked for a firm that supplied Swissair with in-flight food. He and his mate had passes to get into Kloten. The Dutch engineer worked on runway construction. Shall I go on?'

'Airports,' Garrett said. 'Airports and heat-seeking missiles. By God, Mac, I think you may be right!'

'I'm sure of it,' McCaskill said, without pleasure. 'But, as I said, it gets us nowhere. We know we're looking for a multiple terrorist strike. We know where: airports all over Europe. We even know what they plan to use: ground-to-air missiles. But we still don't know when, and you can't keep ten major international airports on indefinite full-security alert.'

'Frankfurt, Zürich, Stockholm, Amsterdam, Brussels, Rome. . . . Wait a minute. What about the New York murders?'

'They don't fit,' McCaskill said flatly. 'You gave us a cleaning woman and a United Nations tour guide. Neither would have access to Kennedy or any other airport, except as a passenger. And it's clear that our friends, whatever their plans are, don't intend to execute them disguised as passengers.'

'What does Langford say about that?'

'Simple,' he says. 'In New York, the target is not the airport. It has to be the United Nations building.'

'The signal,' Garrett said.

'The what?'

'It's all right, Mac. Everything just went click. Langford gets his bubbly. Here's the scenario: Jarhoun's got two people with access to the UN building in New York. What for is another matter: an assassination, a bomb, some kind of attack on the UN building, what, where, how, we don't know. Whatever it is, it will be the signal for the others — they're all probably suicide squads — to either shoot at or shoot down a passenger aircraft.'

'But we don't know when.'

'Not yet we don't. But I'm going to get on to that right now. Do something for me, Mac. Send me over a printout.'

'Already done that. Anything else?'

'I want duplicate copies of the IDs of each of the people who were murdered.'

'No problem,' Mac said. 'What do you want them for?'

'I'll send them to the appropriate security organizations right away: Bundesamt für Verfassungschutz in Cologne, DST in Paris, SIS in Rome and so on. Get them to lay on intensive screening of personnel to locate anyone using those IDs.'

'And if they locate them?'

'Put them on hold. We can't move until we either have them all under surveillance or we know when the attack is to take place. Get that stuff over here as soon as you can, will you? I've got to move fast.'

'Hop to it, then.'

'Har har. Tell Langford I said he's a champion.'

'Don't bother to thank me, will you?'

'It's Glenmorangie you drink, isn't it?'

'Aye,' McCaskill said warily. 'Why d'ye ask?'

'Watch the skies,' Garrett said, and hung up. He picked up the phone again and dialled Liz James. She said Bleke would see him at once. He hurried to the Director's office and Liz showed him straight in.

'Urgent, eh?' Bleke said, by way of greeting. 'Sit down if you like. How's the leg?'

'Itchy,' Garrett said. 'We've got a break on the Jarhoun case.'

He laid out McCaskill's findings and his own conclusions. Bleke listened carefully, then nodded as if making a decision.

'What you're saying is, we have the parameters of the Al Iqab operation now, but we still haven't got enough to nip it in the bud.'

'That's right. As you know, I've got a round-the-clock watch on the PLO safe house in Southall. If Abu-Salem so much as hiccups, we'll know it.'

'Not enough,' Bleke said. 'What we have to do is make

sure that Jarhoun does not succeed in giving the signal they're all waiting for.'

'I've formed my own picture of this woman,' Garrett said. 'Her MO is to lead from the front. Sending the signal will be her big moment. Whatever it is, she'll be doing it herself.'

'You'll go to New York?'

'As soon as I alert the European security services through TREVI,' Garrett replied.

'Any idea where to start looking?'

'DI6 can tell us the likeliest rocks to look under.'

'I'll have a word with Sir Christopher,' Bleke told him. 'Make sure all the doors are opened for you. Anything else you need?'

'Nothing Transport can't organize,' Garrett said. 'I'll get on to them right away. With any luck at all I can be in New York by tomorrow night.'

'Off you hop, then,' Bleke said, with a thin smile.

'You're the second one today,' Garrett said. He was heading for the door when Bleke threw a question after him.

'Hennessy? Nothing,' Garrett replied. 'If you want my reading, he and his squad have gone into deep cover somewhere in Germany. They'll be posing as out-of-work *gästarbeitern* or they'll have already found themselves jobs, road-mending or in the building trade, cash in your hand every Friday, no questions asked. Meanwhile they'll be checking out pubs, dance halls, discos, anywhere Army personnel go. I've given Klaus Prachner in Cologne their dossiers, photographs, everything we had. The Bundesamt is better placed than we are: if anyone can trace Hennessy, they can.'

'You've alerted Army Intelligence? Of course, shouldn't have asked. Well. I'll keep an eye on it. Have a good trip.'

'I'll be in touch,' Garrett said. He went back to his office and called Transport. Arthur Cotton answered on the first ring.

'Arthur, it's Charles Garrett. New York, tomorrow. Can do?'

'I'll need a clearance,' Cotton said. 'Can't get the docket through in time otherwise.'

'Talk to Bleke,' Garrett said. 'He'll okay it. Oh, and Arthur, I'll need to use the apartment in Manhattan. Can you check it's free?'

'And if not?'

'That's up to you.'

'High or low profile?'

'Medium businessman. But Arthur, not the Waldorf. It's full of people on QE2 cruises.'

'Leave it to me.'

Another call, this time to an unlisted number on the 499 exchange. A guarded American voice answered.

'Dick, this is Charles Garrett. I'm off to the home of the brave tomorrow. Any chance of a little help from my friends?'

'You got it.' Dick Snyder was principal deputy to the London station chief of the Central Intelligence Agency.

'I'd like to talk to the top FBI field man in New York on arrival. Your people might want to sit in as well.'

'Can you give me any clues?'

'Scramble,' Garrett said, and pushed the button on his phone. He waited a moment for Snyder to do the same. 'Okay?'

'Fire away.'

'We've got a terrorist group, Middle Eastern in origin, calls itself Al Iqab, leader a woman, Leila Jarhoun. Scenario involves an attack of some sort on the United Nations building in New York. As yet we don't know what, how, or when. I'll get a dossier over to you right away. Fax it over to your people and have Immigration check all entries for the last — let's see — ten days. Not just New York, Dick. All gateways.'

'Okay. Anything else?'

'This woman is going to be hard to find and harder to stop. Tell your people I'll need carte blanche. I'll give them a full briefing when I arrive.'

'I'll tell them,' Snyder said. 'Whether they'll give it to you is another matter. The Bureau can be very territorial about things like this.'

'We'll work something out,' Garrett said briskly. 'Do your best for me.'

'Good as done,' Snyder said. 'I'll call you later.'

Garrett leaned back in his chair and closed his eyes. Once again, he saw the face of Leila Jarhoun behind the windscreen of the big red car, the deep dark eyes glowing with hatred. The phone rang, interrupting his reverie.

'Garrett, it's Pat Miller.'

'What's up, doc?'

'Well, well. For a man who nearly got blown to kingdom come, you're remarkably perky.'

'Nearly is only nearly,' Garrett said. 'That's why I'm perky. What can I do for you?'

'Other way around. I've got that psychological profile you asked for. Leila Jarhoun. Want me to send it over?'

'You're fantastic, doc. How can I thank you?'

'Buy me a drink sometime.'

'I'm chasing off to New York tomorrow. Maybe when I get back.'

'Going to see your lady?'

'That's right,' Garrett said. It was only after he hung up that he realized she had been talking about Jessica Goldman and he had been talking about Leila Jarhoun.

16

Thirty-five thousand feet above Newfoundland, Garrett read for the fifth time the report that Pat Miller had compiled.

From: Patricia Miller, FAPA,
MINISTRY OF DEFENCE,
Central Medical Establishment, Kelvin House,
Cleveland Street, LONDON W1X 9BB.

Telephone 01-218 9000 ext 9856

Charles Garrett, Esq.,   Your reference
Diversified Corporate Facilities,
Lonsdale House,   Our reference
Berkeley Square,   PM (CME)/6/100
LONDON W1H 4WW.   22 April 1989

LEILA JARHOUN

Partial psychological profile

Description: age (estimated) 30; about 5′ 7″, 120 lbs, slender build, dark complexion, black hair and eyes (possibly dark brown). Probable nationality: Palestinian Arab.

Lacking voice and handwriting samples, I can only offer a partial analysis of the subject. In the absence of any indication of religious fervour, her age and nationality suggest the probability that her primary motivation is revenge: she would have been a child at the time of the Six Day War of 1967, and may have experienced dispossession, the loss of immediate family, or both, at the hands of the Israelis: certain of her personality traits suggest her fundamental motivation for revenge to be the death of her father.

She was probably recruited very young; a typical progression would be: dispossession and/or death of family head, refugee camp, identification with and/or physical attachment to a street-gang leader, active participation in anti-Israeli activities (girls and women are used in demonstrations, weapons smuggling, spying on troop movements, etc.). The latter would

201

have been either before or during attendance at University (her fluency in English and probably French suggest higher education). It is possible she was recruited and educated with a view to being trained as a terrorist. Since women do not generally achieve positions of power in Arab society, her leadership of the terrorist cell indicates an unusually strong motivation and personality, probably growing out of an unrecognized need for the love of her father sublimated into an intense desire for attention and admiration from men in general and her peers in particular.

The interrogation dossiers of the two members of her group captured in France provide further revealing aspects of her personality. Both of them use surprisingly similar words to describe her: 'hard', 'unshakable', 'dedicated', 'unafraid'. Taken together with her actions – the assassination attempt on Simion in Paris, the sacrifice of her own people at St Valèry and the bomb attack on Garrett – they offer support for my contention that she is quite ruthless and will go to extreme lengths to protect herself, rationalizing her actions as being necessary for the success of her mission. My preliminary conclusions – I hesitate to be emphatic on such short acquaintance with the subject – are that in Leila Jarhoun we are dealing with a constitutionally psychopathic personality, in whom fundamental inferiority complexes distort, among other things, her attitude to acts of violence.

To simplify: such a personality, while apparently functioning 'normally' is in fact unable to appreciate any concept as abstract as guilt. In other words, no matter what lengths she goes to, she will feel no guilt and have no understanding of what we call conscience. Nor would it be possible to explain to her what such concepts – remorse, regret, guilt, conscience – actually are. Her actions mean no more to her than if she killed a bee that might sting her.

A secondary aspect of this type of personality, the outgrowth of her unrecognized thirst for attention and love, is an inability to form permanent relationships. Although she may have friends, or even lovers, possibly in high places (an alternative but equally possible explanation of her untypical advancement) I would expect that she in fact mistrusts or even hates men, both as individuals and as a sex. Because she is a perfectionist she will tend not to have emotional involvements with any one person in order to avoid 'failure'; if she accepts such an involvement, it will only be on her own terms, with her as the dominant partner.

Where her terrorist activities are concerned, she will always try to inhibit or prevent any action not sanctioned by herself which might result in 'failure' and therefore reflect upon her as a person or a leader. This vanity would be the only psychological weapon that might be successfully used against her. Otherwise, the picture that emerges is of an intelligent, well-trained, highly motivated and completely ruthless survivalist. Operatives dealing with such a personality should be made aware that the subject has no concept of fair play or ethical behaviour, and will unhesitatingly lie, steal, cheat or kill to further her own cause or to stay alive. It may likewise be expected that hostage negotiation techniques will be ineffective; in a critical situation she will sacrifice anyone and anything to effect her own survival. She would see capture as failure; faced with apprehension, it is doubtful that she would permit herself to be taken alive, and in such a situation would in all likelihood seek to ensure the deaths of as many of those responsible as possible.

Patricia Miller, FAPA.

Across the bottom of the report she had scribbled 'And you thought I was just a pretty face!' Garrett smiled as he laid the folder down on the seat alongside his own. Dr Miller had done a great job, bearing in mind how little she had to go on. He closed his eyes and saw again the taut face and wide dark eyes of Leila Jarhoun rushing at him. *Intelligent, well-trained, highly motivated and completely ruthless.* They knew a lot more about her now than they had done at the beginning, yet she was still little more than a cypher. A second request to Mossad for a check on Israeli university records had met with a blank; the secret service could locate no records for anyone named Jarhoun.

He looked out of the window; the sun reflected blindingly on the wing. He could see Fire Island down below, and then they were banking over the suburban tracts of Queens. There was the usual hurry-up-and-wait at the landing bay; Garrett did not follow the knot of businessmen jostling to be first in the immigration line. By prearrangement, a steward took him down to the tarmac via a door let into the landing ramp just to the left of the aircraft exit, and across to a waiting Dodge Aries.

The man standing beside it was short, stocky and smooth shaven, with wide brown eyes that gave his round face a disingenuous look. He wore a brown tweed jacket and a matching hat with a narrow brim, like something out of John Buchan.

'Garrett?' he said, gravel-voiced. 'I'm Irwin Young. FBI chief agent, New York. Can you manage?'

'Just about,' Garrett said. He had expected his wounded leg to be fully healed when they took off the plaster, but that was only the beginning. Another six weeks of physiotherapy were necessary before he got back to something like normal. Even now, the leg was still stiff and the limp still visible.

He slung his bag into the boot and got into the car. Young swung the vehicle around and headed for the security exit alongside the British Airways terminal, where he showed his ID to a security guard who looked as if he could hardly have cared less.

'Asshole,' Young muttered, as he picked up the loop road. 'I could have planted an atom bomb out there for all that shmuck cares.'

Van Wyck Parkway looked the same as always, as if someone had planned to make a garden, said the hell with it and built a six-lane motorway instead. Young drove with a fine competitive élan, changing lanes with an abandon that would have killed him on the M25 in about thirty seconds.

'Where ya stayin'?' he asked Garrett over his shoulder.

'Apartment,' Garrett replied. 'Seventy-ninth at Third Avenue.'

'Ritzy,' Young said. 'Very ritzy.' The traffic was getting heavier as they approached the Grand Central Parkway interchange. Young made an impatient clicking sound and swung off on to Queens Boulevard.

'Pick up the Long Island Expressway at Rego Park,' he explained. 'Take the Queens-Midtown Tunnel in. Okay?'

'Any way you like,' Garrett said. The smaller man grinned and gunned the car past a beaten-up old Pontiac driven by an elderly man.

'Move over, y'old fart!' he growled. He noticed Garrett wince as they cut in inches ahead of the vehicle. 'You nervous in the service, Garrett?'

'Just trying to recall whether I paid my insurance premium before I left,' Garrett said.

'Ya wanna tell me something? How come you got so much clout?'

'Sorry?'

'I talked to the CIA head of station. He said to tell you anything he can do to be of assistance, you call him. That sonofabitch, every time I call him and ask for help, he tells me go piss up a rope. You must have a lot of clout, is what I'm saying.'

'Did you get a briefing on why I'm here?'

'I got it. They said you were asking for carte blanche to operate in New York. That much clout you don't have.'

'Someone said you might get a bit territorial.'

'Territorial, shmeritorial,' Young said, taking the ramp up on to the Long Island Expressway and heading into the thundering lines of traffic as if he was immortal. 'The Bureau don't play second fiddle to nobody.'

'It don't do very convincing Jimmy Cagney impersonations either,' Garrett said.

'Ah, shit,' Young said, grinning. 'I thought I was pretty good in there. Listen, everybody calls me Butch.'

'Charles.'

'Not Chuck, huh? Okay, Charles. Let me tell you where we're at with your lady terrorist. We ran your photographs and description through our computers. I didn't expect her to show up, and I wasn't disappointed. We ran airport checks but nobody seemed to have seen anyone answering her description. No one using the name Jarhoun entered the country in the last three months. So we did it the hard way. We took all the immigration chits and put them through the wringer.'

'Where did that get you?'

'Everybody arriving in the United States has to give an address where they'll be staying. We took a whole month's incoming flights, checked out every passenger that landed. What we were looking for was anyone who wasn't at the address they'd given. Legitimate travellers have no reason to give a false address. Ninety-nine per cent of them go exactly where they say they're going.'

'And?'

'We got sixty-eight possibles. Out of those sixty-eight, only twenty-three were Middle Eastern. Egyptian, Lebanese, lots of Kuwaitis and Saudi Arabians. We ran all their names through the box. Nothing. That was when we lucked out. We asked The Company to doublecheck us. They isolated the landing card of an Egyptian lady, name of Noor Ibrahim. She'd been a low-grade informer for the CIA station chief in Cairo.'

'Had been?'

'Noor Ibrahim is dead,' Young said. 'More than a year ago. So – who's using her passport?'

'It has to be Leila Jarhoun,' Garrett said.

'That's how we figured it,' Young said. 'But wait, it gets better. We also ran a check on all Manhattan hotels, not expecting too much. We came up smelling of roses: she was in the Hilton on Sixth Avenue.'

'Was?'

'She checked in last Tuesday. One-night stay. Paid cash and left.'

'Damn!' Garrett said. 'We could have had her!'

'Something odd about her checking into an hotel. It's not the pattern. That breed usually go to safe houses, cover addresses, somewhere their own people can look after them.'

'If Leila Jarhoun checked into an hotel, she had her own reasons for doing it. Maybe she was up to something she didn't want her people here to know about. Incidentally, did you have any luck with that list of organizations DI6 sent over?'

'Those boys in London know their stuff,' Young said admiringly. 'They had a couple of names in there even we hadn't run across.'

'Do you have the list?'

'Right here.' Young handed a folder back to Garrett. He opened it and scanned the lines of printout.

'There are more than I thought there'd be,' he said.

'I'll be frank with you, Charles, I haven't got the manpower to watch all the ones who ought to be watched. We've got more Arabs right here in New York than they have in Israel. Arab banks, Arab newspapers, Arab investment companies. Restaurants, food stores, bookshops, schools, translation agencies. There's an Arab-American Chamber of Commerce, an Arab League. We've got Saudis and Kuwaitis and Jordanians and Palestininans and Syrians. Doctors, lawyers, oilmen, storekeepers. Most of them are ordinary, God-fearing people who go to work every day and pay their taxes like everyone else. A few of them are terrorist sympathizers. We think we've got most of them spotted, but, of course, there's no way we can be sure. All we can do is keep them under intermittent surveillance and hope Jarhoun will make contact.'

'She may already have done so.'

'I know,' Young said. 'Nothing we can do about that, either.'

'What about the UN building?'

'We've got people standing by there as well. Every one of them has looked at Jarhoun's photograph till their eyes misted over. If she shows, we'll pick her up. Same with the phoney IDs. Anyone uses them, we'll move in.'

'You seem to have covered everything,' Garrett said. 'I'm impressed.'

'That wasn't why we did it,' Young grinned, 'but thanks, anyway. You want to stop anyplace on the way?'

Garrett shook his head. They were approaching the Midtown Tunnel, and he drank in the vista of Manhattan arrayed across the horizon ahead. The tall slim finger of the Empire State Building still stood proud against the sky, but others contested her former supremacy now, the World Trade Center towers silhouetted against the sun, the hunk-of-cheese Citicorp Building, the downtown mausoleums to Mammon, Donald Trump's high-tech triumphs on upper Fifth Avenue.

'New York, New York, it's a hell of a town,' Garrett hummed.

'You've been here before, I take it,' Butch said.

Garrett grinned. 'Funny thing: I always enjoy arriving, but I'm never sad to leave.'

'Used to know a girl who had exactly the same effect on me,' the FBI man said. He swerved around a U-Haul truck and accelerated up Third Avenue, smacking the horn with the flat of his hand. 'Goddam taxis,' he muttered.

They roared up the hill and down to 72nd as if there wasn't another vehicle in Manhattan. The neighbourhood looked much the same: small groceries, tobacconists', a supermarket, a pizza place, the shoe-repairer's opposite the apartment building. Young pulled to a halt outside the bank on the corner.

'You want I should dump your bags and we'll go right on over to my office?' he said. 'Got something to show you down there.' Garrett looked at his watch. Eleven p.m., London time.

'Fine,' he said.

'Be right back,' Young told him. He got Garrett's bag out of the boot and disappeared with it into the lobby. A few minutes later he reappeared: Henry, the doorman, had promised to have it taken up to the apartment, he said. He got back into the driving seat and roared off into the traffic, cut across to 81st and turned left, then left again when they reached Lexington Avenue. He zoomed down the hill, swung left at 56th and headed towards the East River, pulling into a garage entrance beneath an anonymous glass building on the corner of Third Avenue. He showed his ID to a security guard then drove down the ramp, parking the car in a bay with the letters IY painted on the wall in yellow. He got out and jerked a thumb towards the lifts across the garage.

'Where's this?' Garrett asked.

'You'll see.'

They took the lift to the thirty-fifth floor; it opened on to a scene of bustling activity: printers chattering, phones ringing, neatly suited young men and women in white blouses and dark skirts seated at rows of desks with PCs in front of them. Young led the way along a corridor painted and carpeted in neutral shades to a spacious office situated on the corner of the building, with huge windows that gave the room an airy, open feeling.

'This is FBI headquarters?' Garrett said.

'We've got a front office downtown for the public,' Young said. 'But the real work gets done here.'

He must have pushed a button on his desk. A trim young woman with blue eyes and bright blonde hair came in, smiling. She looked a little bit like the young Chrissie Evert.

'Peggy, this is Charles Garrett, all the way from London. Charles, this is my assistant, Peggy Zimmerman.'

'Hi, Mr Garrett,' Peggy said. She noted the stiff way he held his leg but made no comment. 'You want coffee, Mr Young?'

'We both do,' Young said. 'How do you take yours, Charles?'

'Black, one sugar.'

'Coming up,' Peggy said.

'Pretty girl,' Garrett remarked as she went out. Butch Young grinned at him.

'Don't let her hear you say that,' he said. 'She's a qualified Special Agent. Only about five per cent of all agents are females.'

'I'll watch my step.'

Peggy brought them their coffee and left them to it. Young slouched into the big leather chair behind his desk, and Garrett took the one opposite, propping up his leg on a teak coffee table.

'Nothing new on Jarhoun?' Garrett asked.

Young shook his head. 'Didn't think there would be this soon. Look, we know she's in Manhattan. She can't operate in a vacuum. I told you: if she tries to contact any of the known PLO cover organizations we'll pick her up.'

'What about informers?'

'We've tried our own. No luck. I asked the police department to go and do likewise, but they haven't come back to me yet. Those guys have got so much on their plates, I'll be surprised if they ever do. Don't worry. If she hasn't surfaced in twenty-four hours, we're going to flush her out.'

'How do you plan to do that?'

'Peggy!' Young hollered. 'Bring me that mock-up of the *Times*, will you?'

Peggy Zimmerman came back in, carrying a rolled sheet of paper which she handed to Butch Young. He unrolled it and held it where Garrett could see it. It was a dummy front page of the New York paper. Across its entire width marched the bold headline: HAVE YOU SEEN THIS

WOMAN? Beneath it was the composite photograph of Leila Jarhoun.

'We're ready to roll,' Young said. 'A media blitz. Every New York newspaper and magazine will carry this picture. It will be on every newscast from every TV station seen in the metropolitan area. We're offering a ten-thousand-dollar reward. If Leila Jarhoun so much as shows her face on the street, we'll have her.'

'Or drive her so deep underground you'll never find her.'

Young shook his head. 'There's no such place,' he said categorically. 'If she's in Manhattan, we'll get her.'

'When do you plan to launch the blitz?'

'Day after tomorrow, front page of the Sunday *Times*. That suit you?'

'Fine with me,' Garrett said. 'But you won't mind if I follow up a few things of my own?'

Young regarded him levelly, and in that moment, Garrett realized why he was chief of the FBI's New York operation. The brown eyes had become as hard as obsidian.

'Don't confuse polite with soft, Garrett,' Young said. 'I meant what I said. On its own turf, the Bureau doesn't play second fiddle.'

'I believe you. I won't get out of line, I promise. How do we keep in touch?'

'We've got a car for you. Two-way radio, computer. All the comforts of home. What are your plans?'

'Right now? Get something to eat, get over the jet lag, sleep. Tomorrow, I want to talk to the Company man. What's his name?'

'Dave Hughes. I'll give you his direct number. Listen, Garrett, I'm sorry I came on what you'd call territorial just now. . . . Do me a favour, just don't do anything unilateral, okay?'

'Okay, Butch. Where's this car you mentioned?'

'In the basement. Driver's name is Woodring. Woody for short. Want me to come down with you?'

'Not necessary,' Garrett said. 'What kind of a car is it?'

'Blue Dodge Aries, same model as the one I'm driving. I couldn't get a Rolls-Royce.'

'Shame,' Garrett said. 'I'll just have to slum it. I'll check with you first thing tomorrow?'

'Sleep tight,' Young said.

Half an hour later Garrett was in the apartment on 79th Street. It consisted of an L-shaped living room, adjacent bedroom and a galley-style kitchen. It was furnished comfortably but without style. A glass shelf unit held some books nobody would ever read. He threw the papers he'd bought on the sofa: the *Times*, the *New Yorker*. There was a well-stocked drinks cupboard; he took out a heavy crystal glass and poured himself a Jack Daniel's. When in Rome, and all that. He went into the kitchen and checked the refrigerator: milk, bread, a carton of Thomas's English Muffins, butter, one of those assorted packs of honey and jam, half-a-dozen cans of Rolling Rock and two bottles of Sonoma-Cutrer Chardonnay. He sprang some ice from the tray and put it in the bourbon.

'All the comforts of home,' he said to himself, and went back into the lounge. He looked at the phone and then at his watch. Nine o'clock local time. He dialled the number Jessica had left for him in London.

No reply.

Should have called earlier. He thought about going out for something to eat, then thought about walking down to Second Avenue. He decided he wasn't that hungry, and grinned: New York at my feet – well, foot – and I can't be bothered. He poured himself another drink, flipped on the TV, and set it to switch off automatically. A small middle-aged man with bags under his eyes drove a Jaguar saloon to a riverside location. He wore an overcoat and black leather gloves and he talked with an English accent. The bad guys who had the girl hostage were holed up in a warehouse. The small man's assistant, younger, blond, wearing a checked shirt and designer jeans, ran up a lot of stairs. The older man followed more slowly. The young one crashed through a window in a car. The bad guys tried to shoot him. The small middle-aged man shot them. Hooray for our side.

He went to sleep.

* * *

Seventy-one blocks south, in an apartment on 8th Street, Leila Jarhoun was picking up the telephone. A familiar voice spoke her name.

'Asaad!' she said. 'What do you want?'

'I thought you should know at once. An urgent message from the Deputy Director. It is believed in London that the man Garrett is not dead.'

She frowned. 'But that's im—'

'Impossible, were you going to say? I think not.'

'He was killed. It was in the papers.'

'Yes, yes.' Asaad said impatiently. 'I know all that. But the chief of staff in London was not satisfied. Standard checks showed that Garrett's flat was not vacated. More importantly, there was no inquest, no funeral.'

'That doesn't prove anything.'

'By itself, no. But it was abnormal enough to arouse the chief of staff's interest. An intensive investigation was set in motion. No one name Garrett was in any hospital or clinic in London. An all-known-associates check revealed that the woman Jessica Goldman left London for New York the day after the attack. She is attending a three-week seminar at the Institute of Psychology.'

'Jessica Goldman. Is that the woman with whom he spent the night while we had him under observation?'

'The same.'

'His mistress would hardly leave London to attend a course the following day if Garrett were really dead.'

'Precisely.' His voice was dry, precise. 'If Garrett is alive, and all the indications are that he is, he is probably here in Manhattan, looking for you. You may already be under surveillance.'

'No,' she said, with certainty. 'I would have known.'

'What do you propose to do now?'

'What do you mean?'

'You can hardly proceed with your plan.'

'On the contrary. I have already set it in motion.'

'But that is foolhardly in the extreme! They know your intentions, you said so yourself. Our operatives will be apprehended the moment they set foot in the United Nations building!'

'Perhaps,' Leila said.

Asaad was silent for a moment. 'You make it sound as if the UN operation is irrelevant.'

'Do I? It is unintentional.'

'Is there something you are not telling us, Comrade Leila?'

'I have told you everything you need to know, Comrade Asaad,' she riposted. 'Listen to me now. I am leaving this place and going into deep cover.'

'How will we contact you?'

'You will not.'

'I demand to know—'

She hung up and then took the phone off the hook. The fact that Garrett was alive meant that her delaying tactic had not worked; it was a setback, but not a catastrophe. She looked at herself in the mirror and smiled lopsidedly: my secret weapon, she thought grimly. She was well aware of the incredible power of the machinery that was being arrayed against her: the supersophisticated computers, the formidable facilities of the CIA and the FBI, the New York police, the British agency Garrett worked for. She smiled again; despite their power, she had the advantage, for she was fighting the war of the flea. The dog knew she was there, but he could not scratch until she bit.

She went to the closet and threw her clothes into a bag. Then she went into the kitchen and took a clean dishcloth from the drawer, wet it, soaped it, and washed every flat surface in the apartment that she might have touched, as well as handles, knobs, switches, dishes, cutlery and even the bottle in the refrigerator. She stripped the linen from the bed and stuffed it into a plastic shopping bag. She swabbed the phone clean, polished every glass and enamel surface, emptied the pedal bin, checked every drawer. When she was finished she took the rubbish and the bag containing the bedlinen out to the incinerator chute and pushed them in. Then she put on her leather coat, picked up the bag, slammed the door of the apartment behind her and hailed a taxi.

She had the driver drop her at the corner of East 62nd Street and Park. She walked up the quiet, tree-lined street and stopped outside a town house. She looked right and left. There was no one about. She took a bunch of keys from her pocket and went in. As she closed the door of Ibrahim Kutayfan's safe house behind her, she smiled.

Let them find her here.

He was looking for Jessica in an echoing riverside warehouse. A baggy-eyed middle-aged man in an overcoat pointed with a gloved hand. He ran and ran, but he could not find a door. He ran back the way he had come. He saw her walking up an iron staircase and he shouted her name. She did not turn around. He ran up the stairs after her, and when she turned to face him she was Leila Jarhoun, the dark eyes glittering with hatred as she pulled the trigger of the gun.

He shuddered and awoke. The phone was ringing.

'Garrett? Butch Young. We've got action. Get over to the UN building as fast as you can. Your driver will be waiting for you downstairs.'

Garrett looked at his watch. Six-thirty a.m. He got up and dressed, cursing the stiffness in his wounded leg. He gulped a glass of orange juice and hurried down to the lobby, where Woody was pacing to and fro, slapping kid gloves against the seams of his trousers.

Garrett scrambled into the car, and Woody ran around to the driving seat, checked his mirror and surged across 79th in a U-turn that made the tyres squeal, turning right on to Second Avenue just as the lights changed. He was a tight, fast, efficient driver; they reached the staff entrance to the UN Secretariat building on East 43rd Street in something less than ten minutes.

Butch Young was waiting inside, two other men beside him.

'Garrett,' he said. 'Meet Henry Poirot and Dave Larkin, UN Security.'

Poirot was a burly man of about five-ten, with boyishly curly hair and bright inquisitive eyes. Larkin was shorter, with a weightlifter's neck and shoulders. He had reddish hair and very white skin spattered with freckles.

Garrett nodded hello. 'What have we got?' he asked.

'A ringer,' Butch replied. 'Using the ID of Clara Podborski, the cleaning woman who was murdered. Security tabbed her this morning in the Maintenance Department shape-up.'

'Pure luck we made her,' Larkin said. 'Cleaning is contracted out. The firm we use sends in four, five hundred people every day. Easy enough for someone with proper identification to slip in among them.'

'These people are thorough,' Young said. 'They probably know as much about the system as you do. The main thing is, you spotted her.'

'Where is the Maintenance Department?' Garrett asked.

'Right under our feet,' Poirot chimed in. 'There are three levels under this building connecting with the Conference Building.'

'How is the work allocated?'

'The system's fairly simple. The building is divided up into sections and floors. Each floor has a supervisor. Each supervisor selects a team at the shape-up: trash collectors, vacuum cleaners, polishers, mop and bucket ladies, and so on. Each team goes to the building and the floor or section it has been assigned to that morning.'

'It's not always the same?'

'Never. Part of the security pattern: we try to make sure no team polices the same area two days running.'

'So our phoney cleaner couldn't know in advance where she'd be sent?'

'Not a chance.'

'Which means,' Young said, 'that unless she's psychic, she's not where she wants to be, and sooner or later she'll have to make a move. The minute she does, we'll be in business.'

'Where is she now?'

'Right here, in the Secretariat building. Second floor.'

'What happens now?'

'We watch and we wait,' Larkin said. 'Let's get out of the lobby. We can use my office.'

The office was located off the spacious lobby, just behind

and to one side of the reception desks facing the street doors. Poirot and Larkin both carried transceivers that coughed and crackled intermittently.

'What cover have you got on her?' Garrett said.

'A nice loose interchangeable,' Poirot told him. 'Four of my people, working as cleaners.'

'Alpha Four,' a woman's voice said on the transceiver.

'Go ahead.'

'She's talking to the super. He's nodding. Okay, she's leaving the team. Heading for the central corridor.'

'Taking her trolley?'

'Negative.'

'Carrying anything? A package, a box?'

'Negative.'

'Okay, go with her.'

'Ten four.'

'Alpha Three, cover.'

'Ten four. Subject walking north, central corridor.'

'Alpha Two, where are they?'

'Central corridor. Subject asked the supervisor if she could take a ten-minute break. Wants to see her friend who's working in the Legal Department. She's taking the elevator. Oh oh. She's gone past thirty-four. Going to the top, I'd say. Yup, I was right. Thirty-eighth floor.'

'Get up there.'

'Ten four.'

Young turned to Poirot, frowning. 'What's on the 38th floor?' he asked.

'Secretary General's office,' Poirot replied. His radio crackled into life.

'Alpha Four.'

'Go ahead.'

'Subject has gone into the Executive Offices.'

'Anyone else in there?'

'Negative. Offices are unoccupied. They're always cleaned first.'

'Do not follow, repeat, do not follow. Is the subject in sight?'

'Negative.'

'Damn!' Young said. If the surveillance team followed the subject into the empty offices it would tip her off; not going in meant they would not know what she had hidden, or where.

'Walk past the door. Take a look.'

'Ten four.' A moment's wait, and then, 'Nobody in sight.'

'She's gone into the Secretary General's office,' Larkin said to Young. 'Alpha Four, stand by. Wait until she comes out.'

'Ten four.'

They waited a few tense silent minutes.

'Alpha Four. Subject exiting.'

'She seen you?'

'Affirmative.'

'Okay, walk away.'

'Ten four.'

'Alpha Two, can you see the subject?'

'Affirmative. Walking south on central corridor. Past the elevators. Heading for the stairs.'

'Alpha Three, do you have her?'

'Got her. Am following. Descending staircase.'

The little cat-and-mouse game went on for another five minutes. After leaving the thirty-eighth floor, the cleaning woman walked down to the legal department on the thirty-fourth, where she took the lift down to the second floor and reported back to the supervisor there. The supervisor shrugged and waved her in: the woman joined the other cleaners and remained there until seven-thirty, when the bell indicating that the shift was ended was sounded on the PA system. Throughout the building, the hundreds of men and women who made up the cleaning and maintenance task force downed tools and began trooping back to the basement to hand in their polishers and cleaners and tools and mops and brooms and buckets. They filed past the checkout, picked up their time cards and punched the clock, some leaving the building singly, others in groups.

Garrett watched the woman as she came out on to East 43rd Street. She was about fifty, thin and dark-haired, dressed in a cheap coat and white trainers. She hurried up the street to a phone, totally unaware of the surveillance truck that slid alongside the kerb in front of her as she made her call. When she finished she walked rapidly west, turning south on Second, and disappeared from sight. Garrett raised his eyebrows at Young.

'We've got her, don't worry,' Young said. He talked into his radio. 'Mobile, where is the subject?'

'She's waiting at a westbound bus stop, corner of 42nd Street,' the surveillance vehicle reported. 'How do you want to play this, chief?'

'Stay on her,' Young said. 'I want to know where she goes, who she talks to, the works. What about the phone call?'

'We got it,' the agent in the truck told him. 'She said "This is Soraya. I just finished work." '

'That's it?'

'That's it.'

'You get the number she called?'

'No sweat, we were only three feet away. Subscriber is a Keziah Mahoudi, Clinton Street, Brooklyn. That's Little Lebanon, isn't it? We're running her through the computer right now.'

'Put a listener on her phone. Don't wait for the paperwork, just do it. Watchers as well, round the clock. I'll be responsible. Call me when you get something.'

'Ten four.'

'Five'll get you ten Keziah Mahoudi is a cutout,' Young said. 'What was the name of the tour guide who was killed?'

'Annette Hoffmann,' Larkin said.

'Jewish?'

'I think so.'

'Well, someone is going to turn up here for work sometime soon dressed as a tour guide and carrying Annette Hoffmann's ID,' Young said. 'She'll find some excuse for going up to the thirty-eighth floor, genuine or otherwise. Pass the word to your people, Dave. You want to go up there and take a look around?'

'You kidding?' Larkin said. 'Hold the fort, Hank.'

'You got it,' Poirot told him.

The lift whisked them up to the empty thirty-eighth floor. Most of the offices in the Secretariat building were small and functional; movable steel partitions attached to brackets on the superstructure could be shifted quickly to meet changing requirements. The Secretary General's suite was more spacious. They went through a reception area into two outer offices, beyond which lay the larger one used by the Secretary General, with its Austrian wood panelling and furnishings. A Matisse tapestry hung on one wall; on another there were paintings by Albert Marquet and André Dérain.

'What do you think?' Young asked Garrett. 'A bomb?'

'Your watchers said she wasn't carrying anything,' Garrett said. 'My reading is they're doing this in two stages, just in case either of them gets stopped for a security check. The woman posing as Podborski – Soraya – probably brought in either a timer or a detonator. The tour guide will bring in the explosive.'

'I'll buy that. The question is, if Soraya brought in a timer or a detonator, where did she put it?' Young said. 'Where's the wiring, Dave?'

'Ducts under the floor,' Larkin said. 'Phone, electric and signalling connections every six feet. You've also got electric dumb waiters and conveyors to carry mail.'

They lifted every one of the trapdoors giving access to the junction boxes beneath the floor; finding nothing, the three men returned to the outer offices and stared at the rows of desks, the banks of word processors, telexes, laser printers, fax machines and photocopiers. Larkin sighed.

'Be easier to look for a needle in a haystack,' he said. 'Even if we knew what we were looking for. I better evacuate the building, Mr Young. I can't take the chance of there being a bomb in here.'

'Hold it, hold it,' Young said. 'You call an emergency now, and any chance we have of nailing these people goes out the window.

'Look, I want to go with you on this, Mr Young, but I don't dare take the chance,' Larkin said. 'We've got seven thousand people working here. If a bomb went off, there'd be chaos.'

'It won't be out here,' Garrett said. 'It'll be in the Secretary General's office. They're looking for maximum exposure.'

'Right,' Young said. 'Let's take another look.' They checked the desk, the bookcases, the occasional furniture grouped around a glass table. All the drawers were locked. Larkin opened them one by one and they checked through them. Nothing.

Larkin shook his head. 'We need the bomb squad.'

'You heard what your people said, the woman wasn't carrying anything,' Young said. 'My bet is that Garrett's right, she only brought in a timer or a detonator. There's no danger until the tour guide brings in the rest of it, whatever it is.'

'Where does that door lead?' Garrett asked, pointing.

'Private bathroom and dressing room,' Larkin said. Garrett went over to the door, which was standing slightly ajar. The room was brightly lit, functional, sparkling clean.

He checked the cistern, shower head, wall cupboards, the recesses beneath the washbasins. The technique was simple: you looked for something that wasn't as it ought to be: soap still in a wrapper, two deodorizers where one was plenty, a floor tile that wasn't quite flush, a light fitting fractionally askew. He was about to leave the bathroom when something caught his eye. He went across to the metal slot in the wall that housed the tissue box. He put the side of his head against the tiles next to it and squinted along the wall. The holder was slightly proud of its fitting.

With infinitely gentle fingers he eased the metal container out of its slot. He laid the box of tissues on the flat shelf above the sink and peered inside the cavity that housed the fitment.

'Butch,' he said.

Young and Larkin came in. Garrett pointed at the aperture and Larkin shone in a torch. A thin metal tube, about the thickness of a carpenter's pencil, lay against the back wall. Next to it was a tiny LCD clock, the kind that can be stuck on the dashboard of a car.

'Timer and detonator,' Larkin said. 'Nice work, Mr Garrett.'

'How'd you find it?' Young said.

'Hunch,' Garrett said. You had to think like a terrorist. After a while it wasn't too hard to work out the kind of places they would use. There were only so many options.

'Well, it paid off in spades,' Larkin said. 'Now all we need to do is pick up the tour guide when she shows her face.'

'No,' Garrett said. 'We have to let her rig the bomb.'

'We'd be taking a hell of a risk, Charles,' Young said.

'I don't think so. She has to give herself at least enough time to get out of the building: we can disarm it before she's out of the door.'

'Why take the chance?'

'Because we need to know the date and the time of Jarhoun's signal. That's when Al Iqab will make its strikes, all over Europe.'

'We better make damned sure it doesn't go off, then,' Young said. 'Okay, Dave, here's what I want you to do. Get concealed CCTV surveillance cameras rigged up in here. I don't care what you have to do, get it done. I want to be able to watch every single square inch of this bathroom on the monitors. I want videotape rolling round the clock. I want close-ups of that turkey at work that would turn Meryl Streep green with envy. Got it?'

'Got it. How long do we have?'

'When does the next tour guide shift come on?'

Larkin looked at a day-date clock on the nearest desk. Eight-thirty,' he said. 'About an hour.'

Butch Young just looked at him.

'Jesus,' Larkin said, and grabbed a phone.

The rest of the day passed uneventfully. The team shadowing the woman who had posed as Podborski reported that she had returned to her home, an apartment in Spanish Harlem; she had met no one, made no calls, nor left her building. Her real name was Soraya Alvarez. The surveillance team watching Keziah Mahoudi reported no movement; for the moment all anyone could do was wait for something to break.

Background checks on the two women were hardly more encouraging. Alvarez, born Rahim, was a refugee from the Lebanon who had entered the United States in 1974 and married a Puerto Rican dock worker. Keziah Mahoudi was New York-born, her father Palestinian, her mother Lebanese. Married, with two children, she was twenty-nine years old and worked in a local department store as a sales assistant.

'No record,' Young said, slapping the dossier shut with a gesture of impatience. 'Not even a parking ticket.'

'She's probably a cutout,' Garrett said.

'Right,' the FBI man said. 'But if she is, why hasn't she made any contact?'

'Don't worry,' Garrett said, 'she will.'

'Listen, I just thought of something.' Larkin said. 'This woman, she'll be using a tour guide's ID. If she wants to get into the Executive Offices, she has to go for a Saturday or a Sunday. Any other day there'd be too many people who'd want to know what she was doing up there.'

'Jeez, I'm dumb,' Young said. 'Of course. They run tours seven days a week, right?'

'Right,' Larkin said. 'That's why I think she'll go for the weekend.'

Two days later, Keziah Mahoudi took the BMT into Manhattan; she got out at Canal Street and caught a bus to the Public Library on 42nd Street. She spent about fifteen minutes in the reference library before leaving to go directly back to Clifton Street. The agents watching her recognized the techniques of a 'drop' when they saw one; five minutes after Mahoudi walked out, the watcher who had stayed in the library saw a young woman pick up the street directory Mahoudi had left on the reading table and from it take what looked like an ID tag. Within two more hours, she had been identified as Sahar Musaed, a student at NYCU living in a hostel on West 97th Street.

At eight-forty-five the following Saturday morning, Musaed was among the throng of UN staff coming into the Secretariat building at the East 43rd Street entrance. Slender and dark, wearing a tan raincoat, she was small and inconspicuous as she proceeded to the locker rooms in the basement. Instead of going to a locker as the other tour guides did, she disappeared into a toilet cubicle, remaining there until the other guides began hurrying out along the echoing underground corridors that led to the General Assembly building. She emerged wearing the uniform of a UN tour guide, tailing along behind the others until she reached a stairwell. Glancing around quickly, she darted through the fire door and ran up to the first floor of the Secretariat building, silent and empty but for the occasional security guard. Her every movement monitored, Musaed took the lift to the Executive Offices on the thirty-eighth floor. Dave Larkin had done a hell of a job on the closed circuit cameras; they could watch every move she made on the monitors in the security office.

The young woman went into the outer offices, looking about edgily. She crossed to the Secretary General's office and walked straight to the *en-suite* bathroom. Once inside, she removed the tissue-box holder from its slot, placing the box of tissues on the sink top. Reaching inside, she withdrew the tiny timer and the detonator. She took a flat package from her handbag and wadded it into the aperture.

'PE,' Young observed. 'About three pounds of it, I'd say.'

'Jesus,' Larkin said. 'That would blow the whole Executive Suite to bits.'

They watched Musaed set up the timer, link it to the detonator, and fix both to the plastic explosive with tape. She then carefully replaced the tissue box in front of the bomb. Apart from a slight bulge, it looked absolutely normal.

'Imagine trying to find that if you didn't know where to look,' Larkin muttered. He was sweating heavily. 'Jesus!'

'Don't worry, Dave,' Young said. 'I've got half-a-dozen of the Bureau's best bomb men standing by. Just let's have our little pigeon get clear first. We want to see where she goes, and who she calls.'

The dark-haired student in her neat tour guide uniform went out of the empty offices to the corridor, and took a lift back down to the basement. She picked up her raincoat from the toilet where she had left it, and put it on over the uniform. Thus dressed, she walked through to the General Assembly building, up the stairs to the lobby, and across the lobby straight out into the Plaza.

An hour later it was all over.

Garrett and Butch Young left the FBI bomb experts in charge and went down to the coffee shop in the basement of the General Assembly building. Young ate French toast; Garrett settled for an English muffin. The coffee was hot and strong.

'Well,' the FBI man said. 'That's it.'

The bomb had been set to explode the following Wednesday at ten a.m., a time when the Executive Offices would be fully staffed. The damage and loss of life would have been appalling.

'All we need to do now is take Leila Jarhoun off the street,' Garrett said.

'We'll find her,' Young vowed. 'Sooner or later, we'll find her.'

I wonder, Garrett thought. That Leila was still in New York he had not the slightest doubt. Why was another matter.

'What about her people in Europe? The rest of the Al Iqab unit?' Young asked. 'You think they'll locate them?'

'Maybe. They're in deep cover, waiting for that bomb to go off. They won't be easy to find.'

'Maybe we could scare them up a few leads. Pull in Musaed and Mahoudi, put them through the mincer.'

'If you arrest the woman, you'll lose any chance you have of taking Jarhoun.'

'I know,' Young growled. 'Just wishful thinking. Jarhoun could be long gone by now. Out of the country, for all we know.'

'I suppose so,' Garrett said.

'You sound like you're not convinced. Something bothering you?'

'I don't know,' Garrett confessed. 'There's something about all this that bothers me, Butch. It's as if . . . as if the whole thing is irrelevant.'

'Someone wants to blow up the Secretary General of the United Nations and you think it's *irrelevant*?'

'The Assembly isn't in session,' Garrett reminded him. 'The Secretary General is in Africa. But that's not what I mean. This isn't the grandstand play I expected from Leila Jarhoun.'

'Why does it have to be a grandstand play?'

'Because of what it was planned to be – her big moment, the culmination of her jihad. I keep thinking, is that all?'

'All?' Young snorted. 'Listen, blowing the roof off the UN building would do it for me.'

'I suppose you're right. It's just that . . . the way this bomb thing was set up, it's as if she's ignoring the possibility that anything could go wrong with it. As if either she doesn't know we're here, or she doesn't give a damn if we are.'

'Maybe you're crediting her with more sense than she's really got. Maybe she's really as crazy as a bedbug.'

'You could be right. Well, I think we're all through here. You need me for anything else?'

'Nah,' Young said, waving a lordly hand. 'Take the rest of the day off. And Charles—'

Garrett was standing, getting ready to leave.

'Thanks.'

'Any time.'

Ten minutes later, Garrett left the United Nations Plaza. Woody took him back to his apartment, and he told the driver to come back for him around seven. He went up, showered and shaved, and sat by the window, watching the traffic without actually seeing it. After a while, he placed a call to London and reported to Nicholas Bleke.

'Tie it up,' Bleke said. 'I take it you've notified everyone concerned?'

'Everyone. They'll be on full alert on the day, in case there was prearrangement. I'm inclined to believe nothing will happen at all: they're all programmed to go into action only after the big bang.'

'Well, that's the end of it, then,' Bleke said.

'I'm not so sure it is.'

'Not sure? Why?'

'I don't know. Yes I do. Because we didn't take Leila Jarhoun. Because she's still out there somewhere.'

'Leave her to the FBI. You've done all you could.'

'I suppose so.'

'I'd like you back here soon,' Bleke said. 'The Germans think they've got a line on your friend Hennessy. He or somebody very like him stayed in an hotel in Düsseldorf for six days then dropped out of sight.'

'Düsseldorf. That's right in the middle of the Rhine Army.'

'Not to mention the Air Force.'

One day you and I will meet again, Garrett. One day we'll settle this.

'Sounds promising,' Garrett said. 'I'll get back as soon as I can wrap things up here.'

He hung up, his face pensive. Any other time the news that they had a lead on Hennessy would have electrified him, but instead it was like hearing the name of someone he had known vaguely, someone long dead. He could not make it matter while somewhere, deep inside him, his instincts were telling him something about the Leila Jarhoun operation was wrong.

But what?'

Leila, Leila, Leila. The name dinned in his mind like a throbbing drum, the dark eyes blazing in the shadowed corners of his mind. He banished them by ringing Jessica.

It was not an especially joyous reunion. They had dinner at an Afghan restaurant on Second Avenue. The tables were very close together, and Garrett couldn't find a comfortable position to sit.

'What are you doing in New York?'

'You know I can't talk about it. Especially in a place like this.'

'It's a secret, yes, I know. I'll try again. What I meant was, Heavens to Betsy and lawks a-mercy, Mr Garrett, what are *you* doing in New York?'

'Underwhelming you, if that phone call was anything to go by.'

'I just didn't expect to hear your voice. But I'm glad you're here. How is your leg?'

'Still itchy as hell,' he said. 'How's the seminar?'

'It's really interesting. I'm glad I came. Where are you staying?'

'An apartment on 79th Street. And you're in a penthouse on East 64th. We're being Godawful polite, aren't we?'

'Give me a chance, Charles. I'm still trying to get used to you being here. Can I have some coffee?'

'I'm sorry. Would you like Afghan coffee?'

'What's that?'

'Like Turkish.'

'Sounds good. Medium, please.' Garrett signalled the waiter. The coffee was served with Turkish delight and petits fours.

'How long will you be here?' Jessica asked.

'A few more days,' he said. 'I'm not used to this, Jess.'

'To what?'

'The arm's-length treatment.'

'I'm sorry. I told you, I'd just got used to being away from you, and boom, here you are.'

'You weren't missing me, then?'

'I hadn't thought of it like that,' she said, her face serious. 'But now you mention it, no, I don't think I was.'

'Well, thanks.'

'You take everything so literally, Charles. I've been working hard. Engrossed in what I was doing. I haven't had time to miss you.'

'Hit him again, somebody, he's still twitching.'

Jessica took his hands in hers and leaned forward, her eyes close to his own.

'I want to ask you something, Charles. Answer honestly.

When you're out there, doing . . . what you do, do you think about me?'

'Sometimes.'

'How often is sometimes?'

'What is this, Jess?'

'Don't feel badly about it, Charles. You're a single-minded man. The work you do engrosses and fulfils you. I'm the same way. I have a full life, I meet interesting people. A day will go by and I won't have thought about you once. And I bet you're the same.'

'You're wrong.'

'I don't think so. Oh, when we are together we're good together. But it's compartmentalized. I don't like that in you, and I don't like finding it in me.'

'Jess, it will change. Both of us have things to forget. Adjustments to make. Just give it a little time.'

'I am. I will. Oh, Charles, I do want to.'

'Put yourself in my 'ands, me pretty,' he said with a theatrical leer.

'Aha,' she said. 'Having fantasies, are we? Wines 'er and dines 'er and 'as 'er fair white body?'

'Something along those lines.'

'And you with a gammy leg.'

'It's my leg that's damaged, not my libido.'

'So I perceive. But not tonight, Napoleon. This course I'm on is very demanding. I'm going to have an early night.'

'I had exactly the same thing in mind.'

She laughed, and for a moment their accustomed warm intimacy was there again. He took her hand.

'God,' she laughed. 'You're subtle!'

'Ah, well.' He made a wry face. 'It seemed a good idea when I had it.'

'Damn you, Garrett, you're doing it again!' she said.

'What?'

'Being disarming.'

'This isn't turning out anything like I planned,' he said. 'I must really have the clumsies tonight.'

'Oh, Charles!' she laughed, and kissed him. 'You're pouting!'

'Us fellers don't *pout*,' he said. 'We might sulk a little, but we don't *pout*.'

'Come on,' she said, extending a slim hand and standing up. 'Tomorrow's Sunday. Ring me in the morning. We'll have brunch by the waterfall in Trump Tower and you can take me for a walk in the park.'

She kissed him goodbye outside the restaurant, and took a cab home, leaving him standing disconsolately by the edge of the kerb. Woody slid the Aries alongside; the window hummed down.

'Struck out, eh, chief?'

'Looks like it, Woody,' Garrett said. 'Any calls?'

'Only one,' Woody said. 'From Mr Young. He said to remind you not to miss the *Times* tomorrow. That make sense to you?'

'Yes,' Garrett said. And no, he thought. He shook his head. The mind-picture of Leila Jarhoun was still there, the something that he could not define still nagging away at the back of his mind.

Everything he knew about Leila Jarhoun screamed at him that she was far too intelligent to be so obvious, too devious to be so simple, too cunning to have all her eggs in one so easily upset basket. The whole UN operation had been too easy. The question was, had she made it too easy for them? Had they found out precisely what they were supposed to find out, blundering down the well-marked trail she had laid out for them exactly as she intended them to do, baying like demented bloodhounds after nothing more than a dragged carcase?

Take it a step further: if he was right, what did it mean? If the UN was a decoy, then what – or who – was the real target?

It was time to begin.

She had watched the watchers, an unseen third eye on the streets. She had no fear of their recognizing her, and even less that what they found would lead them to her. Soraya Alvarez, Keziah Mahoudi and Sahar Musaed were nothings, donkeys who had been briefed by a cutout who got his instructions via a letter drop from a box at the Grand Central post office. It was the fact that they were under surveillance that was important; it meant her 'plot' had been penetrated, and that the sleeper bomb had been located. They would now conclude the danger was past. Secure in that knowledge, she could now proceed with what she had really come to New York to do.

She dialled the pass-along number in Zürich, her hand trembling slightly with excitement. This was the moment she had been waiting for. She heard the ringing tone, three thousand miles away. After four rings, the recording machine cut in.

'This is Leila. All is well. I have begun.' she said, and hung up.

These were elementary precautions in a world of electronic listening more sophisticated than the average citizen even dreamed. Satellites, turning lazily twenty-two thousand miles above them, could pick up and relay to listening posts on earth – the National Security Agency at Fort Meade, GCHQ in Cheltenham, Pine Springs in Australia and all the rest – any message directed to, or from, a targeted point. Any call made to Kutayfan or any PLO station known to the NSA would automatically be monitored, so a bypass system using apparently innocuous hand-on numbers had been organized. Leila's recorded call would be passed on by unknown hands via similar numbers in Vienna, Athens and Tel Aviv to its ultimate destination. At the same time, the machinery she had set up would begin to turn. Calls would be made to each of the safe houses in the target cities, putting the assault teams on ready. They would all be in position by six o'clock, Greenwich Mean Time.

Her mind went back to the conference at PLO headquarters in Tunis, when the army engineers had pronounced upon the feasibility of her plan. The speaker was a grizzly-haired veteran of a hundred bridge-blowings, a thousand tank traps. He had examined the proposition from every angle, he said. And it could not be done.

'Our calculations indicate that it would take far more C4

231

than could be carried by any one person to achieve the result desired,' he said. 'We are looking at what would be a major work of demolition requiring a highly skilled team.'

The structural core Leila wished to fracture, he reported, was a wrought-iron pylon slightly under thirty yards high, tapering at the top. The corner piers were massive angle girders, each 24 by 27 inches in section, assembled of iron plates half an inch thick and including, at the outer corners, supplementary projecting angle beams for the attachment of the bracing and secondary structure. Such angles, fabricated in pairs to form T-shaped beams, served for the nine levels of horizontal struts and also for the crucial double diagonal bracing that laced the entire pylon into a powerful, rigid trussed unit.

On its upper two levels was hung the more complex trussed asymetrical girder that swung out and rose a further fourteen yards above the top of the truss. In this, angles were combined in pairs and fours to form cross-shaped beams for the cross-braced rising members.

'I estimate it would take several hundred kilos of explosive, strategically placed, to part the anchorings that hold the secondary girder to the main pylon,' he said flatly. 'And that, I suggest, is far more than any one person could put into place and arm without detection.'

'You were not invited to report on what cannot be done, Major, but what can!' Leila snapped, pretending not to see Kutayfan's expression of dismay. 'I trust, therefore, that you and your experts' – she put a sneer on the word – 'have come prepared to suggest a feasible alternative course for me to pursue.'

They had, of course. The whole business was just an exercise to put her in her place. Men tried to do that all the time: it was all part of their damned conspiracy. They did not want a woman to show she could be as good as any of them. Well, she had bent them to her will, and they had come up with what she wanted, a way to achieve the effect she desired, albeit on a smaller, but no less spectacular scale.

She took out from the cupboard the small backpack

Asaad had given her. Inside it was a rolled inch-thick sheet of whitish-grey material that looked a little like Plasticene: about five pounds of C4 plastic explosive, laid alongside a pair of Adidas running shoes with red laces. The laces were actually a thinly rolled strip of detonating cord made from pentaerythritol tetranitrate, mixed with lecithin to stabilize it. Stuffed inside the running shoes was a pair of white tube socks, one in each shoe. In each sock was a squat, ugly German-made phosphorus grenade. She took the grenades out and put them into the pockets of her windcheater. In any other circumstances, she would never have taken the risk of carrying such obviously offensive weapons, but there were no trained security experts looking for bombs where she was going.

She laid the rucksack to one side, picked up the telephone and made a call. A female voice answered.

'Good morning,' she said. 'Is this Jessica Goldman?'

'Yes it is.'

'Oh, hi, Mrs Goldman,' she said. She was a natural mimic: it was a convincing impersonation of the standard nasal New York drawl. 'This is Ruth Carter. Mr Charles Garrett's assistant. He asked me to call you. He said could you meet him at the entrance to the Statue of Liberty, about eleven?'

'The where?'

'He said you'd be surprised.'

'He was right, Miss Carter.'

'He said I was to be sure and tell you it's very important.' She made her voice anxious; it was not difficult.

'I understand. Tell Mr Garrett I'll be there.'

'Have a nice day,' Leila said, with a feral smile.

The idea had occured to her while she was watching the watchers at the United Nations building and realized, with a sudden leaping shock of recognition, that the big man limping across to the blue Dodge Aries outside the General Assembly Building was Charles Garrett. So he had not escaped the grenade attack unscathed. Her fingers touched her face, and she smiled her lopsided smile. It was a partial

233

revenge: she decided, there and then, that Jessica Goldman would provide the rest.

It was as if what she was about to do had been fore-ordained, the means to destroy her enemy delivered to her as a gift. Allah was wise, Allah was great. If, when she telephoned her, Jessica Goldman had hesitated or made an excuse, she would have gone to the apartment on East 64th Street and taken her out at the point of a gun. This way was infinitely better. A small pulse of excitement began to course through her body. This was the day. She tied back her hair and put on a sloppy cotton sweater and a pair of baggy pants that effectively concealed her figure, not to mention the slim Beretta automatic pistol strapped to her calf in a leg holster.

She went out into the sunshine, feeling the welcome warmth of the day. Newspapers were stacked in waist-high piles in front of the newsstand on the corner of Lexington. Her heart pumped as she saw the headline on the front page of the Sunday *Times*.

HAVE YOU SEEN THIS WOMAN?

She picked up the unwieldy bundle of paper and put a dollar on the counter; the man inside the newsstand hardly looked up. She dropped everything except the news section into a litter basket and scanned the rest of the text: how little they seemed to know about her! They had her age wrong, her height wrong. It was all probably this, possibly that. There was a resumé of the events at St Valéry, and what they called the 'bomb outrage' in Paris. There was a reward. She looked at the picture again and laughed harshly.

'Somethin' funny, lady?' the newsstand vendor asked.

'Yes,' she said. 'Very funny.'

She hailed a taxi. The driver who took her down to Battery Park was a thickset man with a pockmarked face who spoke only broken English. The name on the meter was Aram Boyak. He let her out at the Circle Line slip and drove away without so much as a flicker of interest. There were already plenty of people around, even this early in the day, eating ice cream or hamburgers or bagels. It sometimes seemed as if everyone in America ate all the time. No wonder so many of them were gross and ugly.

She made for the pier. As she did, a taxi pulled up to the kerb behind her, and she saw Jessica Goldman get out. Leila went ahead of her to the Circle Line booth and bought a round-trip ticket. Ten minutes later the boat pulled out and headed towards Bedloe's Island, pigeons flying in its wake. Cameras clicked at the statue of Liberty Enlightening the World standing against the sky, her torch bright gold in the morning sun. Leila Jarhoun watched it draw nearer. She felt proud. Strong. Invincible.

'Death to the hated,' she whispered.

The Punishment had begun.

18

Garrett let the phone ring twelve times before he hung up, frowning. Well, maybe she'd gone out to get a newspaper. He waited ten minutes then rang again.

No reply.

He called the car. Woody answered on the second buzz.

'Woody, this is Garrett. Where are you?'

'Outside your building, Mr Garrett.'

'Do something for me, will you? Go over to East 64th and bring Mrs Goldman over here. Could you do that, please?'

He sat by the window, drumming his fingers on the glass table. Fifteen blocks down to 64th. Woody would be there by now. The phone rang; he leaped at it.

It was Bleke.

'Charles, I'm glad I caught you. You were right. The United Nations bomb was a decoy. Jarhoun's people are on the move.'

'What have you got?'

'Abu-Salem, the one in Southall, has made a handover,' Bleke said. 'Last night, about eleven o'clock. The recipient is a complete newcomer. Name of Fuad Hawamda. Lebanese passport. Arrived in London from Athens on Friday. Not known as far as we can make out. We've got watchers on him, of course. He's currently staying at a flat in Hounslow with another Middle Easterner. We're running him through the computer now.'

'Hounslow. Right next to London Airport,' Garrett said. 'That follows. Have you heard from anyone else? Paris, Frankfurt, Brussels?'

'No, nothing yet. What's happening at your end?'

'No sign of Jarhoun. The media campaign breaks today.'

'You sound edgy.'

'I am. I am. Jarhoun isn't through with us yet.'

'I'll keep you posted on developments here. Will you be at this number?'

'No. I'll be on the street, but Young's people will patch you through to me.'

'All right. Keep in touch.'

If the assault teams were forming, then Leila Jarhoun was on the move, too. His hunch had been right: she would want to be centre stage for her big moment. He looked at the calendar. 28 May. The date rang a bell in his memory. What was it?

The phone rang. He snatched it up.

'Mr Garrett, this is Woody. I'm at East 64th. Just talked to the doorman. He said Mrs Goldman went out about a half hour ago.'

'Does he know where she was going?'

'Yes, sir. Apparently she joked about it. She said, you'll never guess where my friend asked me to meet him this bright and sunny Sunday morning. And the door man said, where? And she said, the Statue of Liberty.'

The Statue of Liberty!

Of course, dammit, of course! Symbol of everything America stood for, ikon of freedom, the most highly visible monument in the world! Leila Jarhoun's target was the Statue of Liberty!

'Get back here as fast as you can, Woody. I'll be waiting for you outside.'

'Five minutes,' Woody said.

Garrett broke the connection and then dialled Butch Young's twenty-four-hour number.

'Butch, this is Garrett. The UN bomb was a decoy. Leila Jarhoun is going to bomb the Statue of Liberty.'

'*What?*'

'There isn't time to talk,' Garrett said urgently. 'I've been stupid. We all have. You know what today is?'

'Tell me.'

'PLO Day. The twenty-fifth anniversary of the founding of the PLO. I've just talked to London. Jarhoun's people are on the move. Today is the day.'

'What makes you think Liberty is the target?'

'Someone telephoned Jessica,' Garrett explained. 'Said I wanted her to meet me there. It has to be Jarhoun, Butch. I can feel it in my bones.'

'Who's arguing?' Young said. 'Get on down there. I'll whistle up the people we'll be needing. Meet you at Battery Park as soon as I can.'

'On my way,' Garrett said, and hurried down to the lobby. He went out into 79th Street just as Woody came round the corner of Third Avenue. Garrett was in the car before it had stopped rolling.

'Battery Park!' he snapped. 'Go for the world record!'

'Yeah!' Woody breathed, his eyes lighting up. He switched on the siren and roared away from the pavement, throwing the car into a U-turn to get him back on to the FDR Drive as Garrett rolled down the window and slapped the strobe light on to the roof of the car. The traffic was Sunday morning light, and Woody was able to floor the pedal and put the big car up to its best speed. They roared and banged downtown, sometimes hitting seventy miles an hour. They were at Battery Park in something under twenty minutes.

'Mrs Goldman?'

Jessica, standing in front of the main entrance to the Museum of Immigration, turned in surprise at the sound of a female voice speaking her name. Facing her was a dark-haired woman of about her own height. In spite of herself, Jessica was unable to conceal her reaction to the woman's terrible injuries. One entire side of her face was a repellent mess of scarred weals and raised welts that distorted her entire expression. Dark sunglasses concealed her eyes, giving her an expressionless, masklike look. The mask distorted into a twisted parody of a smile.

'You like my face?' the woman said.

'I beg your pardon?'

'I am Leila Jarhoun.'

Jessica frowned.

'You do not know my name?'

'Should I?'

'Boy!' the girl said, faking exhaustion. 'I'm bushed!'

As she spoke, another couple huffed and puffed up the steps into the small space. They were in their early thirties, by the look of it, casually dressed, the man in a sports shirt and trousers, the woman in a loose-fitting pink blouse and matching cotton jeans.

'Phew!' the man said. 'That's some climb, there.' He looked around, smiling, as if expecting a reply. He was about five-eight, with dark hair and a five o'clock shadow.

'I thought I wasn't goin' ta make it,' the woman said. 'Wow, looka that view, Joe!'

'Here,' the man said. 'Hold the bag. I wanna take some pictures.'

He took a Canon AI with a motor drive out of the grey canvas camera case, then handed the case to the woman. He went to one of the windows and started snapping photographs. The camera went calack, bzzzzz, calack, bzzzzzz.

Leila Jarhoun took hold of Jessica's arm between shoulder and elbow and shoved her over to the left-hand side of the row of windows. She looked down the spiralling stairs; moving figures were coming up towards them. Opening her backpack she took out one of the American M429 Thunderflash grenades, pulled the pin and dropped it downwards. The fuse was a standard Bouchon igniter with a 1.5-second delay. It exploded below with a blinding flash and a deafening blast that reverberated, inside the great copper frame of the statue, like the crack of doom. Way down below someone started screaming.

The people at the windows turned in astonishment to find Leila Jarhoun facing them, the Model 92 Beretta in her hand. She watched their shock and disbelief turning to fear. The Jewish man who had been taking pictures stared at her, frozen in half-turn. His wife made a long, sad, wailing noise.

'All of you, sit down on the floor with your back to the wall!' Leila shouted. 'Down, down!'

She thrust Jessica Goldman away from her towards the others as they scrambled in panic to obey the shouted

241

order. Jessica stumbled across someone's outstretched leg, and fell on to her hands and knees. Someone helped her, she did not know who. Leila now stood in front of all of them, the gun at the ready. A man of about forty was still on his feet. His face set in angry annoyance, he started across towards Leila.

'Now just a damned minute, lady—' he began. Without hesitation Leila shot him through the heart. The explosion was deafening in the confined space. The man's eyes opened very wide and he looked down at his chest and then collapsed on the floor like a heap of washing. His wife, a dumpy woman in a cotton sundress, stared at his body for a long, long moment; then she started shaking her head from side to side and, as a formless shout left her mouth, she leaped at Leila Jarhoun. Leila was ready for her. She hit her across the face with the pistol and the woman reeled sideways, caroming off the handrail of the stairway, and fell to her knees, hands to her broken mouth, mewling with pain. Blood trickled between her fingers. Leila felt neither sympathy nor regret. It was only a face.

The Jewish woman reached across with some tissues, trying to help the woman, who now lay stretched out face down on the floor, sobbing with pain and terror.

'Leave her!' Leila snapped. 'Keep still or I'll kill you!'

The woman drew back like a startled insect, huddling near her husband. He was staring at Leila as if he could not believe what he was seeing. The screaming on the stairs below had stopped. Apart from the snuffling sobs of the woman Leila had hit, there was a weird silence, as though everyone in the world had gone away. They could hear the sound of the wind against the copper skin of the statue, and even the slow, horrid drip of the blood of the dead man lying at the edge of the landing. Gun in hand, Leila stood at the top of the stairway, her back braced against the handrail.

'Listen to me, all of you!' she said, her voice harsh. 'You are prisoners of Al Iqab, The Punishment. You have been chosen by Allah to share a great moment in history, a day of fire that will never be forgotten!'

'You're mad,' Jessica said.

Leila whirled on her like a tiger.

'Did you hear what I said?' she shouted. 'Silence!' She took two steps forwards and put the Beretta against Jessica's temple.

'Do you want to die?'

Jessica closed her eyes and waited. Leila Jarhoun took a deep breath and stepped back, the gun at her shoulder.

'You see, I am generous,' Leila said, breathing heavily. 'I do not kill you. Not yet. We will wait. And we will all die together!'

The eerie silence returned. The young girl in the yellow tank top began to sniffle. The boy put his arm round her. Leila looked at them with contempt. Young, old, Americans were all alike: soft, uncommitted, gutless. Look at them: the callow college boy and his snivelling girlfriend, the Jewish tourist and his wife. The woman she had hit, sitting sullenly with her head down, dabbing at her mashed lips with a bloodsoaked tissue. The fourth couple, a thin, balding man in a seersucker jacket and his spindly wife, narrow-hipped and stoop-shouldered, wire-rimmed glasses glinting in the refracted light. They looked like farmers in a Wyeth painting. Americans. They were worthless, all of them. Self-indulgent, spoiled and arrogant, expecting as a right more from life than most people achieved in a lifetime of backbreaking work.

'You up there!'

A male voice, echoing up the steel stairs.

'You up there, this is Park Security. Come on down out of there!'

'Help!' the spindly woman shrilled. 'Help us, for God's sake there's a crazy woman—'

'Silence!'

Leila stepped forward and hit her contemptuously with the barrel of the gun. The force of the blow rocked the woman's head back hard against the metal wall, knocking her wire-rimmed glasses askew. A bright red bloody welt appeared above her cheekbone where the contact had been made. She lapsed into shocked silence. Her husband glared at Leila, clenching and unclenching his fists, but made no overt move.

'All right, we're coming up!' the voice below yelled.

Leila smiled her twisted smile and dropped another Thunderflash down. The grenade body was soft plastic, the submunition container inside it made of soft foam so as not to produce lethal fragments. She did not want to kill anybody.

Not yet.

Butch Young had five agents with him in the Coastguard cutter that roared them out to Bedloe's Island. Their badges were pinned to their lapels, and each was wearing body armour and carrying riot control equipment. Behind them, a powerful launch carrying a NYPD SWAT team roared in their wake. Garrett had a Point Blank Contour SWAT waistcoat over his shirt; he had selected in Ingram Model 11 9mm Parabellum sub-machine-gun with a sixteen-round magazine from the small arsenal in the FBI truck at Battery Park.

When the launch landed at Bedloe's Island, the FBI agent led his team straight inside the huge mausoleum-like pedestal, where security guards were shepherding visitors out of the museum and into the open air.

'I want all these people out of here!' Young shouted to the police officers piling out of the boat alongside them. 'And no one but authorized personnel are to be allowed to land, understand? The last thing we want out here is a god-dammed media circus!'

'Okay, folks, move on down to the boats!' the Security men shouted. 'Move right along! Come on now, folks, move along please!'

'What is it, what's going on?' a man asked.

'They got a bomb someplace,' another told him.

'Jeez,' the man said. 'Let's get outa here!'

With Garrett at his right shoulder, Young led the phalanx of agents into the now deserted museum building and across to the lifts. The police captain in charge of the SWAT team, whose nameplate proclaimed him to be

Robert Sikking, led his men in a tight wedge behind them. They went up together to the observation deck, where a posse of Park Security guards was gathered at the foot of the staircases.

'All right, who's in charge here?' Young said.

A tall, well-built blond man of about forty stepped forward.

'I guess I am,' he said. 'Joe Hardin, chief of Park Security.' He looked at the bristling array of arms and armour poised behind the FBI agent and frowned. 'What the hell is all this?'

'What's going down here, Joe?'

'We're not sure. Someone up in the head of the statue dropped what appeared to be a stun grenade on some people climbing up the stairs. I sent an officer up there, figuring it was a prank. Kids today, they'll do anything. A woman shouted for help, something about a crazy woman. Then they dropped another flashbang. I whistled up help. I didn't expect the Seventh Cavalry. What's going on?'

'This is no prank, Joe,' Young said. 'We've got a terrorist up there with a bomb and hostages. Any idea how many people she's got with her?'

'No way of knowing.'

'She's in the observatory, right?' Captain Sikking said, easing forward. 'Is there any other way up or down?'

'No,' Hardin said. 'Just the stairways. One up, one down.'

'Jesus,' Young said. 'Tell me something else encouraging.'

'Sorry.' Hardin shrugged. 'This thing wasn't built for tactical exercises.'

'Describe the observatory to me, Joe,' Garrett said.

'Nothing much to describe,' Hardin said. 'The head of the statue is thirteen feet six high. The top half of it is the observatory. Imagine a room shaped like an upturned cup. A floor area, half-moon shaped, with two stairways, one on each side. Each of the stairways goes straight up – or down, whichever way you want to look at it. Each has a simple steel handrail. The whole place isn't much bigger than a small kitchen.'

'Sonofabitch,' Young said. 'No way are we going to get near her without someone getting hurt. I guess we better start thinking about CS, Captain.'

'Got it down below,' Sikking said. 'What we need to know is how much time we got, how many people are up there.' He turned to Hardin. 'How about if we get a helicopter up, could we see inside?'

'I doubt you could get close enough,' Hardin said. 'The windows are pretty small.'

'It's still worth a try,' Young said. 'Maybe he can put limpet mikes down, too.'

Sikking nodded and turned to give orders to one of his men. Transceivers began to cough and crackle.

'Okay,' Young said. 'Let's go take a look. Hardin, you come with me. Captain, I want you and your people down here in reserve for the moment, okay?'

The SWAT squad stood aside to let two of Young's agents take the down staircase. With Joe Hardin leading the way and Young and Garrett behind him, they started climbing, round and round, ever upwards. It was very warm. The lights above the stairs threw strange disorienting shadows in the deep fold of the copper skin of the statue and refracted eerily off the thin flat iron bars connected to the secondary trusswork and the braces with their four huge copper rivets. All at once it got lighter; they could see open space above them.

'This is it,' Hardin said. They stopped on the stairs, the sound of their breathing loud in the solid silence about them. Butch Young leaned over the railing and looked up.

'I don't see anyone,' he said.

He looked through the interlacing forest of metal to the staircase on the other side of the huge steel cage. The thickset agent on the down staircase gave a thumbs-up signal: his men were in position.

'Give me that bullhorn, Davies,' Young said. The agent handed him the loud-hailer and Young switched on.

'You up there!' he shouted. 'This is the FBI!'

The sound blatted off the metal skin of the statue, echoing downwards. There was no response from above.

'Leila Jarhoun!' Young said. 'If you're up there, make yourself known!'

The echoes bounced and died. Still no reply.

'All right, up there, we're coming up!' Young announced. He waved two of his men forward, and they started up the stairs towards the light. On the other side, two agents eased up the down stairway. They had only gone about ten steps when a burst of shots from above spangled and whined off the metalwork about them, driving them back down in clattering haste, their shoulders hunched in reflex.

'Pull back!' Young shouted. 'Get out of range! I don't want anybody killed up here!' Up above them, Leila Jarhoun heard the words and laughed out loud.

Five minutes passed in tense silence. Leila watched the hostages unblinkingly. Long ago, in the camp in the Beka'a valley, they had taught her that there was a point at which hostages began to think again, a moment when the fog of terror enveloping them lifted and they realized, all at once and as if with one mind, that they outnumbered their captor and that if they rushed her, they might overpower her before she killed them all. So she watched them closely, ready to stamp ruthlessly on any little flicker of rebellion before it had time to burst into flame. That was why she had shot the first man to protest, and pistol-whipped the woman. Terror made obedience.

'You up there! Jarhoun!' she heard the man with the bullhorn shout. 'This is Senior Agent Irwin Young, FBI. I am authorized to negotiate with you. Tell us what you want and we'll do our best to meet your demands. There's no reason to kill innocent people.'

'Tell that to the butchers of Israel!' she replied.

'Why are you doing this?' the man shouted. 'What do you want?'

'Nothing!' she shouted back over her shoulder. 'I want nothing.'

'How many people have you got up there?'

'Eight alive,' Leila replied, smiling her distorted smile, 'and one dead!'

'Let's talk about this, Leila. Let's see if we can't work something out.'

Leila did not reply. They had taught her all about negotiation techniques, too. The whole idea was to keep you talking. As long as you were talking, there was a chance: a chance to change the situation, to get into a better position, to disadvantage you, to persuade you out of doing whatever you planned to do, or kill you before you could do it.

'Leila, talk to me!' Young said. Again she ignored the request. She could hear them moving about down there. They had turned out all the lights on the stairs. The interior of the observatory was brightly lit by the sunlight coming through the windows. She knew they would not, dared not, try to storm her position yet. Then would talk until time ran out. Then would come the stun grenades, the CS gas, the head-on SWAT assault.

'Leila Jarhoun!' It was a different voice this time. 'This is Charles Garrett.'

Leila's expression altered; hatred glittered in the dark eyes. 'I thought you would come,' she hissed.

'What have you done with Jessica Goldman?'

'She is here,' Leila said. 'Come and get her if you want her.'

'Let me talk to her.'

'No!'

'Then how do I know you're telling the truth?'

Leila made a gesture with the Beretta, *come here*. Jessica Goldman got up and came over to the head of the stairwell. Another gesture: *talk*.

'Charles, this is Jessica!' she called down into the darkness below, bravely keeping the tremor out of her voice. 'I'm all right. There are eight of us up here. She's already killed one m—'

Leila clamped a hand on her mouth, pulled her back from the top of the stairs and thrust her away.

Garrett and Young were huddled together on the steel stairway perhaps fifty feet below the observatory. Above their heads was a stainless-steel bullet shield on a steel upright, looking not unlike a reflector in a photographic studio. Young had whistled up walkie-talkies and set up a radiophone link with FBI headquarters in Manhattan. He could also talk to the pilot of the helicopter that was moving in on the statue from the blind, New Jersey side to try to fix magnetic limpet microphones to the crown of Liberty's head.

'Leila!' Garrett shouted. 'Let her go. Let this be between just you and me!'

'It is between you and me, Garrett! That is why she is going to die! All of them will die!'

'She's not going to break, Charles,' Young whispered urgently. 'I'm going to tell Sikking to stand by with the CS.'

'She's not a fool, Butch!' Garrett argued. 'She'll have a respirator. You send the SWAT team in, and there'll be a bloodbath up there. You read her profile.'

Young shook his head. 'What do you want me to do?' he said exasperatedly. 'We can't just sit here until her fucking bomb goes off!'

'Let me keep trying,' Garrett urged him. 'If we can just get an idea what the European targets are. . . .' He raised his voice. 'Leila, it's useless! You can't win, no matter what you do!'

'You will see!' Leila shouted back. 'My death today will be the signal for a thousand deaths!'

'No, Leila!' Garrett said. 'Your death will be pointless. You've failed.'

'I will not fail!' she screeched. 'Today is a day of vengeance! A day of fire to mark the birth of the Struggle! Death to the hated, the assassins of Israel!'

Garrett touched Young's arm. The FBI man was already speaking rapidly into his radiophone.

'Hear this. The target is Israeli. Repeat, the target is Israeli. Notify all embassies, airline ticketing offices and personnel in target cities immediately. Notify airport security staffs in all target cities to intensify surveillance on all Israeli locations and personnel.'

'Who are you avenging, Leila?' Garrett was saying through the loud-hailer. 'Your people? Or your father?'

'Do not foul his memory with your words! Do not try to use his death as a weapon against me!'

'What happened to him, Leila? Did the Israelis kill him? In the Six Day War, was it?'

'Yes, they killed him!' she replied. 'They killed my father, as they killed the father of us all. And for that death they will pay in blood and fire across Europe. In one hour! In one hour!'

Butch Young was talking to Captain Sikking now, his voice low and controlled. 'She says an hour. No, I don't know what she's got up there, Captain, but we've got to assume it's a bomb. Ten, fifteen pounds of plastic, a bottle of picatinny disguised as sun-tan lotion, who the fuck knows! Whatever it is it'll probably take the head off the goddammed statue. Just put your people on full alert. I want a thirty-minute countdown, starting now. Got it? Good. Stand by.'

'. . . the others have been arrested,' Garrett was telling the terrorist. 'It's all over. You're just one person, alone. What can you do?'

'You're lying!'

'She's not buying it,' Young said to Garrett.

'Maybe,' Garrett said. 'Maybe not. I'm just trying to get her off balance, Butch. Any way I can.'

'I'm not lying,' he called out. 'We have all your people in London, and Paris and all the other places. We have the missiles and the men who were going to fire them.'

'You lie, you lie, you lie!'

He tried to imagine her up there, tense, alone, uncertain. Go for it, he thought.

'You might as well surrender,' he said. 'There's nothing left to fight for.'

Her answer was a burst of contemptuous laughter and he knew he had failed.

'Wait!' she said. 'Just a little longer, Garrett!'

Down below he could see moving lights. The metal staircase thrummed as the police assault teams began bringing their equipment up: stun guns, AM 180s, Smith and Wesson 210s. Light glanced off fibreglass tactical helmets. He looked up towards the observatory, thinking about Jessica. If the SWAT team did go in, Jessica would be the first one killed.

Diana, anger staining her face.

And what about me? What about the danger I'm in?

You're not in danger. They don't even know who you are.

I don't want to be a hostage, Charles. I couldn't handle being a hostage.

You won't be. I promise you.

As he looked up towards the observatory Leila Jarhoun leaned over the railing and sprayed bullets downwards. He heard them spanging off the metal shield above him, the whanging pound of the explosions coming back off the steel walls, ricochets whining off into the blackness below, shouts.

'Crazy bitch!' Young growled. 'What—'

Garrett stopped him, a hand on the FBI man's forearm. There had been another shot, a lighter bark than that of the automatic Jarhoun was using, followed instantaneously by three shots fired so rapidly as to sound almost like one.

'Someone else is shooting up there,' Garrett said, 'in the observatory!'

Jessica felt perspiration trickling down her back. The air was thick with fear and tension. She could hear metallic sounds on the stairs below; that would be the police assault teams bringing up their equipment: stun guns and Street Sweepers, riot gear and body armour. If they made an assault, Leila Jarhoun would kill them.

She looked at the woman, her scarred face twisted with hatred as she leaned over the steel rail and fired her gun down into the darkness, the whanging pound of the explosions reverberating off the steel walls. Jessica heard the whine of ricochets, shouts of alarm or pain or both.

She could hear her grandfather's voice. *You can't imagine what it was like, child. Unless you were there.*

But you were men. Why didn't you fight them?

251

You don't understand. They had guns. If we had fought, they would have killed us.

But they killed all the Jews anyway.

You don't understand. Only if you'd been there would you understand. You can't fight people with guns.

To her surprise, hatred flooded through her. Come and kill her, she pleaded silently to Garrett on the stairs below. *Kill her.* Leila Jarhoun felt the weight of her eyes and turned towards her, the scarred face twisted in a snarl. 'What are you staring at, bitch?'

Jessica shook her head, shamed by the huge shock of fear that swept through her. She shuddered. Was that how it had been? Had they all been so afraid to die that they would do anything in order to live? No, she thought. I will not let her do this to me. I will not let her make me beg to be allowed to live.

'What . . . what is going to happen to us?' she said.

Leila looked at her in scornful surprise, as one might regard a talking dog. 'Why, you are going to die. What did you think?'

'Why?' Jessica whispered. 'What have we done to you?'

Leila shook her head. 'That doesn't matter.'

'It matters to me,' Jessica said, and this time there was more strength in her voice. I will not be afraid, she told herself. I will not be afraid of this woman.

Leila looked at her in that same disbelieving way. Then she took a fast, sliding step towards Jessica, jamming the muzzle of the gun against her upper lip.

'Would you rather die now?' she hissed. 'Would you like me to kill you right this moment?'

Terror swamped Jessica's entirety; she managed to shake her head. Leila laughed, a harsh sound of contempt, and turned away, going back across to the head of the stairs to resume her watchful vigil. Jessica sat with her head down, drowning in shame at the way her own fear had debilitated her. Was that how it had been for the old people?

Why did they do it?

They hated us, child.

And you? Didn't you hate them?

Oh, yes. We hated them. We hated what they were doing.
Then why didn't you stop them?
They had guns, child. You can't fight people with guns.

They were just ordinary people. It was the guns that gave them the power. They had no right to do what they did, but the guns gave them the right to do it. She thought of Charles Garrett, crouched in the darkness below, a gun in his hand, too. Someone has to do it, he had said. Someone has to make the stand, someone has to say, *no, you will not.* And I said no one had that right, she thought. How different it was when you were alone in your terror, sitting sweating on the steel floor of your execution chamber. Right and wrong became academic. You just prayed for someone to come along and get you out.

We thought at first, it can't go on forever, they'll stop this madness. Then we began to realize there was never going to be any end to it. They were going to kill us all. They were going to exterminate us, like vermin.
Why didn't you fight then?
By then it was too late.

Leila Jarhoun was still staring down into the darkness below, her body tight with tension, the Beretta at her side. Jessica half turned and her hand touched the strap of the rucksack that Leila had placed in the corner to the left of the stairway. She looked at the other hostages. Their faces were glazed with torpor and fear.

Somebody do something, she thought, and then she was angry with herself. The anger hardened into a bitter, searing rage directed against the woman with the gun and, all at once, the anger and the fear coalesced into hatred.

'No!' Jessica shouted. 'No, no, no!' And she grabbed the rucksack and ran at Leila Jarhoun, swinging it in a clumsy, looping arc as Leila turned round, like a cat, the dark eyes narrowed, the Beretta coming up to the firing position. The heavy rucksack caught her on the point of her left shoulder and knocked her sideways against the corner of the steel handrail at the top of the stairs; she screeched with pain as it drove into her ribcage. She fell to her knees, the gun making a heavy sound on the steel floor.

Leila scrambled upright, killing rage blinding her, and in that same moment, the Jewish-looking tourist who had come up the stairs behind her took a 9mm Beretta Model 1951 out of his camera case and shot her. Even as she felt the shock of the bullet in her body, Leila was firing her own gun, three bullets hitting the man in a descending vertical line from the second button of his shirt. He was dead before his body slumped backwards.

A huge wave of nausea and pain surged through Leila's body, misting her eyes. She saw the Jewish woman reaching for the gun and shot her, and as she did, Jessica Goldman swung the rucksack again, this time two-handed, crashing it against the front of Leila's body. She screamed in agony as the force of the blow drove her backwards down the spiral stairway.

Triumphant hatred that she could not control surged through Jessica Goldman, thick hatred like treacle. Garrett was down there somewhere. She wanted to shout out loud. *Kill her, kill the bitch!*

'Charles!' she shouted. 'Charles, she's wounded! She's coming down! Get her, Charles, get her!'

Leila Jarhoun was on the half-landing below. She got to her feet. There was a sharp pain in her hip where she had crashed down the iron stairs, and a sliding wetness to the right of her body below the ribcage. Above her, she heard Jessica Goldman call out, her voice clear and firm. Anger roared in Leila's brain like an explosion. Bitch, bitch! She fired upwards twice, but no cry of pain greeted the shots. She moved down the staircase. In the darkness she sensed, rather than saw, a shape below her, and fired at it. The bullet whacked into a steel stanchion with a noise like the cracking of whip.

'Get back, get back, she's coming down!' someone shouted, and she heard the clanging of feet on the staircase. the steel treads vibrated; she ripped out the empty thirteen-round detachable box magazine and slapped in the spare with the heel of her hand. Red mist swam in front of her eyes.

The bitch! The treacherous bitch! It was unbelievable. Everything ruined by Garrett's whore and one little Jew with a gun. She heard movements below, fired towards them. She heard hoarse shouts, commands. Suddenly the interior of the statue was bathed in unearthly brilliance. Searchlights! She looked away, shielding her eyes so that she would not be dazzled. If they located her with those lights, their marksmen would be able to pick her off like a black bird on a white wall. Her mind spun. Pain hammered through her body.

She was about a third of the way down the staircase now. To her right she saw a small steel door marked *Authorized Personnel Only*. She remembered what it was, and hope flooded through her. There was still a chance, still a chance! She wrenched at the handle but the door was locked. She jammed the barrel of the Beretta up against the key aperture and turned away. When she pulled the trigger there was a huge metallic spanging sound and the gun nearly bounced out of her hand. She tried the handle again. It was still locked but now the door rattled. She put the Beretta against the keyhole and fired again. The explosion flattened her eardrums. This time the door opened.

Sloping up ahead of her was a dark tunnel, with a ladder at its centre ascending at an angle of about sixty degrees. She began climbing into the darkness, her heart thundering in her breast. How far was it? She tried to remember. Forty, fifty feet? Her brain was sluggish; her arms and legs felt like lead. She stopped, clinging to the ladder. Her throat was clogged as if with tar. She spat gobs of blood down into the darkness.

The ladder was cold. Was it her imagination or was it swaying? Spasms of pain hit her body like cramp and she clung to the pitted steel rungs; a moan of agony wrenched itself from her lips. I will not fail, she told herself. I will not fail.

The ladder vibrated, a regular movement that she could feel through the soles of her shoes. Someone was behind her, coming up. She looked back down into the darkness and saw light below her, a torch shining upwards.

'Leila!' someone shouted. 'It's finished!'

Garrett!

'Never!' she screeched. 'Never, never, never!'

She felt the heavy fast movement of his feet on the ladder and forced herself to move. Up and up, up, up. There was light ahead of her now. Not far, not far. She felt blood trickling down her leg. Her belly was numb. Up and up towards light, and then she was in a narrow circular tube of metal with a curiously asymetrical glass roof and large industrial light fittings. The torch! At about the level of the middle of her body she saw a heavy metal bolt. She slid it back and the door opened, and there was a mighty roar of wind. Behind her, light flickered up the shaft of the uplifted arm in whose centre was the ladder she had just climbed. She fired two shots down and heard them carom off the copper skin of the statue as she stepped out on to the narrow balcony around Liberty's torch, three hundred feet above the sea.

Teeth chattering with cold and pain, she threw herself against the central pillar supporting the heavy glass 'flame'. The sky swam in her sight; Manhattan was a blur across the placid water. She shook her head to clear it and, with a scream of defiance, she pulled the pins from the phosphorus grenades, holding them aloft in her hands with her arms outstretched.

'Death to the hated!' she shouted into the tearing wind. 'Death!'

Garrett climbed fast, hand over hand, ignoring the pain in his leg, drawing closer to Leila, close enough to hear her stertorous breathing; it sounded like someone tearing rags. His hand touched a soft slick of thick blood. She was badly hurt. Light above now from the glass dome of the statue's torch. He shone the light upwards, heard two shots that whanged off the rounded skin of the statue. He got to the top of the ladder and was met by the rushing roar of the wind. He gathered himself and then rolled out on the walkway that encircled the torch.

Flat on his belly with the Ingram levelled, he saw her

terrible scarred face, her arms outstretched above her head, the two grenades clutched in her hands. Without a flicker of hesitation he emptied the magazine into Leila's upstretched body. The sixteen heavy slugs drove her against the low, crownlike rail surrounding the torch and off into space. She turned and turned again as she hurtled down, and then the grenades exploded, two flat bangs like gigantic fireworks. Long smoking tendrils of burning phosphorus hung in the midday sunshine and then were gone.

19

'His name was Tsvi Aronson,' Garrett said. 'He was a special agent of Mossad.'

'How the devil did Mossad get involved?' Bleke wondered.

'They're being very coy about the whole thing. My guess is they got on to Jarhoun soon after the first time we requested information on her and her organization.'

'Then why didn't they tell us, or the Americans?'

'I don't need to tell you that they're sometimes considerably less than forthcoming about their operations,' Garrett said. 'Especially where they consider their own people are at risk.'

'So they were on to Jarhoun right from the start?'

'That's the way I see it. That was why every time we asked them for information they stonewalled. They probably had her under surveillance from the moment we alerted them.'

'And this Aronson, and the woman who was with him, were surveillance agents?'

'So I gather. I don't think either of them was prepared for what happened at the Statue of Liberty. But they saved us all a hell of a lot of grief.'

'I get the impression that the Bureau was less than delighted that it was Mossad who saved the day.'

Garrett grinned. 'Butch Young was angry enough to kick his own dog,' he said. 'The Americans have been sensitive about Israeli intelligence operating in the States ever since that Pollard case blew up, a few years ago.'

'Pity we couldn't have taken the woman, all the same,' Bleke said. 'That would have been quite a coup.'

'I didn't have much choice,' Garrett replied. 'I saw the grenades and reacted instinctively. I knew the longest fuse anything has these days is about four and a half seconds, and all I could think was: shut her down.'

'Phosphorus grenades, you said?'

'She would have lit up the Hudson,' Garrett said. 'Blown the torch right off the arm.' He could see it all again in his mind's eye: Leila Jarhoun falling to earth, turning slowly, over, and over, and then below, the bright flat midair crack of the explosion.

A twenty-four-hour embargo which ensured that no news of Leila Jarhoun's death reached the media threw the entire Al Iqab operation into disarray. The teams were in place, waiting for a signal that never came. The difference now was that the security agencies knew what they were looking for, and were able to isolate, surround and capture the eight terrorist teams at each of the target airports without a shot being fired: two men posing as Special Branch officers on 'observation duties' on the western loop of the perimeter road around Heathrow; another pair, using the identification warrants of Frankfurt policemen Peter Heim and Herbert Lichtenfeld, waiting in a car parked on a bridge that carried the Frankfurt airport service road from Zeppelinheim over the Mannheim-Heidelberg autobahn a few miles south of the Frankfurter Kreuz; a third couple posing as civil engineers 'examining' the runway at Amsterdam-Schiphol; another two in a stolen catering van 'waiting to deliver' at Zürich-Kloten. There were others at Paris-Charles de Gaulle, Stockholm-Arlanda, Athens, Rome; the security teams took them all in a clean, bloodless sweep.

Each of the terrorist teams was armed with a Swedish 84mm Carl Gustaf gun carrying a 3kg fin-stabilized, rocket-assisted High Energy Anti-Tank round capable of penetrating 400mm of armour. They were whisked away to maximum security installations and there, systematically, they were broken. In London, Fuad Hawamda and his fellow terrorist, Ali Hassan Shar, were easy meat for the tough dredgers of DI5. With almost the same dispatch, Germany's BfV broke the pair who had masqueraded as *Schutzpolizei*. There was even better news from Paris: not only had the two terrorists arrested there provided DST with comprehensive confessions, but

Eugène Simion was one of the interrogating officers who obtained them.

Bit by bit, the terrifying parameters of the operation Leila Jarhoun had called Al Iqab, The Punishment, emerged. Leila's plan had been simple: murderously simple. Each team was to position itself adjacent to the target airport's runway, somewhere inside the three-hundred-yard range of the weapon, and await the signal that would be relayed to them by car telephone from a local safe house the moment Leila Jarhoun blew the head off the Statue of Liberty. In the five hours remaining of that bloody May Sunday, eight El Al flights were to have been blasted to pieces on takeoff, the first in Athens, the last at one minute before midnight in London, when the Israeli airline's flight LY 318 lifted off, bound for Tel Aviv.

'A victory of sorts, then, Charles,' Bleke said. 'How's that leg of yours, by the way?'

'I doubt I'll ever give Alberto Tomba much trouble in the downhill,' Garrett said. 'But it's a lot better.'

'How about Jessica?'

'She's going to need a little time. But I think she'll be able to come to terms with it.'

I never knew I could hate like that. It's made me take a whole new look at who I am and what I am.

'Glad to hear it,' Bleke said brusquely. 'Have you had a chance to look at the file on Hennessy?'

'Not properly. I gather BfV haven't got him locked in yet.'

'They know where he isn't.'

'Well, it's a start, I suppose,' Garrett said, with a tired grin. 'I'll get on to it.'

He stood up and went across to the door. Bleke watched him go, a small smile touching his lips. I suppose one ought to say 'well done', or something, he thought, as the door closed. He just wasn't the pat-on-the-back type, he supposed.

London was cool after the heat of New York. It was raining as Garrett reached Whitehall Court and went up to his flat. He flicked on the TV. The announcer was saying the usual summer things: cricket rained off, serious doubts about whether Wimbledon would start on time, five-mile tailbacks on the motorway, flight delays at Gatwick. He got a glass from the cupboard and poured himself a large Glenfarclas, gazing without enthusiasm at the floppy disk lying on the computer console next to the Cryptag. He'd have to look at it sometime; but not just yet.

He picked up the phone and dialled. After five rings, the answering machine cut in. He listened to the message and spoke after the tone.

'Tonight I am cooking a spinach soufflé served with a green salad with French dressing, followed by fresh strawberries and cream. The wine is a simple Château Fuissé '83, with espresso and Calvados to follow. A reservation is recommended.'

'A psychologist might conclude that your cookery is a compensatory factor in your make-up,' he heard Jessica say, cutting in on the machine. 'A way of demonstrating – to yourself as much as anyone – that there is a gentler side to your personality.'

'Never thought of it like that,' he said briskly. 'I was just hungry. Will you join me?'

'*Volontiers,*' she said, and a photograph of Irène Level, the one with the dimples, flashed on the screen of his mind. Another casualty in a war nobody knew they were fighting, he thought.

Jessica arrived about half an hour later. She was wearing her Four Seasons trenchcoat and a rain hat that looked as if it ought to have Allan Quartermain underneath it. They ate in the dining alcove by the window and watched the rain turning the streets slate grey.

'This is lovely,' Jessica said. 'I feel warm, safe.'

'A Calvados?'

'Indeed a Calvados.'

The silence was intimate and precious; he did not want to break it. He was happy to sit and look at her face, limned golden in the mellow candlelight.

'Wine comes in at the mouth,' she said. 'And love comes

261

in at the eye. That's all we shall know for truth, before we grow old and die.'

'Yeats?'

'Take me to bed, Charles,' she said, her voice urgent and low. 'Make love to me.'

She was strong and agile and eager, her body rising to meet every thrust of his, her lips hot and seeking. They moved in sinuous arabesques that grew less languid and then less, until they fused in a crescendo of intensity and she cried out in release and joy that ended in soft tears.

'It's all right, Jess,' he said softly. 'It's over. It's time to begin forgetting.'

'How did you know?'

'The poem.'

They lay quietly together in each other's arms for a long while. Later, Jessica got up and went into the other room. He found her sitting curled up on the sofa, staring into the flickering fire. She looked up as he came in and reached out her hand. He sat beside her and stroked her long black hair.

'Will I forget, Charles?' she whispered. 'Will I ever forget?'

'Yes,' he lied. 'You'll forget.'

The telephone rang. He looked at it and then looked at her. At this time of night there was only one person it could possibly be, only one possible reason for him to be ringing. Jessica smiled and touched his face with gentle fingers.

'Go ahead,' she said. 'Answer it.'